A CELESTIAL SHIFTERS STORY

NIKA

TJALARA DRAPER

www.tjalaradraper.com

Edited by: Kirstin Andrews

Cover design by: Deranged Doctor Design

Chapter background image design by: baimo on pngtree

Chapter heading image design by: skullvector on pngtree

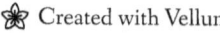 Created with Vellum

To my Mother,
Where would I be without you? Not pursuing a career in being a professional daydreamer and writing all about my imaginings, that's for sure!

Thanks so much for everything you've done for me, and for all you've had to put up with—the good, the bad, and the downright ugly.

I am who I am today because of your strength and determination. Many thanks!
xxx

Note From the Author

Hello Wonderful Reader!

Thank you so much for taking the time to pick up this book and give the story a bit of a looksy.

I know, I know, of all the characters in the Celestial Shifters world, why write Nika's spinoff book first? (I'm hearing you Sagan fans!! 😂) I've been having the same thought, I never planned to write her spinoff, so Nika's story was a bit of a surprise, even for myself. To be honest she wasn't even one of my favourite characters, and yet this somehow just happened. I decided to just follow the muse with this one.

It all came about while I was right in the thick of writing the third book in my Celestial Shifters series when things were staring to get a little muddy with some of the storyline. In short, I realised I needed to get Nika's story thread a little more clearer and I was trying to develop her backstory a little for my own benefit. NekMinute! I'm hitting 20k words with Nika's story and it didn't take long for me to decide to just go ahead and write the rest of the story as it was developing in my mind.

Note From the Author

I'm surprised by how much I've started to like Nika more since writing her story, and it turns out I had such a blast writing this book. So I really hope you enjoy reading Nika's story as much as I've enjoyed writing it!

Oh! And another note, for those of you who have already read the first two books in my Celestial Shifters series, the time line for Nika's story happens after Shards of Venus and directly before Flames of Mars.

Thanks again lovely readers!

Happy Reading!! xx

Chapter One

"Nika! Look out!"

A bright magenta flash explodes across my vision.

For a second, gravity disintegrates as I'm flung backward, pure agony slicing and radiating through my lower abdomen. My muscles tense right before my back collides with the ground; the jarring impact is marrow deep.

Winded, I try my best to inhale, but my breath hitches. Sharp, searing pain brutalizes my entire being. Is my stomach on fire? It feels as if lava has been poured directly into my insides.

My world is still spinning from the blast. Quill and Hestus, my two older brothers, run over to me—at least, I think they do. The magenta light has already cleared, but an overwhelming afterglow flickers across my closed lids each time I blink.

"Nika!"

My brothers continue screaming, calling my name, but the blast has ruptured my eardrum. Their voices sound muted against the high-pitched ringing in my ears.

All I can focus on is the pain—the infernal, gut-wrenching pain. In all my years of being a hunter, I've never experienced anything like this. I grind my teeth, willing the torture to end.

The stench of scalding flesh makes me want to gag. Smoke pollutes the flavor of each shallow breath I take. My lungs scream for air, but I can't force them to draw in enough oxygen.

Pain. So much pain.

When I clutch at my stomach, my hands come away coated in something warm and sticky.

"We've got to stop the bleeding!" one of my brothers yells.

A small groan escapes my lips as large hands press down on my burning abdomen. Writhing, I roll over onto my side, and a new color engulfs my vision.

Scarlet red.

For a heartbeat, I can't comprehend it. The color is wrong. We're supposed to be hunting shifters. Red blood isn't a usual occurrence during a hunt, because shifter blood isn't red.

"Nika? Can you hear me?"

I nod. The small movement brings another flare of blazing torment, and it's all I can do not to scream. If I start, I'll never be able to stop.

Arms wrap around me, and one of my brothers lifts me off the ground.

"Heavens above! Nika, are you okay?" says a new voice.

"Get lost, Troy!" barks Quill.

Troy's fair-skinned, freckled face comes into my periphery, his features screwed up in concern. "Nika? Nika, can you hear me?"

Quill slams a hand into Troy's chest, shoving him back, but Troy continues to shout my name over and over.

"Shut up, Troy!" snarls Hestus. "Don't you dare come any closer! You've already caused enough damage."

The jostling of my body as I'm being carried is excruciating. Either I'm going to start my eternity of screaming, or I'm going to pass out. But if I embrace unconsciousness now, I don't know if I'll have the courage to ever wake up. Not if it means facing this pain again.

"Nika? Answer me!" demands Troy, ignoring my brothers' warnings. "Please! Someone, tell me she's not dead."

"*Shut up!*" Quill's tone holds a sinister promise.

I'm laid down on a hard surface, and my brothers disappear from view, revealing the vast skyscape above. Bright stars glitter against a black velvet sky. How can such a twinkly, merry scene exist during a time like this?

"Put pressure here!" orders Quill.

Hands press down on my wound again. It's like a thousand knives dicing up my insides.

Finally, I scream.

And scream and scream.

"Hestus, quick! Get the Ylixium!"

A few moments later, a foul-tasting liquid pours into my open mouth. My gag reflexes kick in, and I spit and splutter the pearl-white fluid all over myself. I recognize the flavor of Ylixium, a medicinal elixir meant to accelerate my healing, but the excruciating pain eclipses any conviction that the thick, cool liquid is powerful enough to help.

"Drink it, Nika!" Quill orders, forcing more Ylixium into my mouth.

I choke on another gulp of the ghastly stuff. The cough jolts my body, and I scream again as the agony surges.

"Be careful, Quill, don't drown her." Hestus holds my head up, allowing me to clear my lungs and chug down more Ylixium.

Quill shoves the vial with the remaining pearly liquid at Hestus. "Here, pour the rest of this on her stomach."

Hestus nods and snatches the vial.

The torture in my lower torso still rages, but it's soon replaced with an icy chill. For a second, there's pure relief—though that doesn't stop me from bracing for what I know is coming. Sure enough, the icy chill builds into a frosty burn, and once again I'm screaming.

"What are you doing to her?" Troy's panicked shouts rival my own until—*crack!*—Quill smashes a fist into the side of Troy's head.

The pain, the trauma, the horror of imagining the state of my abdomen finally push me beyond all comprehension. Quill's raging bellows are the last thing I hear before it all turns black and silent.

"You did this to her, Troy! You did this to her! *You did this...!*"

Chapter Two

"Nika? Are you awake?"

A dull ache weasels its way into my consciousness.

"Nika? Can you hear me?"

"Hm?"

"Hey, Nika. Welcome back to the land of the living."

"Mom? Is that you?" My croaky voice rasps like sandpaper against my vocal cords.

"No, it's Francine."

Francine? I frown. Why is the barracks doctor here? Where's my mom?

Then despair floods through me as the memories roll in.

My mother's dead, has been for ten years now. It was so hard for twelve-year-old me to process at the time.

I almost scoff. Who am I kidding? Even after ten years, who wants to accept their own mother's death?

"Do you think you can sit up for me?" Francine asks.

Pushing thoughts of my mother aside, I do my best to oblige when hands take hold of my shoulders to help raise me up.

The moment I move, a sharp ache in my abdomen flares

to life. My eyes snap wide open. White surrounds me—white sheets, white walls, white ceiling, white bandages—but I hardly see any of it. All I can focus on is the stab of pain as I gasp and clutch at my lower torso.

"Easy," says Francine in a low, soothing voice. "Slowly now."

Moments later, Francine has me sitting up, pillows propped against my back.

"Better?" she asks.

I give a slow nod. The severity of the pain starts to ebb, but it takes a few more moments before my body actually begins to relax.

A tube is attached to a cannula taped to the back of my hand, and a pulse oximeter pinches the tip of one of my fingers, keeping a record of my heart rate. Its consistent beep comes from a nearby monitor, where numbers and squiggles flash across a display screen.

I look over at Francine, who's rummaging around on the trolley by my bed. She studies me with eyes dull in color but sharp with intelligence, her raven hair pulled back into a tight bun on the top of her head. If not for the white doctor's coat hanging crisply on her frame, one could almost mistake her for a clichéd ballerina—beautiful, petite, graceful.

I've heard the other hunters gossiping about Francine in the cafeteria, but the vulgar whispers cease the moment she's within earshot. Regardless of the lustful brag-talk, no one is brave enough to risk getting on her bad side. Maybe it's because the infirmary doctors in our barracks aren't subject to the same ethics of doctors out in the real world. In any case, she's somehow managed to gain a lot of respect without throat-punching someone.

While Francine examines my wounds, she fills me in on what happened in a soft voice. Not that I need her to. I remember most of it. Even so, I remain silent as she fills in the gaps left by my delirium and shock.

"The Luxium grenade caused a lot of burns and lacerations to your lower abdomen."

Burns and lacerations feels like an understatement. A Luxium core is an energy source we hunters harvest from the Magneii shifters. Not only do they power a lot of our hunting equipment and facilities, but they're the source of the Magneii's fire and magma abilities.

It's no wonder the Luxium grenade felt as if the pit of Hell itself had opened up in my abdomen.

"Your brothers didn't hesitate to administer a dose of Ylixium," continues Francine, "which, as expected, kept you alive and kickstarted the healing process while they hurried to bring you back to the barracks. We rushed you to surgery upon arrival. As far as I'm concerned, the surgery was successful. However..."

My eyes dart to her at the hesitation. With practiced restraint, I keep my expression neutral. "However, what?"

Francine doesn't make eye contact, busying herself with smoothing the nonexistent wrinkles on her white coat. Finally, she clasps her hands in front of her, her stance rigid and all emotion absent from her face. "With the extent of your injuries, the Ylixium and the surgery could only do so much. The window of losing you was closing fast, so some compromises had to be made."

"What kind of compromises?"

"There's no easy way to say this. There was extensive damage to sections of your intestines, as well as to your uterus and ovaries. Fortunately, we were able to salvage what was left of your intestines, and the need for a colostomy bag was avoided. However, as much as we tried, the damage in other areas was irreparable. I'm sorry to say, a hysterectomy and removal of your ovaries was necessary."

"Wait..." I flounder, waiting for my bewilderment to clear enough for me to comprehend her words. "A hysterectomy? But then, that would mean I can't..." The words burn on my lips; I don't have the courage to speak them out loud.

"I'm sorry, Nika." Francine rests a hand on my forearm. Her hand is icy to the touch, yet it can't ease the fiery agony that sears straight through my soul. "I'm sorry to say that the prospect of you having children is no longer possible."

My world falls out from under me.

...the prospect of you having children is no longer possible...

...no longer possible.

...no longer possible.

My calm facade starts to crack.

I am going to scream.

I am going to kick and punch anything within reach.

I am going to cry—something I haven't done since my mother passed away. The sensation rises up from my belly and burns along my throat like acid.

But instead of crying, I lean over the edge of the bed and vomit all over the floor.

Francine rushes to find a vomit bag and calls for someone to get a mop and bucket. The flurry of action is a welcome distraction. Anything to get my mind off what I've just been told, and also to stop Francine from looking at me with such pity.

Fifteen minutes later, the floor is scrubbed and sterilized. Clean sheets are put on the bed, and I'm given some water to rinse my mouth.

Quill and Hestus barrel through the door just as the attendant wheels the mop and bucket out.

"Hey, Nika!" Hestus, my second-oldest brother, greets me with a relieved smile.

"Finally, you're awake," says my oldest brother, Quill. The two walk over to my bedside. "About time, sis. We thought you were dead."

"Quill!" Hestus turns on him with a glare.

"What? It's true," says Quill. "I'm serious, Nika, we all thought you were a goner. Your intestines were all over the place. I swear I could see the bones in your lower spine through the hole in your stomach. And there was so much blood it was like—*ooph*."

Hestus jabs him in the ribs with his elbow. "Shut up, Quill. The last thing Nika needs is a reminder."

"Oh." Quill finally has the courtesy to look a smidge sheepish.

"Excuse me, Nika?"

The three of us turn to Francine, who's hovering behind the boys. Quill and Hestus move aside to allow her to step closer to me.

"I need to go check up on the other patients. You'll buzz if you need me, right?" She gestures to a button on the wall by the head of my bed.

"Sure." I shrug, then grit my teeth when the motion jostles my abdomen.

"Great," says Francine with a smile. She grasps my wrist and gives it a slight squeeze. "Not all is lost. You're going to be just fine," she adds in a low voice, but I'm unwilling to accept the sentiment. The room falls into silence for a few moments when I don't bother to respond.

"What was that about?" Hestus quirks an eyebrow after Francine leaves—thankfully without making more of a scene.

I wave a nonchalant hand. "It's nothing."

9

Quill and Hestus glance at each other. I can just imagine the bets they're planning to place on what Francine was referring to. Hopefully neither of their guesses will come close to the truth.

With tentative adjustments, I settle back into the mound of pillows behind me, then glance between my two brothers. The older dark haired, the younger fair. One bulky and broad, the other lean and toned. One brutally honest, the other tactfully intuitive. Total opposites, yet equally deadly on the hunting field.

But there are still days I want to punch both their lights out.

I look around the room. "Where's Dad?"

Hestus huffs out a deep breath. "He left on an impromptu hunting expedition, looking for an Yranum colony."

I snort my derision. Figures. Anything to avoid parenting responsibilities. "Didn't he just come back from one?"

They both nod.

I roll my eyes. I don't know why I keep bothering to assume our father wants anything to do with us—with me in particular. "I know the Yranum blood supplies are getting more scarce as the years go by, but I didn't realize it was getting *that* rare to warrant so many Yranum hunts in such a short period of time."

"Uncle Matthias is back," says Quill. "Dad's trying to avoid getting roped into another one of Uncle Matthias's 'adventures to the end of the rainbow.'" Quill's voice rises an octave, as if narrating a kiddie cartoon.

"Ah... now that makes more sense." Still, I can't stop my shoulders from sagging; the disappointment is bone deep—it's almost a part of me now. My father wasn't present much during my childhood. His lack of concern for Quill, Hestus, and me became even more evident when my mother passed away.

Shoving that old resentment away, I ask with heavy sarcasm, "What is Uncle Matthias after this time? A herd of unicorns?"

"Not quite," says Hestus. "He's back to being obsessed with tracking down the mythological winged shifters."

"He's got Axel out there now recruiting the gullible for their next expedition," says Quill.

I sigh in disbelief. "After his last few failed expeditions, he'd have a better chance finding recruits for a mission to Jupiter."

"No kidding." Hestus shakes his head. "Remember what happened to Curtis?"

"Don't tell me you still believe those rumors?" says Quill.

"Here we go again." I stifle a groan and settle farther back into my pillows, anticipating the same old argument I've heard over and over for the last eight months.

"Why not?" Hestus ignores my remark and takes Quill's bait—hook, line, and sinker. "You don't think Uncle Matthias is capable of killing Curtis?"

"I don't know..." A corner of Quill's mouth tweaks in contemplation.

"Think about it, Quill," says Hestus. "How many times did you see Curtis bested in the sparring rounds in training? Not to mention, Curtis already had four colors in his hunting amulet, and I bet he would have had his fifth by now if he hadn't been blindsided."

"Hmm..." Quill pauses for a second. "Don't get me wrong, Curtis was an avid hunter. But even the best of us can make fatal mistakes in the hunting field. And as for

Uncle Matthias, well, we can't really argue that he's borderline psycho, but breaking the hunter code?"

"Curtis had his head cut clean off." Hestus enunciates each syllable, as if speaking to an imbecile. "Curtis—a hunter. A *human* hunter. What do you think the hunter code, '*We don't kill our own,*' means? We don't kill humans, and we definitely don't kill hunters."

Quill snorts. "Come on. It could just as well have been a shifter who cut Curtis's head off. Hunters die all the time. It's not uncommon for fewer people to return after a hunting mission."

"Curtis returned all right, just minus a head," I add.

"True, but shifters aren't exactly in the habit of lopping heads off," says Hestus, ignoring me. "If anything, Uncle Matthias seems to be making a habit of losing people in these expeditions of his. Besides, there were half a dozen hunters—*witnesses*—there, and I've heard at least two of them say it was definitely Uncle Matthias who chopped Curtis's head off, not one of the Veniri shifters."

"We've all heard the rumors, Hestus," I say. "And anyway, the Grimvast twins don't count. We all know how those two like to talk up a story. Whether they were eyewitnesses or not, we can't exactly take their word as gospel."

"Still"—Hestus crosses his arms—"you can't deny Uncle Matthias is more unhinged than normal."

"That's one thing I agree with." Quill scratches at his chin. "You know, I thought Uncle Matthias went a little nuts when Lyla-Rose was killed, but I just put it down to him being a grieving father, you know?"

"Yeah, but he's gone waaay downhill with the crazy, especially since Sagan..." Hestus's eyes glaze over, and he stares into the distance.

A pang of emotion hits me in the chest at the mention of

Lyla-Rose and her older brother, Sagan. I eye both my brothers and huff out a sigh. "So I'm assuming there's still no word from Sagan?"

Both shake their heads, their expressions hardening.

"Nothing," confirms Hestus.

Quill groans. "Just get over it, Nika. Sagan's been missing for months. If our cousin wants to take the coward's way out of this life and take off without even a 'see ya later, mate,' then he can be my guest."

"Don't ever call him a coward," I growl. "He's proven over and over again that he's better than the rest of us put together."

"We don't even know for sure what happened," Hestus interjects. "He just disappeared without a trace after he helped that slith. There's a chance he might actually be in trouble."

"Sagan? In trouble? Highly unlikely." Quill scoffs. "One, Sagan's not stupid enough to help any shifters escape, let alone a slith. And two, Uncle Matthias was the one leading the hunters who went looking for Sagan. And it was Uncle Matthias who told us that Sagan ran off."

I frown. "Yeah, but how much do you trust what Uncle Matthias says?"

"What's not to trust? It's Uncle Matthias." Quill throws his hands up in exasperation. "Yeah, he's a little nuts, but why would he lie about his own son?"

"You know, I've always wondered what's so special about that slith," Hestus muses. "Out of all the sliths we've captured over the years, why did Sagan choose to help that one escape?"

"Don't be stupid," Quill snaps. "If you guys think Sagan would kill one of his own and then choose a slith over us, then you're both more deluded than I thought."

Hestus and I share a glance. I'm almost relieved to see Hestus's furrowed brows mirror my own suspicion over the situation.

"You both need to get over it and accept that he's gone. If Sagan's not back by now, then he's never coming back," says Quill.

I wind and unwind a loop of IV line around my finger. Sagan is one of the strongest people I've ever known. He's too strong and capable to just be killed or to keel over and die. Even Quill used the word *gone*, not *dead*.

On the other hand, it's been about eight months since the three of us saw our favorite cousin. The last we heard, he disappeared from the barracks on the same night, coincidentally, a Veniri shifter also went missing from one of the harvesting rooms. Sagan's father, Matthias, and his sidekick Axel, along with a band of Uncle Matthias's hunter buddies, went in search of Sagan and the missing Veniri. When they returned to the barracks, all carried with them the faint stench of smoke and kerosene, as well as three live Veniri in tow, but no Sagan.

Whatever went down, Uncle Matthias and his cronies have been tight-lipped on the details.

Speculation among the hunters birthed a few scenarios, some involving Sagan turning his back on the hunter life and setting up shop as a small-time hitman in a suburban neighborhood. Other rumors—whispered with more caution—suggest that Matthias's jealousy over his son's notorious reputation finally came to a head. After all, the only way a hunter knows how to deal with a problem is to eliminate it, one way or another.

I'm not one to play the gossip game; usually I don't care what the latest harebrained rumor going around is. But it makes my blood boil when stories of Sagan's alleged murder are spread around with enthusiastic exaggeration. I, for one, don't believe Sagan could have been bested by that seedy hunter Axel, who always skulks around with his crystal trident, ready and waiting to kiss Uncle Matthias's butt.

If I'm being honest, though, the stories of Sagan leaving to start a brand-new happy life away from the hunters stings a little more.

I quickly lost count of how many times I went searching for him after he went missing. I looked everywhere I could imagine he might hide out, starting with a small cavern we used to play in during our annual Branstone family camping trip out in the middle of a national park. I searched that cavern from top to bottom, even broadening my search to the surrounding wilderness, but there was no sign he'd been there.

Still I searched.

I persuaded Quill and Hestus to help me look on a few occasions. Days turned into weeks and then into months, and still I found nothing to prove Sagan was alive and well. It became hard to convince my brothers to continue helping me.

Maybe Sagan is dead...

I give a slight shake of my head. No, I still can't bring myself to entertain that thought. It's Sagan, after all. If anyone could disappear without leaving even a trace of their shadow behind, it would be him.

But he promised not to leave me behind.

I shut down that errant thought. I can't afford to fantasize about running away, especially not in front of my brothers. They'd be able to discern my weakness too easily.

"Here, Nika."

I blink, breaking out of my reverie, and look up to find Hestus holding his hand out.

"They had to take this off you when you went in for surgery."

In his palm is my hunter amulet. The black metal chain spills down between his fingers. For a moment, I'm startled that I didn't notice it missing. I never take my hunting amulet off; most hunters don't. How else are we supposed to flaunt our blood colors and brag about our skill level?

I take it from him. The black metal is still warm from being in Hestus's pocket.

Instead of immediately putting it on, I admire it for a moment. Our Branstone family crest makes up the amulet's detailed design, and embedded in the crest are ten tiny glass vials. The filled vials give off a subtle glow, even in the daylight—silver blood from a Lycan shifter, teal blood from a Veniri shifter, magenta from a Magneii shifter... and orange?

I raise an eyebrow and look up at my brothers.

"I took the liberty of filling the vial with the Jiovis blood for you while you were in surgery," says Hestus.

I'm slightly shocked at the kind gesture. There's not exactly room for many endearments in a hunter family, and judging by the slight scowl on Quill's face, he doesn't approve of Hestus tilting the amulet competition in my favor. Quill was probably hoping my hunting accident caused everyone to forget I was, in fact, the one who killed the Jiovis shifter during our last hunt.

I filled my third vial the same night Quill and Hestus filled their third. Memories of that night still send a shiver down my spine, an echo of the supercharged adrenaline that was pumping through my veins. That night was rich with shifter killings.

As much as a small part of me is proud every time my brothers fill another of their vials, I never admit it out loud.

From the moment we were all initiated and received our hunting amulets, it's been a race to see who can fill all ten of their vials first. And it's a race I intend to win.

Yeah, yeah, good luck with that, sneers the cynical side of me. In the hunter world, three vials is when other hunters start paying attention to you. With five, you can class yourself a small-time hero in your own barracks. If you're lucky enough to survive long enough to fill eight vials, you basically become a legend; not just your own barracks but hunter barracks all over the country know and respect your name.

But ten vials?

I almost scoff. Ten vials is unheard of, next to impossible. I've never met anyone with seven vials filled, let alone ten.

And yet, I only have six more to fill.

I brush my thumb over the cool glass of my latest blood sample. The glowing liquid shines with the bright orange from a Jiovis shifter.

The Jiovis shifters are like walking, talking metal statues with shifter energies connected to Jupiter. Before my last hunt, I'd only ever seen one at a distance, but it's well known that to hunt one down, you have to be extra vigilant against their electrical abilities.

Vivid memories flicker like a strobe light in my mind as I recall the events of my latest hunt. The hunt was even more tantalizing than usual, as I'd outwitted and outmaneuvered my brothers to claim the kill shot for myself.

Those memories should be ones of glory when I think of them, worthy of boasting about to anyone within hearing range. I should be joyous. I should be goading my brothers with incessant gloating. I claimed my fourth color on my amulet before they did.

Except that my memories of claiming the Jiovis kill are tainted now, overshadowed by my encounter with Troy's ill-aimed Luxium grenade. A flash of magenta light washes through my mind, and bile once again rises and burns the back of my throat.

...having children is no longer possible.

For most of my life, I believed filling the vials in my hunting amulet would be my greatest goal. Hunting shifters and filling vials is all I've ever known; it's all that's been expected of me. Since my mother's death, throwing myself into the hunting frenzy along with the others has been easy. It's the one thing that stopped the grief of my mother's death from consuming me completely.

But now, with Francine's shocking revelation, I've had a sudden perspective shift. A different lifelong dream I've imagined for myself—a soul-deep hope I've never dared to speak aloud—will never become a reality.

As I tenderly lay a hand over my abdomen, I can't help but wonder if my latest and greatest achievement in filling my fourth vial was worth the very permanent payoff.

Squeezing my eyes shut, I try my best to banish Francine's echoing voice from my mind. Instead, I trace each empty glass vial with a finger. I imagine how radiant my amulet would look with the luminescent blood of all ten shifter species, and I force myself to revive the determination to achieve all my dreams.

But not all your dreams are going to come true now, whispers a brutal thought. Another echo of Francine's voice warbles through my mind as a stab of agony shoots through my abdomen, as if to ensure I never forget.

My fingers tighten around my amulet, and the edges cut into my flesh, not quite hard enough to draw blood. Every inch of my body tenses as I begin to panic. No matter how hard I try, I can't shake the tormenting voice.

...*having children is no longer possible.*

My teeth bite down on my tongue, flooding my mouth with saliva, pain, and blood. My life, my future, is no longer as clear as I once thought it to be. There's only one thing I know for sure.

I will not cry.

Chapter Three

HEAVENS ABOVE, it's good to finally be done with my last physical therapy session. Francine always inconveniently booked them during the general training and sparring times over the last four weeks.

Once I was discharged from the infirmary, Francine stayed pretty involved in my rehabilitation by organizing a stringent schedule of light exercise, massages, pain management, laser therapy to reduce scar tissue, and a whole bunch of other stuff to restore my body back to hunting condition. Yet if you ask me, Francine just wanted to flex her authority as the head doctor of our barracks. A few too many times, she threatened to revoke my role as a hunter and reduce me to permanent service duties if I tried to rejoin the general hunting schedule prematurely.

This was the first time in my hunting career I was harmed quite seriously. My rehabilitation would have been drawn out for much longer if not for my semiregular doses of Ylixium, under Francine's strict supervision. Constant eye checks were a must to ensure my irises weren't showing any indication of bleaching—the telltale sign of an Ylixium addict, and also a warning that the Ylixium buildup in the body is reaching toxic levels. Thankfully, no grueling detox was required for me.

Of everything I went through during my four weeks of rehabilitation, the "rest" times turned out to be the worst. It was all I could do to keep from going insane during the long periods of silence with only the torturous echoes of Francine's voice for company, whispering about what had been taken from me.

The moment my rehab is done and Francine sets me free, I make a beeline to my personal sleeping hub on the far side of the barracks. My room is located in a special division set apart for the hunting families who established the barracks several generations ago. The area also has an exclusive gym, heated indoor pool, recreational room, and dining area, but my brothers and I generally prefer to mingle with the rest of the riff-raff in the common areas. And whenever I get sick of those morons, I'm always relieved to have my own private space to return to.

As soon as I enter my room, I'm overcome with the desire to lie down on my own bed and hide out in the only place I feel safe. Fighting the temptation, I stay only long enough to have a quick shower in my en suite and change into my black hunting leathers. I've been cooped up long enough in the barracks; it's about time I get back out on a hunt.

I check my watch and *tsk*. It's late afternoon, about half an hour shy of sunset. The daily training session is well and truly over, and hunters will soon be gearing up for the upcoming evening hunt.

Quill and Hestus visited me a handful of times during my rehab when it suited them. Most times Hestus came bearing sweet treats he'd snagged from the cafeteria. My brothers didn't come to visit me today, but I'm pretty sure I'll find them in one of the weapons rooms around this time.

I weave my way through the passageways toward the other side of the barracks. Much like the several other barracks scattered around the country, ours is built like a large bunker within the side of a mountain out in the desert. The closest signs of civilization are at least an hour's drive away.

The internal footprint of our barracks is equal to the span of several football fields. In addition to the sleeping quarters, the cafeteria, and the infirmary, our barracks holds everything a person needs to lead a substantial hunting career, with training rooms, weapons rooms, the vehicle foyer, and even the harvesting rooms for extracting and processing the loot from our prey. Not only is the barracks our home away from home; it's our work place, leisure land, hospital, and crisis center all rolled into one. Everyone earns their place by training and hunting to add to the barracks' wealth and prestige.

Everyone, that is, except me for the past four weeks. I've done diddly-squat to earn my place, leeching food, medication, and whatever else was necessary to get back out hunting.

For a second my FOMO kicks in, and I have the irrational thought that my brothers and the rest of their hunting crew have already left without me.

My impatience drives me to take a shortcut through the labyrinth of harvesting and shifter holding rooms instead of going all the way around as I usually do. I'd never admit it to anyone, but the harvesting area of the barracks really creeps me out. The tortured wails of the shifters and endless begging for mercy have starred in my nightmares on more than one occasion.

Killing or knocking a shifter unconscious is, without a doubt, something I'm good at. I'll be the first to admit I'm far from being a saint, but one has to be some kind of high-functioning sadist to be involved in the harvesting department of our hunting empire.

Faint, guttural screams start to drift out to me the closer I get to the harvesting rooms. Holding back a wince, I pick up some speed, though not too much; I don't want to give anyone the impression I can't handle this place. With every step I take, the harrowing screams grow louder, like a twisted, disturbed choir.

Some shifters need to remain alive while they're stripped of their profitable parts. One example is the reptilian-like Veniri with their Diamantium bones and spikes. The Veniri have the toughest hide of all the shifters, and ironically, only their own crystal shards pierce through their scaly flesh—like a hot knife through cotton candy. It's practically a no-brainer for hunters to utilize the Diamantium in all kinds of melee weapons.

Another wretched scream warbles down the empty hallways. I'll never understand why the harvesters don't just inject the shifters with some kind of anesthetic instead of putting up with that continual ruckus.

Itching to clamp my hands over my ears, I turn a corner and find myself in a hallway lined with doors. Most are closed, except one that's slightly ajar. I'm about to walk past when a voice from beyond the door shouts out a curse.

I've never been one to eavesdrop, but for some reason, I can't make myself move away. Something about the tone of the conversation catches my attention.

Another loud expletive rings out.

"*Damn that slith queen,*" the same voice seethes. "Damn that scaly demon to the fiery pit of Hell!"

The hairs on the back of my neck rise when I realize who's speaking. Uncle Matthias. I'd know that sly voice anywhere.

A thunk follows, like the sound of a fist slamming against a table.

"She thinks she can deny me the rest of those tomes," continues Uncle Matthias. "You just wait. I'll get the rest of those tomes. And her spangle too! No matter how much she denies it, I know she's got it. I'll wrench it out of her dead hand if I have to and raze her pitiful queendom to the ground."

I frown. Tomes? Spangle? What the heck is he babbling on about?

"Yeah, but how are we going to do that?" That gravelly voice has to belong to Axel—no surprise there. Wherever Uncle Matthias is, that seedy hunter lingers close by like a fetid odor. "We're still no closer to finding the slith queendom than before we started making deals with those scaled sliths. And now we've lost our leverage, especially since we haven't come through with any of her bounties— which she *loves* reminding us of each time we see her."

Again I frown. Axel has to be joking, right? Hunters never take on a bounty job from a shifter. We hunt them; we don't work *for* them. What is Uncle Matthias doing making deals with a shifter—and with a *Veniri queen* of all beings? On top of that, what could the Veniri possibly have that can't be taken by force?

"What I really wanna know," continues Axel, "is what that Violet girl, Gloria Chambers, and that Nathan slith have done that's so bad the slith queen comes to the likes of us to hunt them down. What's so special about those three?"

"That's none of my concern. And don't remind me

about *Nathan Delano*," says Uncle Matthias with undiluted venom in his voice.

Axel *tsk*s. "You gotta stop letting that slith get to you. He's locked up on Tempecrest Island, although why you put him and those other two sliths there instead of just gutting them and harvesting their bones, I'll never understand."

My eyebrows fly up. Sliths at Tempecrest? Now that's interesting.

Tempecrest Island is basically the devil's playground and a high-end gambling addict's dream. Of all the different shifter species out there, Lycans are the ones we hunters encounter the most. Nine times out of ten, their silver blood is the first color added to a hunter's amulet. Ultimately, though, there are only so many of those werewolf shifters a hunter can kill before the thrill starts to get old.

A few generations ago, the most depraved hunters gathered up a surplus horde of Lycans and tossed them into an abandoned island prison they'd remodeled into a gladiatorial arena. Despite the fact that the hunters are meant to be a secret society, it didn't take long for the most twisted billionaires and perverted trust fund kids to hear about the Lycan gladiators and start throwing their fortunes at Tempecrest. With the frequent spilling of silver blood and the promise of a spectacular show, the hunter empire gained a new and extremely lucrative source of revenue. The high-stakes winnings have even tempted Quill and Hestus to waste their earnings on some big-name Lycan fighters.

I've never taken much of an interest in the goings on of Tempecrest, but I'm still shocked to find myself in agreement with Axel. Why have slith gladiators? Lycan leather is still salvageable even after a spectacle worthy of Maximus Meridius, but every other shifter is much more profitable with as few broken bones, severed limbs, and puncture wounds as possible.

"I don't see why you should be complaining, Axel," says Uncle Matthias. "Don't pretend you haven't been cashing in on those sliths at Tempecrest."

Axel chuckles. "What can I say? I'm an opportunist. And who knew Nathan and that other slith—Thane, I think his name is—would prove to be gladiator superstars? Although I'm surprised that slippery slith Kronan has lasted as long as he has."

"So you admit it, I was right to throw those three into Tempecrest."

"Perhaps, but I also think you should call it what it is— at least to yourself."

Uncle Matthias hesitates before asking, "And what is that?"

"Revenge. You're pissed off your son chose that slith over you, but with Sagan still missing, you can't punish him, so you're punishing Nathan. And death by harvest isn't good enough for that slith. You want his suffering dragged out for as long as possible because your son turned on you."

"He didn't just turn on me," Uncle Matthias spits. "When that boy helped that slith escape, he turned his back on the entire hunter legacy. Everything that I, my family, and my ancestors built—Sagan tossed it all away. And for what? All for a slith."

My jaw nearly drops on the floor. So it's true after all. Sagan *did* help that slith escape. But why? Before more questions begin to rattle through my brain, I focus back on the conversation within the room.

"Hmm... If you ask me, it still doesn't add up. Perhaps Sagan had other reasons for helping the slith," says Axel. "Regardless, he's not here to explain himself."

"I don't need an explanation," growls Matthias. "That boy has taken every chance to humiliate me and desecrate everything I do. He may as well have laughed in my face when I tried to bring him in on my search for the winged shifters."

A heavy sigh follows, although I'm not sure if it's from Uncle Matthias or Axel.

"Getting anyone to believe in the myth of the winged shifters has been a challenge," says Axel.

"But it's not a myth!" Something crashes to the floor.

"I know, I know," says Axel, his placating voice undercut by chagrin. "We just need to prove it so that everyone else can believe—"

"But we have the proof! You want proof? I'll show you the proof."

My eyebrows shoot skyward. Is Uncle Matthias serious? He has proof that winged shifters actually exist?

This I have to see.

Cautiously, I lean in to peek around the door. The room beyond is the size of a small office. Someone's shoved a desk aside to make way for piles of stacked papers, documents, and random boxes overflowing with various items I can't quite make out. The walls, however, are covered from ceiling to floor with maps, newspaper articles, and hand-sketched drawings. I recognize the archaic depictions of humans with wings stretching out from their backs. Quill and Hestus are right; Uncle Matthias *is* obsessed.

Axel, with his scruffy gray beard, looks more like the poster child for a local biker gang. He stands to one side of the room while his weapon of choice, an obnoxious Diamantium trident, leans against the wall just out of arm's reach. Like every other hunter, Axel is dressed from head to toe in hunter-black Lycan leathers. He crosses his arms over his chest and slowly taps his foot as Uncle Matthias hauls over a suitcase.

After gently laying the suitcase on the floor, Uncle Matthias heaves out a massive golden tome. By the way he almost buckles under the weight of it, I can only assume the entire thing is made of actual gold. Colored gemstones embedded in the pages sparkle each time Uncle Matthias flips a solid page.

He stabs a finger at a two-page spread. "Here's your proof!"

From this angle, I can't make out the finer details, but the familiar shapes look very much like the Egyptian-esque profile drawings pinned to the wall behind the two men. The image appears to be of a woman with outstretched arms, and from her shoulders fan a pair of magnificent feathered wings.

None of the stories I've heard about the mythological winged shifters can fully confirm what they looked like, but one thing all the stories agree on is that their wings were made of feathers, each one royal blue, emerald green, and tipped with shining gold. Sure enough, all three of those colors shine brilliantly on the golden page in Uncle Matthias's tome.

Disappointment crashes through me. How is a stupid image of a woman with cosplay wings in a gaudy, ancient-looking tome proof of anything?

Axel begins to voice exactly what I'm thinking when a hand clamps on my shoulder.

"Nika?"

Heart pounding, I spin and come face-to-face with Troy.

At the sight of him, my initial shock morphs into hatred and anger. Flashes of that unfortunate hunting night strobe through my mind—Troy's face, his Luxium grenade, the almighty explosion of magenta fire, the most severe pain I've ever experienced ripping through my body.

A small, rational part of me reasons that Troy had no intention of harming me. Yet the consequences of his misjudgment can never be erased, and Francine's voice echoing through my skull only pours fuel on the raging inferno of emotion.

...having children is no longer possible.

My hands close into fists.

Troy glances at the door he caught me peeking through. He's clearly figured out I'm being a shady eavesdropper, but when his eyes find mine, every inch of his demeanor switches from judgment to judged.

Troy tugs on his earlobe. "It's, uh... good to see you're out of the infirmary."

"No thanks to you," I hiss through clenched teeth.

Troy winces. "Listen, I've been meaning to come and see you, but..." He shuffles from one foot to the other. "About that night, with the grenade... I didn't think you'd—"

Crack.

Troy's head snaps to the side.

My chest heaves with shallow, ragged breaths, and my knuckles are already beginning to throb from my hook punch. But the pain in my hand pales in comparison to the agony I've suffered in my body and am still suffering in my soul.

Clutching his cheek, Troy regards me with shock, then his eyes quickly narrow in anger.

The temptation to strike him again is almost overwhelming, but I know if I do, I won't stop until I've beaten him to a pulp.

"If you ever come near me again, *I will kill you.*" My shaky voice is low, almost a whisper.

Troy's expression turns calculated. He was initiated into our barracks only about eight months ago, and if I had to guess, I'd say he's two or three years younger than me— perhaps about nineteen or twenty. For some reason, he also has some kind of fascination with Quill and Hestus. He never hid the fact that he looks up to them, and after a lot of nagging on Troy's part, my brothers finally allowed him to hunt with us.

Unfortunately for Troy, he still isn't high enough in the ranks for anything he says to hold much sway.

A series of emotions flickers across Troy's features; I can almost hear the gears cranking in his mind.

If he walks away now, he'll worry I'll spread the report of his cowardice to the rest of the hunters. If he retaliates with his own violence, then no matter the outcome, he risks my brothers hunting him down for revenge—not necessarily to defend my honor, but to defend the Branstone name and legacy.

I register a scattering of faint bruises over his face and neck. My brothers never mentioned Troy's name during my rehabilitation, but I've no doubt Troy's collection of bruises are a reminder of the punishment Quill and Hestus dealt out while I was recovering. And considering it's been a couple weeks since the incident, either no one was kind enough to give him some Ylixium vials to speed up the healing process, or Troy isn't ruthless enough to steal his own.

For several long, rib-cracking heartbeats, Troy stands as still as a statue. Then his narrow gaze focuses on something behind me.

I toss a glance over my shoulder to find Uncle Matthias

and Axel standing in the now wide-open doorway. Both hold bemused expressions, laced with the all-too-familiar hunter bloodlust—yet there's something else in the way Uncle Matthias looks at me, and only me.

In contrast to Axel's leathers, Uncle Matthias is dressed in a crisp gunmetal-gray suit, and he keeps his salt-and-pepper hair cropped short and tidy, matching his trimmed goatee. The formal attire gives him a dignified yet much more sinister air than his biker-bearded acquaintance.

The thought that my uncle's guessed I was peeking in on their private conversation makes my stomach drop. For an uncomfortably long moment, his eyes stay fixed on me.

Then his mouth curls up into a predatory grin that sends ice-cold chills down my spine.

"Is this boy bothering you, Nika?"

It takes me a moment to grasp Uncle Matthias's question. No one has ever asked me that, especially not Uncle Matthias. He believes the bullied deserve to suffer—the result of their own weakness in not standing up for themselves.

With practiced ease, my face smooths into impassivity. "Uncle Matthias, I didn't realize you were back."

Uncle Matthias raises an eyebrow, no doubt noticing I avoided his question.

"How was your mission?" I almost cringe. What is wrong with me? I'm not one for small talk, let alone encouraging Uncle Matthias to warble on about his psychotic obsessions. But I can't deny that my situation with Troy is sensitive, and deflection seems better than having Uncle Matthias and Axel bear witness to my near meltdown.

"My *mission* was fine, thank you." There's a hard edge to his voice, but his disturbing grin never falters.

"Uh, pardon me, Mr. Branstone. I'm Troy, and I heard

31

you were planning another expedition and interested in recruiting—"

"Who are you?" My uncle turns his penetrating gaze on Troy.

"I'm, um... I'm Troy, Mr. Branstone." Troy drops his hand from his jaw and reaches out to offer a handshake.

Axel grins as Uncle Matthias stares at Troy's hand as if it's carrying Ebola.

"Troy?" My uncle pauses. "I think I've heard of you. You're one of this year's new recruits to the barracks. If I'm not mistaken, I've also heard a little story about an unfortunate incident involving a Luxium grenade. Correct?" The glint in Uncle Matthias's eye turns flinty.

Troy's gulp is audible, and his mottled face turns a pallid gray. After a beat, he drops his hand and shuffles from one foot to the other.

"I think you've mistaken him for someone else," I blurt, then almost shake my head in startled confusion. What on earth made me say that?

The shock on Troy's face almost reflects what I feel on the inside.

Uncle Matthias slowly returns his attention to me. "Oh, really?"

Before I can think it through, I nod.

The expressions on Uncle Matthias's and Axel's faces confirm neither believe my lame-ass confession. But only then do I realize two things.

First, I don't need anyone stepping in on my hostility with Troy, especially not Uncle Matthias. I definitely *do not* want to owe a debt to the likes of him. Besides, I highly suspect my brothers have already dealt with Troy. If I feel inclined to take it any further, that's for me to decide.

Second, I can't deny I hate Troy with every fiber of my

being, but that doesn't mean I want to put him on Uncle Matthias's radar. An influx of memories from my childhood, particularly the ones of Uncle Matthias training Sagan, induce a slight wave of nausea.

I discovered long ago that my uncle is capable of much more than what I can—or want—to even comprehend.

Still, I'm not quite sure if it's fear of my uncle or fear of what will happen to Troy that drives me to continue with the blatant lie.

"You're thinking of another Troy." I cast my face in a confident mask, my eyes never wavering from Uncle Matthias's steely gaze.

Finally, Uncle Matthias releases a chuckle. "It's not often I'm wrong, and yet, who am I to question my own niece?" He shifts his cool gaze back to Troy. "It seems our friend... Troy is a little lost and needs some help finding his way in the barracks." He gestures to Axel. "Would you mind being of assistance?"

Before I can react, Axel swoops in and wraps a heavy arm around Troy's shoulders, not giving him much choice but to walk with the burly, gray-bearded hunter down the hallway.

Before the two disappear around the corner, I'm sure I hear Axel begin his well-known spiel for recruiting the gullible for Uncle Matthias's fruitless expeditions. The interaction seems casual enough, but it doesn't stop a shudder from running through me. Why do I feel like Axel is leading a lamb to the slaughter?

"Nika? Did you hear what I said?"

I blink. Before I can worry any more about Troy, I'm once again caught in Uncle Matthias's unnerving gaze. "You said something?"

Uncle Matthias's smile doesn't quite reach his eyes. "I

was saying, I've been hearing about your exploits while I've been away. You've got four colors now, huh? You know I could use someone like you—"

"Uh, thanks, Uncle Matthias, but I'm still recovering from my last hunting trip." The words tumble out of my mouth. I take a backward step and point my thumb over my shoulder. "I've also got to get going. I'm running late to meet up with my brothers."

Uncle Matthias regards me with an arched eyebrow as I take another step back. "Of course. I wouldn't want to keep you from your brothers. But next time you're free, Nika, I'd love to have a little chat."

I only just stop myself from cringing; I can only guess what his idea of a "little chat" entails. Not trusting myself to say anything further, I give a final nod and turn my back on him.

The harrowing screams of the harvesting chambers grow louder as I speed-walk through, yet I can't help but think I'd rather deal with this auditory nightmare than one more second with Uncle Matthias.

Chapter Four

"WELL, well. Look who's decided to grace us with her presence." Deshawn Grimvast elbows his brother Jakai as I approach them.

"Long time no see, Branstone." Jakai continues to load up his bandolier with crystal throwing daggers, but his teeth flash in a mischievous grin. "So you've finally decided to drag your lazy ass out from rehab, huh?"

"Aww," I coo, "don't tell me you guys have missed me kicking your asses in every hunt."

"As if." Deshawn scoffs. "Why they call you the Branstone Iron Maiden is a mystery to me. We know the truth, Nika. You're not as badass as you make everyone else believe."

"Oh, really?" I step up to Deshawn. The jerk is half a head taller than me, and I have to crane my neck to glare down my nose at him. "So if you guys are so 'badass,' then why haven't either of you earned any new colors in the four weeks I've been away?"

Jakai's and Deshawn's grins falter as I make a show of looking down at their amulets, both with only two vials filled. I tut and pull my lips into an overemphasized "poor baby" pout.

Jakai's expression clouds over into nonchalance. It's a mask to cover his humiliation—something I easily recognize. I've had a lot of practice with my own masquerade; it takes one to know one.

As for his brother, a muscle twitches in Deshawn's jaw, and a corner of his mouth curls up in a sneer.

Good. My fists clench at my sides. All I need is a single flinch from Deshawn, and this sparring match is on.

I'm ready for a pre-hunt warm-up.

Francine may have made me promise I wouldn't go hunting for at least another week to ensure my internal wounds fully healed, but what she doesn't know won't kill her. And killing is all I'm good at. Who else would I be if not a hunter? Besides, I no longer have the option to be anything else—at least not what I might have aspired to be.

The hollow ache in my chest has become unbearable, overshadowing any lingering twinges of physical pain. Without hunting as an outlet over the past four weeks, my seething anger has turned into its own special kind of torture—but at least the fury is easier to handle than the endless void of despair. When my mother died, I learned the hard way that grief and sadness are not emotions welcome in a barracks; hunters don't deal well with problems that can't be solved with weapons or fists.

But weapons and fists are still my favorite distractions—anything to escape this internal agony. I need to hit something. I'm well past due.

Deshawn studies me with narrowed eyes, but I'm not going to strike first. That would be too easy. Unfortunately for me, though, I picked the wrong target. I should have known Deshawn isn't the type to go on the offensive.

A few heartbeats pass, and Deshawn and I are still in a staring showdown, which is a mistake. It's given my mind room to dredge up what I'm trying to avoid.

...having children is no longer possible.

I bite down, and a familiar pain shoots through my tongue. My new habit hasn't yet allowed my tongue to heal, but the pain in my mouth is nothing compared to the growing, much deeper ache threatening to consume me.

My eyes begin to sting, but with practiced control, I force the sensation away. *I will not cry.* Especially in the weapons room with half a dozen other hunters stocking up for the night's excursion.

"Hey, Nika. Think fast."

Instinct takes over, and I catch the sheathed crystal throwing dagger Jakai has launched at my head.

He snorts a laugh. "Well, look at that. Branstone still has the reflexes. But does she still have what it takes to keep up with the rest of us out on the hunting grounds?"

Deshawn huffs in frustration at his brother's interruption. When my attention returns to him, he leans closer, scrutinizing me up and down with deep brown eyes. If I didn't know better, I'd think the guy's assessing me like a choice piece of steak.

I slam my palm into his chest, and he stumbles back a couple feet. "Shove off, Grimvast," I growl.

"What's the matter, dollface?" Deshawn taunts. "Worried you'll get hurt before you get a chance to go hunting again?"

"Worry about yourself," I warn. "We all know you couldn't track down a shifter if it was biting you on the ass. And another thing—*don't call me dollface*."

Jakai guffaws.

Deshawn flicks a glance at his brother and then at Quill

and Hestus, who've joined in with the laughter. The angry smolder in Deshawn's eyes fizzles into humiliation, then finally lands on resentment. "Watch yourself, Branstone," he says to me. "Or it might be your ass I mistake as shifter prey tonight."

I sneer. "Yeah, yeah. You'd have to get your head out of your own ass first."

Jakai hoots out another laugh as I push past his brother, making sure to clip him hard on the shoulder as I do. Deshawn's answering shove sends a shock of pain through my abdomen. I grit my teeth to force down a startled yelp, then continue over to the wall of net launchers.

"Why'd you do that?" I hear Deshawn hiss to his brother.

"I was saving your ass."

"As if, bro. I totally had her. The Branstone Iron Maiden was mine. At least she was until you threw a dagger at her head."

Jakai sniggers. "Whatever, bro. From where I was standing, she was locked and loaded to rip your head off. A second longer and you were going to get slammed."

"As if. I would have taken her down."

With a casualness I'm not quite feeling, I make a show of examining the dagger Jakai hurled at me, all while pretending I can't hear him continue to scold his brother for not being careful with the girl who's still recovering from a Luxium grenade blast.

"What's the big deal?" Deshawn retorts with hushed indignance. "She's a Branstone. It's not like they can't take what they dish."

"True," says Jakai. "But not all the other Branstones have been hit with a Luxium grenade and lived to tell the tale. Cut Nika some slack. She might have some sweet, honest-to-goodness luck on her side, but from what Hestus said, she's acquired some major damage."

Jakai then lowers his voice, and I don't quite catch the rest of what he says.

Right then, Hestus and Quill come over to me. Quill homes in on the net launchers, while Hestus regards me with a knowing look before subtly glancing over at the Grimvast twins. No doubt he overheard what they're saying.

"So, you couldn't help but squeal to the twins about me, huh?" I toss the sheathed throwing knife onto the weapons station in front of me. It lands with a dull thud on the green-tinged metal surface. "Is everyone now gossiping about poor little Nika?"

Hestus doesn't reply, but I can't stand the way he's looking at me. Why can't he be more like Quill—self-centered and ignorant instead of intuitive?

Breaking eye contact, I grab a few net canisters from the canister drawer.

"How are you feeling?" Hestus asks.

"Fine." I force the word out as flatly as possible before shoving my net launcher into one of the empty hunting packs.

Quill's over at the next station, loading up a bandolier with more Diamantium throwing blades than necessary. He's a lousy shot when it comes to throwing knives, so I suppose he needs more than his fair share. I don't know why he insists on using that type of weapon. Brute strength and aggressive bludgeoning are his forte, not anything that requires stealth and finesse.

"Here you go, Quill." I unhook three more throwing daggers from the wall brackets and place them on the counter in front of him. "The more you have, the better the odds at least one will hit your target."

Quill throws me a glare that's enough to make anyone else quiver in their boots. The Grimvast twins chuckle behind us, and Quill unleashes his rage on them in a torrent of verbal abuse. Hestus just gives me an accusatory look and shakes his head.

With a shrug, I grab my backpack and head to the next station. But when my eyes land on the weapons stacked neatly on the shelves, a small gasp escapes my lips.

The rows of Luxium grenades seem to taunt me, each one about half the height and half the diameter of a soda can. The small viewing window in each glows with the distinct magenta light of an inferno-fueled Luxium—the energy core extracted from a Magneii shifter's skull.

The collection sits in unassuming silence, but I'm not fooled. I know what they're capable of—the ear-splitting blast, the blinding light, the searing hellfire, and the devastating carnage. It all replays in my mind as though it happened only a few minutes ago.

I place a hand on my belly, just above the adhesive wound dressings beneath my shirt.

"Uh, I don't think we need any of those tonight," says Hestus. With a gentle nudge, he moves me on to the next weapons station.

Chapter Five

Quill parks the Land Rover Defender by an overflowing dumpster at the back of an abandoned warehouse. Once he turns the engine off and the headlights wink out, our world is immersed in the dark of night, only to be reilluminated by the interior light when I open my door. Three other black Defenders pull up alongside us. A succession of car doors being opened and slammed shut echo around the surrounding warehouses like an offbeat percussion rhythm.

A cool breeze sweeps over my face, bringing with it the fetid stench of garbage mixed with diesel fumes and the subtle undercurrent of promised rain. My light brown curls bounce around my face. For a split second, I regret not bringing a band to tie my hair up, but there are more important things to worry about right now.

The adhesive wound dressings tug a bit on my lower abdomen as I walk around to the back of the car. Hestus glances at me, a hint of concern in his eyes as he looks down at my hand over my stomach.

"I'm fine," I growl in a low voice.

"See, Hestus? I told you she's fine," says Quill. "Now

stop hovering over her like a mother hen. It's about time she got back out hunting."

Hestus just shakes his head before helping Quill unload the gear.

I look up at the sky. The moon glimmers brightly, its beams igniting the nearby clouds with silver outlines. A few stars twinkle between the clouds, but the haze from the city's nightlife a few blocks away has muted the rest of the nighttime glory.

I glance down at my watch: one thirty on a Saturday morning. The clubbers and the boozers still have hours left in them before they'll trickle away to sleep off the events of their raucous night. In the gathering around me, on the other hand, not a bottle of rum or fishnet stocking is in sight. Every clear-headed, adrenaline-pumped hunter is focused on preparing and distributing the weapons cache from the back of every vehicle.

"So what's the prey?" I ask, reaching into the car to retrieve my backpack.

"Lycan, as always," says Quill. "The scouts reckon they caught sight of some Veniri and Magneii too."

"I heard there was a Sathoi spotted hiding in the area as well," adds Jakai as he and his twin stride over to join us.

"Sathoi?" My eyes widen. Lycan, Veniri, and even a few Magneii shifters can be expected to be found during a hunt. The rest of the shifter races are more of a rarity, some because of their nonconfrontational nature and epic hiding skills. Others are a little more slippery and adept at blending into the world of humans. Even coming across the Jiovis shifter a few weeks ago was lucky. Regardless of the warlike culture those metalloid shifters have, it's still quite an effort to track them down.

As for the chances of hunting a Sathoi, neither my

brothers nor I have seen one of those shifters associated with Saturn in the flesh—at least, not out on the hunting field.

Both Hestus's and Quill's eyes glitter with the thought of filling a vial in their amulet with the absinthe-green blood from one of those insectile or fungi-like Sathoi shifters. I know that's what they're imagining, because it's exactly what I'm imagining.

Deshawn groans. "Great. Thanks to you and your big mouth, Jakai, there's now going to be a race for the Sathoi."

"Race? Against you two?" I scoff and pat the top of Deshawn's head; his crop of tight dark curls bounce under my hand. "You think a little too highly of yourself, don't you think?"

"You got a problem, Branstone?" Deshawn leans toward me, his face creased in anger.

Jakai rolls his eyes. "Deshawn, don't."

Deshawn ignores his brother and continues to stare me down, rolling his shoulders back to make himself appear bigger.

Why do all these hulking hunters have to be at least half a head taller than me? I crane my neck to look up at him, then plaster an expression of pure innocence on my face. These tough guys hate that from a chick like me.

Before I can voice my brewing insults, Hestus steps up to my side. "Come on, Nika, no need to make the Grimvast twins feel incompetent."

"Yeah, that's our job." Quill sniggers.

Deshawn hurls a few choice insults at Quill before he finally heeds his brother's order to help finish unloading their car. Only then do I register my hand at my hip, over my holstered crystal dagger. My other hand is in my jacket pocket, my fingers already threaded through my Diamantium-tipped knuckle-duster.

I turn my glare on Hestus. "How many times do I have to tell you not to do that? I had it under control."

"Sure you did." Hestus sighs; it's an old argument. "You don't have to keep picking a fight with people just to prove you're a badass, Nika."

"Please, I would hardly call that a fight. Besides, it's not my fault Deshawn has low self-control. It's his follow-through that's lacking."

Hestus snorts, not bothering to conceal exactly what he thinks of my lame-ass remarks. He grabs a small satchel of snacks and tosses it to me. "Why don't you just channel whatever it is you're trying to prove onto the prey out there tonight."

He elbows me good-naturedly before busying himself with buckling on his bandolier.

For half a minute no one talks as buckles are clipped, straps are tightened, net launchers are double- and triple-inspected, and Diamantium daggers are holstered.

Just as we're all about ready, the faint roar of a car engine starts to grow louder, and a glossy cherry-red Jeep pulls around the corner of the abandoned warehouse. Another red Jeep follows close on its bumper, and another after that. The three Jeeps park by the dumpsters, lining up with our hunting group's four black Defenders.

Deshawn and Jakai rejoin us as the Jeeps' engines turn off.

"Who invited them?" Jakai groans.

Quill juts his chin at the newcomers spilling out of the vehicles. "It's Stellan Ragefire and his crew."

"Duh," says Jakai. "I know a Ragefire when I see one."

"Especially that tall guy with the dark brown hair and

green shirt." Deshawn points. "That's Elias Ragefire, Stellan's son."

"The real question is, what are they doing here?" Jakai crosses his arms. "Their barracks is three states over. This hunting ground isn't in their territory."

"What do they think this is? A free for all? It's bad enough hunting alongside you Branstones." Deshawn jabs a finger in Hestus's chest.

"Some of their scouts called in the Lycan sightings for tonight's hunt," explains Hestus. "Also, they're staying at our barracks for a few weeks. Something about renegotiating the peace and trade agreements with Uncle Matthias and the rest of the leadership. With all their travels, they've missed out on a few days of hunting. Instead of heading straight to our barracks, they've opted to hunt with us first."

"What could they possibly want to negotiate with our barracks?" Jakai's brows furrow in concern.

"Who cares?" snorts Quill. "I don't give a crap about barracks politics, or the Ragefires."

"Agreed," I say. I don't bother looking over at the Ragefires and their crew as I cherry-pick a few final items out of my backpack and toss it back into the Defender. "Are you dudes going to be fluttering your eyelashes at the Ragefires all night, or are we going hunting?"

"Sure, let's go," Deshawn gruffs. "We'd better get a head start on the Ragefires and their crew. But I'm warning you about that Elias Ragefire—watch your back with that pile of slith crap. He's a sly one."

I *tsk* through my teeth. "Sheesh, it doesn't take much for you Grimvasts to tremble in your boots."

"Whatever, Nika. Don't say I didn't warn you. You'll only have your Branstone arrogance to blame if Elias ends up stealing your prey out from under your nose." Deshawn glowers at me one final time before turning his back and sauntering off with the other three.

I roll my eyes. What a moron. I'm not even going to bother feigning innocence if I "accidentally" land one of my crystal daggers in his ass.

Before I go join the others, I throw a glance over my shoulder at the newcomers, who are still doing their final weapons prep by their Jeeps.

There are about eight hunters in all, of varying ages. I easily recognize Stellan. It's never hard to spot a leader or a second-in-command of a barracks. Those guys want to be known to every barracks in the country.

I also spot the guy Deshawn singled out.

Sure enough, underneath his black hunting jacket, Elias Ragefire is wearing an almost fluorescent lime-green T-shirt with a puking emoji on the front. What kind of idiot wears lime green on a hunt? He may as well have a neon sign over his head saying, *Here I am shifters. You better run screaming.*

Elias has grown a lot since the last time I saw him. I recall a few scattered memories of him from when we were children, on the semifrequent occasions his family and my family interacted. The guy used to be a ruffnut of a kid, just tearing around the place like a whirlwind. He always had a short fuse, but he learned not to mess with me the day he kicked me in the shin when I was about eight. It didn't matter that he was a year or two older than me. I may have ended up with a bruised leg, but he ended up with a black eye and a bloody nose before he went screaming for his mommy.

I didn't see the Ragefire family much during my teens. A few scatterings of noteworthy gossip made its way to our barracks, but I didn't take much notice—although I did feel a small pang of sadness a few years ago when I heard Elias's mother passed away. It was weird, because I didn't know the woman all that well; I hadn't even seen her in at least eight years. I probably wouldn't have recognized Elias himself if Deshawn hadn't said something, and I doubt he remembers who I am.

Something bumps into my shoulder, and I turn to find Hestus grinning at me as if he's just busted me picking my nose.

I frown at him. "What?"

He inclines his head at the hunters by the Jeeps. "Who's fluttering their eyelashes at Elias Ragefire now?"

"As if." I elbow him in the chest. "Come on, let's catch up to the others before the Grimvasts think they've got a chance at hunting down any prey tonight."

Chapter Six

MOVING SWIFTLY, yet ensuring my heavy combat boots make as little sound as possible, I turn into the dark alley.

"Are you sure it went this way?" Hestus whispers.

"Yeah, Nika, are you sure? I didn't see anything." Trust Quill to always echo Hestus questioning me whenever I try to take the lead.

"Yes," I hiss. "Now shut up, and get out of my way." I push past my two brothers and stop for a moment, squinting into the night.

The Grimvast twins took off by themselves ages ago, which is convenient. I don't think I could've put up with much more of their whining and arguing with everything I suggested. Their bickering has to be what's scaring away all the prey tonight.

Thankfully, my brothers are smart enough to wait in silence as I focus all my attention on the shadowy alley in front of us.

Anticipation grows into a tangible mass in my chest, almost like a balloon about to pop. I place my hand on the hilt of my Diamantium dagger, ready to yank the blade free at a moment's notice.

For the most part, I'm still a little unsure what kind of shifter we're hunting, but I know we're on the right track. My instincts are fluttering inside me like butterflies whispering secrets. Growing up in a multigenerational family of hunters, I've learned to listen to those instincts and trust their wisdom.

I chance reaching for my flashlight. With the press of a button, a white beam illuminates a dingy alley littered with trash and graffiti—and nothing else. I strain my ears for any kind of subtle sound that may give away our prey's location, but the only noise comes from a cool breeze rustling some scraps of paper.

Quill's obnoxious tone echoes through the alley. "I knew it. Nothing but a dead end."

"I'm telling you, I saw something," I growl. "If we just wait a few minutes, we could—"

"No way." Quill gives a sharp shake of his head, not even bothering to stay quiet. "I'm not interested in waiting just to find out this was all in your head. There's no way I'm going home empty-handed tonight. It's about damn time I filled my next vial."

I have to resist the urge to sucker punch him; his cry of agony would only scare away any other potential prey in our vicinity. And then, of course, he'd blame me for a bust-up of a hunting night and complain in the car the entire way back to the barracks.

"Too bad. It did seem like you were onto something," says Hestus, his tone a little softer than Quill's. Patting me on the shoulder, he adds, "Just forget it, sis."

"We should go find the others before all the good prey are taken," says Quill.

I stop myself just short of stomping my foot like a toddler. "Are you serious? Come on, guys." The whining tone of my voice almost makes me cringe, but I don't bother to get rid of it. "Sagan wouldn't give up so easily."

Maybe I've gone too far with that comment. Both Hestus and Quill cast severe expressions my way—Hestus's etched with worry, Quill's screwed up with anger.

"Does it look like Sagan is here?" Quill says in a low voice.

Sarcasm would usually be my response for a dumb question like that, but Quill turns his back before I can respond.

"I'm not interested in talking about our cousin again, Nika," he says. "I'm here to hunt. Come on, let's find the Grimvasts."

"Screw the Grimvasts." The frustration behind my words cracks like a whip and echoes down the alley; so much for trying not to scare the prey away. "I'm telling you, I know we're onto something. And it went this way."

"Oh yeah?" Quill darts a glance over his shoulder into the alley, then looks back at me, his eyes half-lidded with disbelief. "I don't see anything."

"What kind of shifter do you think you saw, Nika?" Hestus asks.

"I'm not sure."

Quill folds his arms, his meaty biceps stretching the tight black pullover. "Did you *actually* see a shifter? Are you sure it wasn't just a giant rat?"

"It wasn't a rat. And... I didn't actually see something. Just a flicker from the corner of my eye. But trust me, I can almost feel—"

Quill's loud groan drowns out the rest of my sentence. "Come on! Again with your 'I can feel it' crap? Just admit you're wrong, Nika. Now, let's go find the others. The last thing I want is those Ragefires showing us up and ruining everything. Besides"—he holds up the amulet hanging on a black chain around his neck—"like I said, I'm not going home empty-handed, and standing here gawking at an empty alley isn't going to get anyone's vials filled. *So let's go.*"

He spins on his heel and stalks off without waiting for a response.

I turn to Hestus. "You believe me, don't you, Hess?" I hate the edge of desperation in the words. I'm always conscious of never giving other hunters a reason to think of me as a weakling, but with Hestus, every now and then I allow myself to drop the "tough chick" act a little. Sometimes it works to make him more compliant, and for some reason, I'm especially determined to prove I'm right tonight. Blame it on my weeks of being out of the hunting game— I've got to try to play catch-up.

Hestus regards me, his face pinched in a wince. "Maybe we'll have better luck catching up with the others." With a sympathetic shrug, he turns and follows Quill.

My jaw drops, my glare burning into my brothers' backs. It's all I can do not to grab a handful of throwing daggers and toss them at the back of their heads. "Fine! Go chase after your buddies. I was going to share the credit for this kill, maybe even allow one of you to claim it to fill your itty-bitty vial. But you can forget it now."

"Yeah, yeah," Quill calls over his shoulder. "Whatever, Nika. Just so you know, filling your vial with concrete dust or trash water from a dark alley doesn't count." His heckling laugh fades as he and Hestus round the corner and disappear from sight.

I growl through gritted teeth.

Jerks! Some days it sucks having brothers.

I yank my Diamantium crystal dagger from its holster and turn to scowl into the alley, meticulously sweeping the beam of my flashlight to take in every detail. My instincts still raise the hairs on the back of my neck. There is something here, I'm dead sure of it. But if that's the case, what am I missing? What am I not seeing?

The dead end is about sixteen feet from where I stand. The walls on either side are about seven feet apart, made of concrete bricks heavily decorated with graffiti tags and slogans. They're too high for any kind of shifter to climb up and over, and there are no doors or windows for one to escape through. There isn't even a manhole in the ground. A few scattered piles of soggy cardboard boxes cover the asphalt, but none are high enough or wide enough for a shifter to hide behind.

But I could have sworn I caught a flicker of movement from the corner of my eye as something ran into this alley...

After another slow sweep of my flashlight, I can't deny my eyes aren't being deceived. It's just as empty of shifters as it was before.

My shoulders droop. Maybe my brothers are right. Am I *that* desperate to fill another vial I'm now hallucinating shifters? I pat my hand over my chest, right where my amulet is hiding under my shirt.

Perhaps it's time to face facts and go catch up to my brothers.

And yet... my instincts still niggle.

I cast my gaze along the top of the ten-foot cement wall at the end of the alley. Maybe I'm underestimating a shifter's ability to escape over the top of the wall. A Veniri probably could clear that height if they gouged their crystal shards into the bricks to volley themselves up and over, but I've never known a Veniri to scale walls.

Lycans perhaps would attempt climbing the wall, but again, their silver claws would leave gouge marks. As far as I can tell, there are no telltale grooves in the bricks to suggest any kind of escape.

So if the shifter didn't climb the wall, then where did it go? How did it get out?

I narrow my eyes. I have heard rumors of a gorgon-like race of Veniri overseas with the ability to camouflage into their surroundings, but if you look hard enough, the camouflage always produces a giveaway flicker of distortion, as if looking through steam. There's no sign of a rippling steam-like distortion within the alley.

Besides, what are the odds a European Veniri is here by itself in this country? Even if that is the case, is it really worth this much effort? I've already scored my Veniri blood trophy.

Fishing out my amulet from under my shirt, I spy the small vial filled with illuminated Veniri blood. The teal is radiant among the silver, magenta, and orange samples. I go on to mentally list the empty vials—the missing colors: gold, absinthe green, pearl white, purple, black...

Wait a second!

My attention jolts back to the empty alley.

Of course! Black!

A buzz of excitement sparks deep in my belly.

If I'm correct, that would totally explain why I can't see the shifter, even if they're standing right in front of my face.

I want to kick myself. Why didn't I think of it before— especially before Quill and Hestus left?

You didn't think of it because the odds of finding a shifter with black blood are like winning the lottery, says a small voice in the back of my mind.

With that, skepticism creeps over me, eclipsing the rush of excitement. Can I seriously be that lucky? No one I know has black in their amulet. Just imagine all the hunters back at the barracks turning green with furious envy once they see black in mine.

A victorious grin pricks at the corners of my mouth. This will serve Quill and Hestus right for once again not trusting me.

Don't get too cocky, pipes up the small voice again. *You'll have to capture the shifter first.*

Trying to appear nonchalant, I tuck my amulet back into my shirt, then slowly reach into a pocket in my utility belt. I fetch a tool I've never used before but have always wanted to: a small flashlight that fits snugly in my palm. With the item still behind my back, I feel for the switch with my thumb.

Adrenaline tingles through me, along with an edge of doubt. What if this is all just wishful thinking? What if this special flashlight doesn't work?

But what if it does? says the small voice.

I bite the inside of my lip. Only one way to find out.

In a quick, fluid motion, I press the button and swing the flashlight in front of me. A rippling beam of black-tinted light streams out into the alley—it's almost an *absence* of light and yet, at the same time, a shimmering ray of darkness. For a second, disappointment bites into my anticipation when the far-right corner looks exactly the same as before. But as I slowly pan the beam to the other side, my breath hitches in the back of my throat.

The beam of darklight catches the edge of a figure, much like how ultraviolet light reveals invisible ink. Before I can make out what I'm looking at, a flurry of movement springs forward, knocking into me as it rushes past.

"Damn it!" I growl.

The collision causes me to stumble and drop the dark-light. It clatters to the grubby concrete, the beam flickering around uselessly while the damn shifter runs under the cover of invisibility.

"Oh, no you don't!" I give chase, scooping the darklight up on the way. "Get back here, you Meruvo."

All my senses kick into overdrive as my mind swirls with excitement.

No. Freaking. Way.

I'm hunting down a Meruvo!

I'm hunting down an actual shifter who derives its energies from the light of Mercury.

Screw Quill and Hestus for doubting me. And screw the Grimvast twins for always trying to undermine and humiliate me. I'm going to shoot through to legendary status with this Meruvo prey.

I pause for a second once I'm back out on the quiet road. A desperate pounding of footsteps recedes to the left.

I dart left.

Pumping my legs to keep up, I shine my shimmery beam of darklight ahead. Thanks to the ingenuity of our forefathers in the hunting world, the condensed beam of Mercurian light brings my prey into view. The shifter flickers in and out of visibility while I struggle to keep the beam steady.

My thighs and calves begin to burn, but I force my legs to run harder, willing myself to close the gap as I imagine the dirty, envious looks on all the other hunters' faces back at the barracks. No one will dare to call me "goldilocks" or "dollface" ever again... although I suppose hunting down this prey won't do much to put an end to the "Branstone Iron Maiden" label.

But it's not just picturing their jealousy that's driving me forward; I'm reveling in the thrill of the hunt—the rush of wind in my hair and the surge of adrenaline in my veins. Thanks to a lifetime of training, muscle memory and instinct take over. Within seconds, I'm almost on the shifter's heels.

The Meruvo skitters to one side, then to the other, almost as if it's trying to confuse me and dodge the Mercurian stream of light. I almost laugh out loud. What an amateur. Does this shifter think it's my first night out on the hunt? No matter how much the shifter dodges and weaves, my reflexes keep up; my Mercurian beam keeps the wretched Meruvo in sight.

The shifter shoots a glance over its shoulder at me but staggers and trips, almost colliding into a power pole. It takes a second to recover, but it continues to flicker and weave while sprinting.

I grin, unholster my crystal dagger, and hold it tight. The shifter's lapse is my gain; I'm now getting close to stabbing range.

The creature's movements grow more erratic, more desperate. It must be getting tired. It must know its end is imminent.

I think of whipping out my atomizer of Myst—a strong sleeping concoction formulated from the Sathoi shifters who secrete poison Viscid—but I dismiss that thought in an instant. Only lazy, cowardly hunters use Myst to capture their prey. Besides, if I hunt down this Meruvo without Myst, no hunter will ever question my hunting skills ever again.

I push myself harder.

Only two feet between myself and the Meruvo.

Then one and a half.

The Meruvo ducks around the corner of a building.

I'm so close I can almost taste my victory. In the almost fifty years since my great-grandfather established our hunter barracks, I, Nika Branstone, will be the first—

I halt.

A jolt of pain shudders up my legs at the sudden stop.

What the hell?

Where is the Meruvo?

Chapter Seven

My DARKLIGHT BEAM catches nothing but empty air. I jerk the beam from side to side. Human or shifter, there isn't a soul in sight.

With a frown, I scrutinize every flicker of movement, every rustle of trash tossed by the breeze, every minor input from my senses. The effort to slow my rapid breathing and pounding heart for the sake of silence is a challenge.

A chorus of faint raucous shouts and celebratory cheers makes me flinch. Other hunters must be close by, maybe a street or two over, and they've clearly caught whatever shifter they were after. I swear under my breath, certain I can make out Quill's boisterous whoops.

Gritting my teeth, I block out the distraction. No way am I going to lose my prey now.

I chance taking a few steps forward, then pause halfway through the fifth. In the same way my instincts alerted me to a shifter hiding in the alley—when Quill and Hestus couldn't sense anything—the deep, familiar knowing within my soul tells me I've taken one step too many.

I backtrack half a step and look around: brick wall on

one side, another on the other side of the road. No windows or openings are close enough for the Meruvo to have escaped through in the seconds it was out of my sight.

Instinct spikes as a thought hits me. Slowly, I turn my attention up, scanning the crisscrossing metal rafters of a warehouse awning about three feet above my head.

My roaming stream of darklight brushes across an intersection of rafters slightly to my left. A disembodied voice hisses a curse just as the beam brings the perching shifter into the land of the visible.

At closer proximity, the sight of the shifter almost takes my breath away. I've heard stories, even seen illustrated renditions of the Meruvo in their shifted form, but it's nothing compared to seeing one up close with my own eyes.

The figure before me is humanoid, I'm guessing female. Booted feet balance on a round metal beam, and her posture is crouched, legs bent, hands wrapped around the cross-wires of the overhead structure. The edges of her body are strangely undefined, hidden by a slight rippling distortion that gives the impression she'll once again blink out of sight without a moment's notice. Even without the Mercurian light, the Meruvo reportedly emit a telltale ripple in the air around them in their invisible shifted form. Apparently, though, it takes a lot of practice to discern the ripples, and only the exclusive Meruvo hunters are adept in spotting them.

The Meruvo above me is almost like a living spacescape. Starlight speckles her flesh in myriad constellations and galaxies of nebulous colors, which slowly orbit through the midnight black and deep navies of her skin tones—although, whether skin or the night sky made tangible, I'm not quite sure.

For a creature so gracefully ethereal, a pair of ripped tie-dye cutoff shorts, a sequined crop top, and mid-shin silver holographic boots seem very much out of place. Perhaps the Meruvo started the night rave hopping in the city a few blocks away—in human form, of course—and somehow found herself in the midst of a hunting ground. At least, that's the best explanation I can come up with to explain her music-video-girl getup.

But I'm not here to play fashion police. It took me only a few seconds to assess my prey perching in the rafters, and I've already created a plan of attack to kill her and claim a sample of her blood for my hunter amulet.

Exhilaration shudders through me, and I grin. "You're mine."

A fierce expression crosses over her empyreal face at my declaration.

Without giving any further warning, I lunge.

I catch a lower rafter in the crook of my elbow and simultaneously slice my other arm toward the Meruvo. My Diamantium dagger arcs through the air in a flash of rainbow fractal light and slashes through a silver holographic boot as if it were made of rice paper.

The Meruvo's shrill cry slices through my eardrums. She launches herself away and lands on the next rafter, then continues without stopping, jumping from one rafter to the next.

I take a precious second to glance at my Diamantium dagger, where a drop of black blood gleams on the crystal tip. My heart rate kicks up a notch. Never have I seen with my own eyes the black blood of the Mercurian shifters. But the blood sample on my dagger doesn't count for my amulet —not unless I actually kill the shifter.

I roll my neck in frustration. Placing the handle of my dagger in my mouth and holding my Mercurian flashlight tight, I swing the rest of my body up into the awning. The Meruvo is only about four rafters ahead when I continue my chase. I have to rely on my sense of hearing as I jump and swing through the web of metal poles, unable to keep my darklight beam steady.

My instincts urge me to go faster, vaulting over each metal beam with precision, keeping hot on the Meruvo's heels. She casts a fearful glance back at me every now and then but never once reduces speed.

Regardless of her lithe efforts, though, I'm gaining on her. Before long, I'm once again in dagger-swiping range.

But the Meruvo has reached the end of the warehouse and, consequently, the end of the awning. For a second I assume she'll jump back to the ground and take a left or right at the T-intersection at the end of the building, but instead, she launches herself off the last metal beam. Her ethereal body dazzles in midair as she flies over the road, kicking a leg out in front of her. Then her boot crashes through the second-story window of the warehouse on the other side.

Shards of razor-edged glass tinkle down onto the pavement as the Meruvo glides into the darkness beyond the window.

I can't help but be impressed. That was a magnificent jump.

But it won't deter my pursuit.

Half a second later, I hurl myself from the edge of the awning and into the open air. The effort jars my abdomen, and the adhesive wound dressings tug on my skin, but my adrenaline-fueled high masks the pain. I force myself to focus on the task at hand.

Gravity disappears for a single heartbeat as I soar toward the jagged maw of the broken window. I note another sample of black blood on the glass-fanged opening as I sail through.

My calculations must have been off by a hair's breadth, because glass shards nick both my right shoulder and ankle on the way in. Again, no pain registers, either because of the acute thrill of the hunt or because of my protective hunting leathers; I'll figure it out later.

Darkness engulfs me.

Anticipating the impact, I land and tumble to a stop on the concrete floor. My darklight faintly lights up a nonde-script room, empty and dusty from neglect. The Meruvo's receding footsteps echo out the doorway opposite from the window we just entered.

I spring back onto my feet and once again give chase. The door leads out onto a concrete walkway that looks down on some type of factory floor, about a quarter the length of a football field. Several rows of monolithic machinery loom in undistinguished black mounds, lined with silver from the moonlight streaming in from the skylights. I have no idea what the machines are and can't begin to imagine what they produced long before this place was abandoned.

A clamor yanks my attention to a spiral metal staircase leading down to the factory floor. I'm starting to regret not using Myst when I had the chance. This Meruvo is proving more cunning than I expected—another reason why these shifters are super rare to catch. But if I want my grand prize, standing here like a sookie-lah-lah isn't going to get the job done. If I don't get my ass moving, I'll lose the shifter in that maze of ominous machinery.

Forget the stairs. I have no time.

I glance over the rail. The scrabbling of disembodied feet reaches the last few steps, and I calculate the path she'll have to take to disappear into the labyrinth of machines. If I time it just right, I'll have her.

With a flick of my legs, I vault over the railing. My stomach lurches into my throat as I sail down, but my Mercurian beam remains steady enough to bring my target into view, just where I predicted.

With expert accuracy, I land on top of the Meruvo.

The impact knocks the air from my lungs, but the simultaneous *ooph!* from the Meruvo tells me she's also winded. She gasps for breath as she tries to wriggle out of my grasp.

Not wasting a second, I hunker down and trap her beneath me. My legs lock on either side of her body, my Diamantium dagger digs into her throat, and my Mercurian darklight shines directly into her face.

Now that I'm all up in her personal space, the galaxies and nebula clouds within her flesh are even more mesmerizing—but it's her eyes that captivate me most. Even more than the brightest stars in her complexion, her eyes are radiant. They're fully mottled black, without whites, although a brilliant white edge circles her irises. As for the irises themselves... I can't help but suck in a breath of wonderment. It's as if I'm looking at the birth of two starbursts. When her eyes dart around, every now and then a stream of light flashes outward and then fades a few inches from her face, similar to glare off a disco ball.

It isn't as if I'm glamoured or romantically enraptured with this creature; I've just never seen anything like her before. Despite my fascination, never once do I forget my mission—or that this otherworldly shifter is my prey.

"Please." The fear and desperation in the Meruvo's expression are unmistakable. "Please don't kill me, hunter. I'll... I'll give you my wish."

For a moment, I'm tempted by her offer—I hate to admit

just how tempted. The wish I'd ask for is immediate and soul deep, especially as the infirmary doctor's voice once again echoes through my brain.

...the prospect of you having children is no longer possible.

Images flicker across my mind's eye. In one, I'm nursing a tiny baby wrapped in a blanket that also belonged to me as a baby. That image morphs into another where I'm smiling down at a small girl holding my hand. The girl, about the age of five, has a full head of light brown curls, and her big doll-like eyes are the same color as mine. The images continue, one after the other, as the young girl, the figment of my desires, eventually grows into a young woman.

I squeeze my eyes shut, holding back the burning tears that threaten to spill down my cheeks.

Despite my delusions, I force an unkind laugh. "Nice try. Like I'd fall for that one."

"Honest!" The Meruvo grips my forearm where it's braced across her chest, pinning her to the floor. "I can see in your eyes you have a deep yearning for something that will make you complete. Tell me what you want, hunter. I can make your wish come true." She holds up a finger. "But only if you let me go."

With a scoff, I narrow my eyes into a glare. "Do you think I was born yesterday? What's the point of bargaining away your single wish if you'll forfeit your life anyway?"

Despite the indifferent words, my wishful dreams *scream* inside me to be made a reality. Dominating skepticism alone keeps me from giving in to the Meruvo's persuasion. Few hunters may have encountered these shifters, but the stories are notorious. When cornered, a Meruvo begins to spin fancy words and tantalizing promises, bargaining with the one thing that would be valuable to anyone—fulfillment of their captor's deepest desire.

If only it were that simple. These Mercurian shifters may have the power to grant a wish, but that mighty power comes from their very essence. They pay the price of a wish with their life.

Supposedly, for such a fatal trade to occur, the Meruvo's wish has to be sanctioned by their own unadulterated want. Worship and bribery, sadistic torture, gentle persuasion, and even romantic relationships are never enough to convince a Meruvo to relinquish their wish. They themselves have to *want* with every fiber of their being for the wish to come true before they die at the behest of another.

Stories of the Meruvo shifters circulate through the barracks like fairy tales, yet it's rare for any story to end with a wish being granted. The Meruvo's infamous resistance is unbreakable, even right up until they die in chains of old age or torture.

Whatever kind of trick this Meruvo is trying to pull, it won't work. Besides, I'm self-aware enough to know I couldn't face the inevitable failure if I tried to force my wish to come true. Better for my ego and my heart to claim my kill and my small glory now.

I raise my dagger.

Horror strikes the Meruvo's ethereal face.

Before my dagger descends an inch, an odd noise comes from somewhere in the machinery at my right. My head snaps to the side, only to find stillness and silence in the dimly moonlit forest of metal.

The Meruvo doesn't hesitate to take advantage of my second-long attention lapse. With a raging grunt and a buck of her hips, the shifter knocks my dagger arm away and flips me off of her body. I don't even have time to grit out a curse before she's dashing down a dark aisle of machinery.

Ensuring my beam of darklight stays dead center on the Meruvo's receding back, I jump to my feet.

The shifter nimbly weaves and darts left and right, with me once again on her heels. But this time, instead of exhilaration, fury fills my pursuit. The way this shifter keeps eluding capture is quickly getting old—I'm ready for this hunt to be over.

The Meruvo once again swings to the left. A split second later I move to follow when—*wham!*

A large, dark blur hammers into me. I fly sideways, my cry of surprise melding with the grunt of a deep voice. Winded, I struggle against a tangle of fumbling limbs and agonized curses as the random guy and I tumble along the cold, hard concrete.

When we finally come to a stop, my legs are pinned under the weight of a male human body.

"Get off, moron!" I kick, wriggling out from underneath whoever this idiot is.

"Hey! Watch it!" comes his reply after a choice kick to his jaw.

Ignoring his protests, I scramble back onto my feet. With my hands braced on my knees, I allow myself a moment to heave in a few deep breaths before panning my beam of darklight in the direction I last saw the Meruvo.

Damn it!

I swing my darklight beam back around and come face-to-face with a puking emoji on a bright lime-green T-shirt. My glare sweeps up to meet honey-brown eyes.

"What are you, some kind of stupid?" I hiss.

Chapter Eight

Elias freaking Ragefire rubs at his jaw where I kicked him.

"What?" The hunter blinks, as if mystified by my anger and confused by the darklight beam in his face.

I balk. "Are you serious?" My arm sweeps out, gesturing to the now empty aisle between the mystery machines. "I almost had it! But thanks to you"—I stab an accusing finger in his face—"my prey is probably long gone."

He drops his hand from his jaw. "Oh."

"'Oh'? Is that all you have to say? 'Oh'?" My fingers curl, itching to wrap around his neck. He's only about five inches taller than me, but I still hate how much I have to look up at him. "I was a dagger slice away from filling my next vial before your mammoth self crashed into me."

"Okay, okay." He glances at my balled fists. "I'm sorry I messed up your kill."

A hiss escapes through my clenched jaw; my disappointment and frustration are almost tangible enough to stab my dagger into. "Sorry isn't going to cut it, moron. You should just... you should..." *He should what?* I'm out of insults, but my rage won't let him off the hook just yet. "Just go back to wherever it is you came from, and leave the real hunting to the experts." With that, I swing around and stalk off. If I'm lucky, I still might be able to track down the Meruvo.

An amused chuckle follows me. "Experts, huh? What makes you think... Oh, wait a second..." He catches up, and out of the corner of my eye, I see him look me up and down. "Supercilious expression, check. Pig-headed confidence, check. Quick to deflect blame, check... I'd say you've got to be a Branstone."

I pause mid-step, then round on him. "Excuse me, I am not supercilious or pig-headed, and I'm certainly not the one to blame for the shifter escaping. You're the one who—"

The rest of my words are drowned out by the hunter's victorious laugh. "Yep. Definitely a Branstone." He half closes an eye, his expression changing as he looks at me again with the new perspective. "Hold up, I think I know you. You're Nika, right?"

I answer with a scoff and continue walking, busying myself with sweeping my Mercurian beam in every dark crevice I pass.

"I'm right, aren't I? You're Nika." Again, he hurries to catch up to me. "You might remember we used to hang out when we were kids. I'm pretty sure you once gave me a decent shiner, although I'm a bit fuzzy on whether I deserved it or not."

"Get lost, Ragefire. I'm not here to play 'let's take a trip down memory lane.' But just for the record, you definitely deserved that black eye."

"Ah, so you do remember me." Elias's low laugh

rumbles deep in his chest. "Nice to know I left some kind of impression."

"Don't fawn over yourself too much. The only impression made in this scenario is my bootprint on your face."

He rubs his jaw again but lets out another deep laugh, this time loud enough to echo through the jungle of machinery.

My lip curls in a sneer. "You've got three seconds to get lost before I claim *your* blood as my trophy for tonight. I think red will make a nice addition to the rest of the colors on my amulet."

The expression Elias gives me isn't nearly intimidated enough. He glances at the spot where my amulet is hiding under my shirt, almost as if he's amused with the thought of his blood being displayed there.

"You're exactly as I remember you," he finally says. "Confident, fiery, tenacious, although perhaps a little less... innocent. And yet"—his eyes drift, focusing on something unseen—"who of us is still innocent these days?"

What the heck did he mean by that? I frown, surprise lancing through me at how much that comment bothers me. For a moment, all merriment withdraws from his gaze, leaving an anguish so vivid I swear I'm at risk of drowning in his sorrow.

After a heartbeat, I roll my eyes. "Whatever. I don't have time for this. I've got a shifter to track down."

"Right, we can't forget what we came here for."

I arch an eyebrow. The harsh inflection in his tone piques my curiosity, but after a beat, he grins, making me question if I simply imagined it.

Elias gestures to the darklight in my hand. "So, Meruvo's on the menu tonight, huh?"

Adrenaline once again seeps into my veins. Great, this

is just what I need. It's bad enough having to deal with this slippery Meruvo shifter without another hunter thinking he can claim my rightful kill.

"Nope, I'm hunting rabbit," I say in my best condescending tone. Best-case scenario, he'll just assume I'm an overachieving hunter who thinks a Mercurian darklight is necessary for hunting down a Lycan or something.

Much to my chagrin, his smirk intensifies. "But I thought it was duck season."

"What?" My eyebrow shoots up again.

"You know, 'it's rabbit season, no, it's duck season'..." He waves his hand in the air, as if that aids his ludicrous explanation. When I continue my deadpan stare, he adds, "Seriously? You've never heard of it? But it's a classic."

I huff in frustration and spin on my heel. What's the likelihood of salvaging any kind of kill before tonight is over?

As I make my way down one of the center aisles, the dull ache of my lower abdomen starts to become more pronounced. I probably should have taken another dose of the pearl-white Ylixium before going on a hunt, but I'm already wary of how much I've consumed since the Luxium grenade. The last thing I need to deal with right now is an Ylixium detox.

Yet in this moment, I really wish I'd thrown caution to the wind and taken another dose, especially when my shoulder starts to ache, another pain throbs down my left side, and my ankle twinges. I'm not sure which of the night's events caused my ailments. Jumping through a window, tussling with a Meruvo, and being crash-tackled by Elias Ragefire are all contenders. In the end it doesn't matter. Whatever the case, that feisty little Meruvo has some severe payback waiting for her.

Of course, there's no point trying to hide the fact that I'm after a Meruvo; Elias clearly knows. Even as a kid, he wasn't really the gullible type. All I have to do is make sure I claim the Meruvo kill before he does. No big deal, right?

I increase my speed, still panning my darklight left and right, all while trying really hard to ignore the thud of heavy boots behind me. I pause every now and then, searching, listening, waiting for a tug on my instinct. If I were a shifter running from a hunter, where would I hide?

Thud, thud, thud.

I'm at risk of cracking a tooth from grinding my teeth. How the heck am I supposed to concentrate with this neanderthal hulking after me?

Thud, thud, thud.

I swing to face him.

Elias halts, mere inches from crashing into me.

"Are you lost or something?" I demand.

His brow furrows. "No."

"Then try harder."

I don't like the smile he gives me—mischief mixed with a challenge. The temptation to punch that stupid grin off his stupid face is almost impossible to ignore, but after a second I groan and shake my head. I'm not going to fall for his juvenile baiting.

He holds up both his hands. "How about a proposition? I'm feeling bad for interrupting your kill. Maybe I can help you track the shifter down?"

"What do you mean, 'help' me?" I grip my dagger tighter, eyeing several places I can stab him if he dares to suggest we split the kill. No one would be stupid enough to believe we tracked down two Meruvo shifters in one hunt.

He opens his mouth to answer, but before he can utter a word, I slap a hand over his mouth.

"Shh!" I hiss. He grabs at my hand, mumbling his protest, but I dig my fingers into his jaw. "Quiet. I think I hear something."

Elias grows still.

Holding my breath, I focus my senses on our surroundings. There it is again, that subtle noise I heard.

Elias's eyes shift to a spot beyond my shoulder. So I'm not imagining things—he can hear it too.

Another slight scuffle pricks at my ears. My instinct flares back to life, along with a spike of adrenaline-fueled excitement.

"It's still here." My words are just above a whisper.

I drop my hand from Elias's mouth and place a finger on my lips, warning him to stay quiet. In response, he slowly pulls out an atomizer of Myst.

I give him a mocking eye roll and mouth, "Cheater."

Elias shrugs, but a corner of his mouth quirks into a smug grin. I shake my head. If I'm lucky, the idiot will accidentally Myst himself, leaving me to hunt the Meruvo alone.

Not willing to delay any further, I make sure I'm half a step ahead of Elias as I move forward and crane my head around the corner of a machine.

A few heartbeats pass.

"Anything?" Elias whispers, just over my shoulder.

I shake my head.

"Maybe it's gone." This time he doesn't bother to whisper.

I shoot another warning glare at him, but he only raises his eyebrows as if to say, *What's the problem?* Is this numbskull trying to be the worst hunter ever? If crimson blood were worth the loot, I swear I'd have carved open his veins long ago.

I can't stand this anymore. I'm going to track down this Meruvo and drag its body back to the barracks if it's the last thing I do.

Another sound catches my ear. This time it's a soft hiss, like a startled intake of breath.

My heart rate quickens. Did I just see a slight distortion in the air about five feet ahead? Or am I imagining things?

Learning from my previous mistakes, I try my best to appear nonchalant as my attention narrows on a shadowed area in the corner of my eye. A plan forms in my mind, and if I can pull it off, there's a chance I'll ditch Elias and claim my kill in one fell swoop.

I adjust my grip on my Diamantium dagger and brace myself for a kill strike. Then, casually, I move my darklight beam in the opposite direction of where I heard the gasp. "What's that over there?" I stage-whisper.

Elias's head whips in the direction I point. "Did you see something? Was it the Meruvo?"

"Yeah. I'm pretty sure it was the Meruvo."

I charge.

Elias takes the bait and also bolts. Within two steps, he's overtaken me.

I almost scoff out loud when I skid to a stop. Typical male hunters always needing to charge ahead—proof that they can't handle the idea of being out-skilled by a woman.

When Elias disappears into the dark void of the machinery aisle, I dodge in the other direction. This time, instead of using my darklight to confirm my target, I drop it on the floor, whip my pneumatic dart gun out of its holster, and pull the trigger in one fluid motion. With a blast of pressurized air, a Diamantium-tipped bolt half the length and thickness of a ballpoint pen shoots from the gun. A strand of strong wire trails out from behind the dart, leading back to the gun still in my hand.

A split second later, an almighty screech of agony shatters the silence.

The wire pulls taut, and the dart gun almost jerks out of my grasp. Holding the weapon tight, I yank it back hard.

"*Gotcha!*" My grin is triumphant. The slippery little sucker won't deny me my sample of black blood this time.

I pounce. My deliberate aim lands me perfectly on the screaming shifter. Without the aid of the darklight, I can't see her at all; my arms appear to be wrapped around thin air, yet the invisible body beneath my tight grip is just as tangible as my own. The Meruvo bucks and thrashes, threatening to break free of my hold.

I almost hoot with exhilaration, much like my brothers do each time they best their prey.

"I'm coming!" bellows Elias from an aisle or two over.

I don't bother to respond. Grunting with the effort, I wrap my legs around my captive and raise my dagger.

"Let me help," comes Elias's call, now a few feet away.

Before I can tell him to get lost, a sudden numbness envelops me. The descent of my blade hitches. My hand and arm suddenly grow heavy and fall to my side. The dagger clatters to the floor, missing my mark entirely.

"What the...?" My speech turns sluggish as my mouth and jaw become numb. One moment, I'm seemingly hovering a few feet in the air on top of the Meruvo; the next, my entire body goes slack. Gravity takes hold, and I tumble into an ungraceful heap on the ground.

For half a confusing moment, I can't understand why I'm unable to move any part of my body.

Elias's face comes into view, looming over me. His

expression is a mixture of concern and something else I can't quite decipher.

"Oops" is all he says.

Only then do I spot the atomizer still in his hand.

A furious rage flares deep in my center. The stupid, *stupid* moron just doused me with Myst.

Chapter Nine

Hunters part for me like the Red Sea did for Moses when I stomp down the hallway from the infirmary.

"Where is he?" I demand.

Two hunters point toward the cafeteria, careful to keep out of arm-swinging distance.

I pivot toward the direction they point, half glad and half insanely pissed they know exactly who I'm talking about. If they know who I'm after, that means word has already spread and everyone knows about my humiliation.

Red fury clouds the edges of my vision, and my heavy boots thunk with dire warning as I storm down the hallway. The moment I barge through the double doors of the cafeteria, aromas of bacon, eggs, and pancakes with maple syrup flood my senses. My stomach growls, and a torrent of saliva fills my mouth in eager response to the appetizing breakfast menu.

But my rage eclipses my hunger. I'm here for one thing.

Animated conversation echoes throughout the cafeteria. Hunters of all ages jostle through lines and crowd the seating area, all still abuzz and ravaged with hunger from their night's work. I take half a second to scan the tables before one in the middle draws my attention.

My brothers, Quill and Hestus, see me first. Both wear expressions of mild caution, but that doesn't stop me from locking my sights on the person seated two chairs away from them. As I make a beeline for the table, my fingers thread through the Diamantium-tipped knuckle-duster my Uncle Matthias gave me one Christmas.

"Told ya she'd have her knuckle-duster," says Hestus, elbowing Quill. "You owe me fifty bucks."

I ignore my brothers' exchange of cash, my focus never leaving my mark. Elias is in the midst of a spirited conversation with three other hunters at the table. One I recognize, but the other two—a guy with a mohawk and some chick with pink streaks in her midnight hair—must be a part of the Ragefire entourage.

When I'm just a few feet away, Elias finally catches sight of me. He cracks a smile, laugh lines enlivening his features.

"Hey. Look who's up." He gestures for me to join them, pointing to an empty chair.

The other hunters at the table who have their backs to me turn, and the eyes of the ones from my barracks grow wide. Everyone from the Ragefire crew—all of them but Elias, that is—exchange confused glances.

Conversation at the closest surrounding tables begins to fade out as the attention slowly turns to me.

"Oh, crap." The hunter in the chair nearest to me hastens to vacate her seat to get out of my firing line.

Without hesitation, I stomp a heavy boot onto the now empty chair, then step up onto the table. Cutlery and plates clatter, followed by a few cries of protest.

Only then does Elias's grin drop. "Nika, are you all right? You seem a little—"

I land a power kick right in the middle of his chest, which sends both him and his chair flying backward. Arms and legs flail as Elias's chair tips over and slams him onto the floor. The back of his skull hits the ground with a loud *crack.*

The guy hardly has a chance to wince with pain before I jump off the table. Landing one foot by his side, I slam my knee into his diaphragm. He jolts as air gushes from his lungs, but to my slight surprise, he still doesn't cry out.

I clutch a handful of his shirt. The knuckle-duster, glittering over my fist, hovers inches above his face. "I should gut you for getting in the way of my kill," I spit out. "Because of you, my prey got away."

"Phew," wheezes Elias. "For a second there, I thought you were pissed because I doused you in Myst."

Hunters all around murmur. A few softly snigger.

Again, red flashes over my vision. I throw a bare-knuckled punch into his jaw with my other fist.

Crack.

"That's for the Myst." I drive another punch into his face. "You doused me with enough Myst to tranquilize a herd of elephants."

I may not have been able to move a muscle after my Myst shower, but I'd still been conscious when Elias carried me back to the rest of the hunters, and throughout their jeers during the whole car ride home. The humiliation continued back at the barracks when Elias once again picked me up and paraded me through the corridors of the bunker all the way to the infirmary, where I had to wait another three hours for the Myst to wear off.

My cheeks burn, betraying the residual shame of it all.

Crack. I slam another punch into Elias's jaw.

A small groan of pain escapes him.

I can't help but be impressed he lasted this long. I may not have the brute power my two older brothers inherited, but my father and Uncle Matthias have taught me how to inflict enough damage that even Quill and Hestus flinch whenever I charge at them in training.

I raise my bare-knuckled fist for another strike, but pause. My lungs heave with shallow breaths, barely audible over the raucous shouts and taunts from the hunters gathered around to watch me turn Elias's cheek into mincemeat. They're practically baying for me to hit him again. I glance up at the faces around me, most of them wide-eyed and half-glazed with that familiar hunter bloodlust.

Yet the bloodlust is absent from Elias's eyes. He doesn't try to clutch at his cheek or shield his face from me either. There's no hint of resentment. He doesn't even look angry! Instead the expression on his face is... *what?*

It's as if he understands exactly how humiliated I feel.

I recoil just an inch. I've never had anyone look at me like that before, especially not after I've pummeled them with my fists and threatened to disembowel them. I can't fully decipher the rest of the emotions in his eyes, yet somehow, Elias's gaze washes over me like a balm.

I lean back farther with a frown, trying to maintain a grasp on the vicious fury that's leaching out of me.

What is with this guy? He's looking at me as if he... cares about—

No! I can't finish that thought—can't even entertain the possibility. I'm still reeling from the last time my brothers thought it would be hilarious to trick me into thinking someone liked me as more than just a friend, only to metaphorically kick my feet out from under me in front of the rest of the barracks. Granted, that mortifying moment happened almost seven years ago when I was fifteen, but it scarred me enough that I'd never risk a similar situation.

I bolt to my feet, burying any assumptions I might have made about Elias's enigmatic gaze under a heap of incredulity. Standing over him, I muster up my dirtiest glare. "Next time I tell you to get lost, you'd better, or I won't be joking when I come to claim a sample of your blood for my amulet."

Elias doesn't respond. Part of me wants him to—to shout at me and spew hateful names—but another, more fragile side of me is glad he doesn't. Instead he slightly tilts his head, his expression still soft, and those honey-brown eyes hold me captive.

A rush of fear surges through me. I don't know what Elias thinks he's seeing, but I can no longer take the scrutiny. I need to get out of here before any more cracks in my facade start to show.

Turning my back on him, I stride through the hunters now jeering at Elias for getting his butt whooped.

"Damn it," Quill cusses as I walk past. "I figured she would at least give him five punches. Since when has she ever stopped at three?"

"Ha ha!" taunts Hestus. "I was right again! Pay up, Quill."

I barge through the cafeteria double doors with less gusto than before, and they swing shut behind me, drowning out the swell of discordant voices. My brothers will likely start arguing, Quill trying to come up with another bet to win his money back, while the rest of the dining hunters debrief over the scene I caused.

I round a corner, thankful to find the corridor empty. It's at that moment I notice the ache in one of my hands. I hold it out in front of me, palm down, to see fresh bruises blotching the skin over my knuckles. Startled, I realize I never used the knuckle-duster on Elias as I'd intended. It certainly would have diced his face up and landed him in the infirmary longer than I was in my Myst-induced coma.

I hold up my other hand; the knuckle-duster glitters under the hallway's white fluorescent lights. My blinged-up knuckles are slightly shaking with the residual adrenaline, but not nearly as much as my other hand. My bare hand shakes almost uncontrollably.

What the hell is wrong with me? I went in there prepared to slice Elias's face open with my Diamantium knuckle-duster. What caused me to do otherwise?

Confusion mixes with the already surging turmoil of my humiliation and frustration. Saltwater prickles my eyes, but I refuse to let any of the tears fall.

Get yourself under control, Nika!

Blinking furiously, I increase my speed. I need to get back to my room—no one can see me like this. In the realm of hunters, emotion is nothing but a weakness.

"Nika!"

Stunned, I half turn. When I see who's calling after me, the feelings I'm trying so hard to suppress crash over me all over again.

Damn it. Not him!

I turn back the way I'm heading, adjusting my speed to appear indifferent rather than what I really am: desperate to escape.

"Nika! Wait up!"

I once again curse Elias's long legs; he's caught up way too quickly. "Get lost," I growl.

"Nika, please. Slow down." Elias jumps in front of me, his large frame blocking my path to the corridor's exit. He calmly holds up his hands. "I'm not here to start anything. I just want to talk."

"I've got nothing to say to you."

I try to move around him, but he steps into my path.

"Please. Just hear me out?"

The plea in his tone makes me curious despite myself. I take a moment to study his expression, trying to decipher what his intentions really are.

Now, under the bright lights of the barracks rather than the darkness of an abandoned factory, I notice how much Elias has changed since we were kids. Long gone is the plump boyish cheeks he used to have; adolescence has sharpened his features, granting him a distinguished jawline and defined cheekbones. His honey-brown eyes are more piercing, more wizened.

Or perhaps it's just the dark bruises forming along his jaw and the side of his face that make his features seem notable.

I drop my gaze to the highly detailed design of a rainbow chameleon on the front of his dark purple shirt. It sports the caption "When I grow up, I want to be a chameleon" in neon blue.

Again, what kind of hunter wears such bright colors? Everyone I know only wears hunter black.

"Please, Nika. I promise it will only take a minute."

I refuse to look away from the chameleon. "You have one minute."

"Okay." Elias drops his hands, then fumbles for the zipper tag on his unzipped black hoodie. "I just wanted to apologize for ruining your hunt last night."

My eyebrows shoot up. "You what?"

"I said I'm sorry for ruining—"

"I heard what you said. It's just..." Since when do

hunters ever say sorry? I've never heard anyone utter any kind of apology—ever.

Unless...

My glare returns, along with a wave of mortification. "Did Quill or Hestus put you up to this? I swear, if I find out my brothers have bribed someone else to make me think he has a crush on me, I'm going to break every bone—"

"No, that's not it at all." Elias slices his hands like an X through the air. "This has nothing to do with your brothers. I haven't even spoken to them since I arrived at your barracks."

I stare at him long and hard, searching for any evidence of falsehood. "Then why are you apologizing to me?"

Elias's eyebrows rise slightly, surprise and confusion evident in his expression. "Tell me, is it just you, or does everyone in this barracks consider an apology to be a threat?" His gaze drops to my hand at my waist.

Only then do I realize I have my hand resting on the hilt of my dagger, my finger ready to unclip it from its holster. I casually let my hand fall to my side and shrug. "Force of habit."

Elias hesitates for a beat, perhaps to ensure I'm not going to reach for another weapon. He's already zoned in on the knuckle-duster I'm still wearing. For a split second I have an overwhelming urge to yank it off.

Elias rakes a hand through his short wavy brown—almost black—hair. "At the barracks I come from, an apology is just an apology. No strings attached. No hidden agenda. No insincerity." After a pause, he quirks an eyebrow. "And another thing. If I have a crush on a girl, I have the balls to tell her myself without needing any kind of bribe."

The intensity in his gaze stirs something in my ribcage. I

quickly shove that feeling down, but my cheeks still warm without my permission. Like a coward, I break eye contact to stare once again at the chameleon on his shirt.

A sudden wave of self-consciousness sweeps through me. *Damn it!* I was still paralyzed in the infirmary while all the other hunters showered and dressed before breakfast. I'm still in my hunting gear, now caked in the stink of dried sweat and smeared with dirt and grime from last night's hunt. Hopefully, Elias hasn't noticed any kind of stench I might be emitting. And when was the last time I ran a brush through my hair?

I awkwardly fold my arms. "Yeah, well, the barracks you come from also seems to think wearing bright colors on a hunt is suitable," I say, feeling myself start to ramble. "Seriously, dude? Next time you should just rock up to a hunt dressed in a bedazzled tie-dye shirt with the slogan 'My favorite color is glitter.' Then you won't have to rely on your crap hunting skills to snag a kill, because all your glittery rainbows will blind the shifters long enough for you to catch them."

A few seconds of silence pass as Elias regards me, his eyes twinkling with humor. The ghost of a grin twitches at the corners of his mouth.

Again, it doesn't take long for the intensity of that look to become too much for me.

"I've got to go," I blurt. "I need a shower and a nap before training this afternoon."

I step around him, but jolt a little when my arm brushes against his.

"I'll see you at training," he calls after me.

Biting the inside of my cheeks, I try my best to ignore the flutter in my chest and the rush of... something I'm not quite familiar with.

Chapter Ten

I DASH THROUGH THE HALLWAY, darting around the corner and into the next corridor.

Damn that alarm clock. After finally getting some much-needed sleep, I slept right through my alarm. That's never happened before.

My face screws up into a scowl. I'm going to blame Elias and his pathetic aim with a Myst atomizer. Surely I have some residual Myst in my system. Now I'm running half an hour late to training—which sucks! Chances are I've already missed out on all the good sparring opponents, and it's no fun sparring against those who are already wiped out from their previous rounds.

I'm zipping myself into some clean hunting leathers and buckling up my weapons belt as I run, but at least I had the foresight to shower and braid my hair before I went to bed. When I woke up and realized I'd slept in, I was already dressed—well, half-dressed—and out the door within a minute.

My boots thunder down the hallway. Not a soul is in sight, which isn't surprising. Everyone's either still sleeping or at training. I growl in frustration and push myself to run faster. Almost there—just four more junctions to go.

When I reach the end of the hall, I fling myself left at the T-intersection.

Thwump!

I reel back, stumbling a few steps, but manage to steady myself before I fall on my ass.

"Heavens above, what in the—" I cut myself off when I register who I ran into. I'm smack bang in the middle of a group of four hunters. The guy at the front of the group I recognize from breakfast; he was seated next to Elias at the cafeteria. The others look vaguely familiar too—probably also part of the Ragefire posse. All four appear young, maybe fifteen or sixteen. Only the leader looks as if he could pass as an eighteen-year-old.

I scowl at the group, but when I go to push past, they form a barricade to block my way.

"We've been looking all over for you," says the leader.

"It's about time too," mumbles the tall guy behind him, who then receives an elbow to the ribs from the chick next to him.

"What?" he protests. "It's taken us hours to find her."

"Shut up," hisses the chick.

My senses now on high alert, I assess the group with narrowed eyes. "Congratulations, you found me. So what, now you're waiting on a gold star?"

The leader regards me with a cool gaze, then shrugs. "We just thought we'd have a word with you. Especially after the little scene you caused in the cafeteria this morning."

"Really?" Placing my hands on my hips, I give him a slow blink. "How special am I that it takes four of you to 'have a word' with itty-bitty me?"

The leader's mouth twists into a malicious smirk. He swaggers forward, but I refuse to take one step back from this power-tripping adolescent. My gaze on him remains steady, even as I take note of the other three's movements behind him.

"I bet you didn't think you were so 'itty-bitty' attacking the likes of Elias Ragefire," says the leader. He takes another small step. One more and he'll be right up in my face.

"Aww, did I hurt Elias's feelings?" I stick out my bottom lip in a mock pout.

The thug leader gives me a dark scowl. "The hunters in this barracks might think it's appropriate to humiliate one of us in front of everyone, but in *our* barracks, we look out for our own."

"Yeah." The chick brushes a strand of pink-streaked hair behind her ear. "You Branstones are gonna learn you don't mess with the Ragefires. You'll be sorry you even looked at Elias."

"Oh, really? And which one of you is a Ragefire?"

The tall guy at the back shuffles from one foot to the other, and the chick exchanges a glance with the other guy, who has a green-tipped mohawk.

I sneer. "So much for all your 'don't mess with a Ragefire' bullcrap."

"I'm warning you, Branstone." The leader's shoulders bunch with a rising ferocity. "Elias is ten times—fifty times—the hunter a Branstone scum like you could ever wish to be. So you better watch what you say about Elias, or else—"

"Or else what? If this guy is such a big shot, then where is he, huh?" I mockingly look around. "He's not man enough to confront me himself? He's got to send four kids out instead?" I *tsk* and shake my head. "Poor Elias, he's really scraping the bottom of the barrel."

A muscle in the leader's eyebrow twitches.

"Come on, Bandit," coaxes the tall guy, shooting a quick glance over his shoulder. "Let's just get this over with. The others will be done training soon."

I give the group my best knowing smile. "Oh, I get it now. You're not here for Elias at all." I make an exaggerated show of inspecting their hunter amulets. All four have their silver vials filled; only the chick and the leader also have teal. "Hmm... two colors, huh? It totally proves how badass you are that you had to wait until everyone is busy training to come find me. But then, I suppose the story will be that much more entertaining when I tell everyone how I beat all four of your pathetic asses."

The leader stares me down, but the acidity in his expression hitches when he glances at where my amulet is hiding under my black leather jacket. A few tense heart-beats pass before his curiosity gets the best of him. "How many colors do you have?"

With a challenging grin, I say, "Come and find out."

The change in his eyes takes only a millisecond, what-ever restraint he had left obliterated.

"Dex!" he orders with a snap of his fingers.

Mohawk charges.

But I'm ready.

Mohawk is smart enough to at least come at me with his Diamantium dagger. His first strike might even have gutted me if I didn't dodge at the last second. Unfazed, Mohawk follows up with another nimble, lightning-fast swipe, then another and another. The leader, the chick, and Tall Guy take a few steps back as Mohawk's dagger slices around in a deadly frenzy. There's no question as to why this guy is the champion of this amateur group.

I duck and weave, the dagger's crystal tip coming ever

closer to my face. I'm sure Mohawk has nicked my cheek, but with adrenaline coursing through my body, I don't yet register the telltale sting of a cut. I'll worry about that later.

Just as Mohawk's dagger sails through the air with fatal precision, I take hold of his dagger arm, redirect his blade, and bring my knee straight into his diaphragm. Air gushes from his lungs. As soon as he doubles over, I meet his face with another knee and enough force to knock him out cold.

His head snaps back. Blood sprays from his nose. His dagger clatters to the ground, and then he collapses in a clumsy bundle.

The kid was good, I'll give him that, although there isn't much about his skill to make me think he was raised a hunter. It isn't uncommon for hunters to recruit those who don't have much going for them in the real world, as long as they show enough potential to become a worthy trainee.

With Mohawk down, I turn my attention to the other three. Tall Guy is wide-eyed and slack-jawed. The chick narrows her eyes at me. The leader's scowl is still set in determination and rage.

"Bandit, look at her amulet," says the chick.

All three sets of eyes land on the amulet now swinging freely from my neck.

"Four colors," says Tall Guy, his voice lowered in reverence or fear, I'm not sure which. "Bandit, I don't think we should—"

"Just shut up," spits the leader. "She needs to know her place. Besides, she's just one girl."

"And she's just a Branstone," says the chick. "We take her down now, everyone will know how putrid the Branstones really are."

"Yeah, but look what she did to Dex. Not only that, she's got four colors, dude. *Four freaking colors.*"

"Stop being such a coward," Bandit says to the tall guy, then to me he adds, "You're finished, Branstone." He brandishes a crystal dagger. The chick follows suit, and a second later, the tall guy reluctantly pulls out his own Diamantium blade.

I grin viciously at the three as they deliberate their chances. My body is practically buzzing with bloodlust. It looks as though I won't miss out on a decent sparring match after all.

I pull out my Diamantium-tipped knuckle-duster. The second I thread my fingers through it, the three charge.

Just as the leader is upon me, I slam my boot square into his chest. He flies back and collides with the chick behind him. Leaving those two to sprawl on the ground, I duck the tall guy's incoming blade, swipe my foot out, and kick his legs out from under him. He hits the deck with a heavy thud and a strangled yelp.

The other two have recovered, and I redirect my attention to them, lunging into their tumult with familiar delight.

All erratic emotions and turbulent thoughts grow still in my mind, and my body melds into the weapon I've spent a lifetime training it to be. My arms, legs, torso—every inch of my body bends, ducks, swoops, and slices through the air as my Diamantium-tipped knuckle-duster carves through black hunting leathers and eventually flesh.

All three try their best to claim a piece of me, but they're no match for my instincts. My bare fist collides, cartilage crunches. Cries ring out, curses hiss, and crimson droplets splatter.

With my blinged-up knuckles, I slash and stab at every opening I see. In a matter of seconds I've eliminated Tall Guy from the foray. He retreats back down the hall in a diced-up mess, whimpering about the new boo-boos over his face, neck, and arms.

Bandit and the chick, however, are proving to have a little more gumption than I originally anticipated. The two circle around me with speed and finesse, their Diamantium blades slicing a few nicks and cuts over my arms and torso. Nothing deep enough to be concerned about, but the two are relentless. I have no doubt with a bit more training, these two will turn into a force to be reckoned with.

Among the rush of adrenaline, a new emotion rears its head—one I'm unfamiliar with while fighting. It takes me a moment to recognize it, but when I do, shock quickly follows the realization.

No way. It can't be envy I'm experiencing... can it? What about these two amateur hunters would call forth that reaction?

I try to take more careful, deliberate notice of how they work. The two are clearly compatible as a team. Whether in a romantic relationship or not, they're a mighty duo, the yin to each other's yang. Where Bandit's skill is lacking, the chick fills the void, and vice versa.

Envy stabs at me again when the question creeps into my head: What must that be like—to have a companion adequate enough to be my equal, someone who fulfills my shortcomings, not just in hunting and fighting but in other areas of my life?

Granted, Quill and Hestus do look out for me in their own twisted way, but they're more of a duo than we are a trio. I'm just the little sister they allow to tag along whenever it suits them.

For the longest time, I convinced myself I was better off alone anyway. This situation with Bandit and his minions is the perfect example of why: Every hunter has something to prove against a Branstone—our reputation has spread far and wide. It's more than difficult to trust anyone.

Bandit, his chick, and I continue our vicious battle of crystal shards, ebbing and flowing around each other in a three-part tango. I'm thoroughly enjoying the challenge of taking the two thugs down, although I'm working hard to only maim, not kill. Humans don't have Diamantium bones like the Veniri, tough hides like the Lycans, or Luxium power cores like the Magneii. The death of these two would be of no benefit to me, and I don't need the inconvenience of having to explain why a cleanup is needed in hallway twelve.

Swipe. Block. Lunge. Parry. Slash.

We fall into a steady rhythm. My knuckle-duster is doing a great job of tearing up my opponents. Their shirts and other clothing not made of Lycan leather are already in shreds. Lycan leather is the ultimate protective hunting armor, flexible and tough. As much as Diamantium blades can slice through just about anything, it still takes a few deliberate strikes to cut through Lycan leather.

Seconds grind into minutes. Breaths heave harder, and splashes of red pepper Bandit and the chick. But the two still aren't quitting. I don't blame them. They have their reputations at stake, not just with their barracks but also with mine. As hunters with two colors in their amulet, taking down a hunter with four colors would certainly boost their reputations. If I were in their shoes, I'd continue fighting right up until the bitter end, especially with Tall Guy running off with his tail between his legs and Mohawk still passed out on the floor a few feet away.

Desperation forces their kicks to come harder, and daggers to swipe faster, albeit with a little less precision than before. I soon realize my own fatigue is beginning to set in. If these two are planning to wear me out for a guaranteed KO, it's working.

The chick swoops under my right hook, but my power kick to her lower ribs connects with enough force I swear I hear a bone crack. She wails and clutches her side, stumbling back to allow Bandit to take her place. Without hesitation, Bandit jumps in to try to gain the upper hand.

Sweat streams down his brow, mingling with the bloodied lacerations all over his face. His gasps for air have grown heavy from exertion, and his movements are noticeably languid.

Ha! I would guess this guy has less than half a minute left before I best him. Then it will take nothing to finish off his little girlfriend, if it turns out she isn't smart enough to tap out.

I almost grin in triumph. I'm going to reign supreme in this battle.

No sooner does that thought cross my mind than I have a lapse in judgment and trip over Mohawk's leg.

Damn my stupid, stupid arrogance.

Bandit takes swift advantage of my stumble and crash-tackles me to the ground. The move costs him his dagger though, which flies out of his hand and skitters across the floor. We scramble, him trying his best to stay out of swinging distance of my knuckle-duster while trying to retrieve his weapon.

After several seconds, he gives up on the dagger and switches tactics. Grabbing my other arm, he jars my elbow in a lock. I grit my teeth as the joint bends the wrong way.

Bandit is just out of reach of my free arm; any further attempt to punch him with my blingy knuckles will only put further strain on my locked-up elbow. The hunter may be younger than me, but he's still strong.

I kick my legs and buck my body—any attempt to loosen his grip before things in my elbow start to snap.

"Help me!" Bandit calls out to the chick.

With a wince, the chick obliges, stepping over Mohawk's body and steering clear of my kicking legs.

"Give up, Branstone," Bandit orders.

"*Never*," I hiss through my teeth.

Bandit bears down on my arm; the ligaments and tendons are a hairsbreadth away from tearing. My elbow screams in pain. I bite down, refusing to cry out at the grind of cartilage and bone.

"You're done. Just tap out, Branstone."

"Over my dead body." I've got one last thing up my sleeve. It's a dirty trick, but I've never been one to play by the rules.

I yank my pneumatic dart gun from its holster at my waist at the same moment the chick draws her arm back to throw her dagger at me.

Time freezes. Her arm halts in the air and her eyes grow wide at the sight of my dart gun aimed at her face. Sweat mixed with blood trickles down her brow, plastering strands of her pink-streaked midnight hair to her cheeks.

I can practically hear the gears working in her mind: there's no way her dagger will hit me before my dart slices through her eye socket.

"You shoot her, and I'll break your arm," promises Bandit.

I scoff. "A broken arm I can live with."

A burst of pressurized air echoes through the corridor—at the same time a scream bursts past my lips as the kid snaps my elbow back.

Chapter Eleven

"IS SHE AWAKE YET?"

"Just like the previous twenty times you asked, Peony, no, she's not awake. Now move away from her before you wake her," replies a hushed familiar voice.

The first, younger voice responds with a dramatic sigh. "When will she wake up?"

"I still don't know. Nothing's changed since the last time you asked. Now, I'm just going to check on your chicken nuggets. I'm going to be gone for one minute. Can I trust you to stay quiet?"

"Mm-hmm."

"Peony?"

"I said 'mm-hmm.'"

Someone gives a soft chuckle, the sound followed by fading footsteps.

Several silent heartbeats pass, and then my body jostles, almost as if someone is climbing onto the bed with me. Whether I'm ready to wake or not, my eyes fly open. I half flinch at the smiling round face, rosy cheeks, and big blue eyes looming mere inches from my nose.

"Hello," says the girl hovering over me. Two dolls with mussed hair appear next to her. "Wanna play dolls with me?"

"Peony! What are you doing? What did I just say?"

A guy runs into the room and hauls the child away from me. While the girl protests, I sit up.

It takes me a second to register three things. First, a dull ache throbs in my arm, along with a collection of other faint aches in my torso, legs, and back; second, the air around me smells like stale chicken nuggets; and third, I'm in one of the guest rooms of the barracks. When I realize whose guest room I'm in, I feel all blood drain from my face.

Oh no, this can't be happening.

"Hey, look who's up," says Elias Ragefire, grinning down at me.

In one fell swoop, I kick my legs over the side of the bed and stand up. I start to make a direct exit through the door, only to have the room spin and the beechwood-print linoleum fly directly toward my face.

Aw nuts, I stood up way too fast.

"Whoa, careful." Arms swoop in and catch me before I have the chance to face-plant.

"Don't." I try to squirm out of Elias's embrace, but as soon as he relaxes his hold, my knees buckle, and I slump ungracefully to the floor. I toss out a few more swats at the arms holding my shoulders, but only when it's evident gravity has taken me as far as I can go does Elias finally release me.

It takes a few moments of me leaning back against the bed for the room's spinning to slow down. With relief, I stretch my legs out on the floor, fighting back a groan at my stiff joints. Apparently that action is an invitation for the little girl to swoop in like a ninja and plonk onto my lap.

"Peony, what are you doing?" Elias hisses.

"Hi, you haven't said if you want to play dolls with me yet," she says, blatantly ignoring Elias and smiling up at me with bubbling enthusiasm. Without giving me time to respond, she quickly follows up with "I'm Peony. What's your name?"

Shock eclipses the remainder of my dizziness. I hold completely still, as if a giant rattlesnake landed in my lap instead of a cute-as-pie little girl. "Uh... I'm Nika."

Peony gives me a gap-toothed smile, holds up two dolls in my face, and chatters at a hundred miles an hour. "Hi, Nika. Wanna play dolls with me? You can play with the purple one—her name's Princess Giggles. And I'll play with Queen Cupcake—she's the pink one. If you want you can brush their hair—I don't mind. Oh! Do you know how to braid hair? Elias has tried, but he's terrible." Peony ends with gagging noises to further express her opinion of Elias's hairstyling skills.

"Okay, that's enough," interjects Elias. "Let's not freak Nika out too much. She's hurt, remember?"

Peony frowns at Elias. "But I thought you gave her the magic potion?"

"Yes, but it still needs a little more time before she's all better."

"Oh." Peony directs her interrogating eyes back at me. "Do you feel better yet?"

I nod slowly, not sure I want to face the consequences of saying otherwise.

"See, she's all better." Peony gives Elias a triumphant grin.

"Still, we should give Nika some space. One needs a little more time before being pounced on and forced to interact with Princess Giggles and Queen Cupcake." He reaches over to lift Peony off my lap.

"Aww, but I wanna play dolls with Nika."

Elias stifles a laugh. "As much as I would *love* to see Nika playing with dolls, she still needs to rest."

"Aww, but—"

"Peony, Nika needs a few minutes, okay?" Elias's tone is firm but affectionate at the same time. "How about you go and eat your chicken nuggets before they get cold?"

"Okay." Peony's bottom lip droops with defeat. "Can I watch cartoons while I'm eating?"

"You sure can." Elias carries the small girl and her two dolls over to the doorway. "But make sure you eat all your chicken nuggets."

"Fine," Peony says with a heavy sigh. Elias places her on the floor, and she runs out of view. As much as I'm still stunned by the gusto that tiny human has, I'm surprised how sorry I am to see her leave.

When Elias turns back to me, I raise an eyebrow. "Magic potion?"

"It's easier for her to say magic potion than Ylixium." He smiles. "For a while there, you were fading in and out of consciousness, so I gave you the Ylixium to help with the pain and speed up the healing."

"Right." I nod with understanding.

Elias crouches down in front of me, a forearm resting casually on his knee and his head slightly tilted to one side. "How are you feeling?"

"Fine." I go to put my hand on my now pounding head, only to find my arm caught up in a sling. "What happened?" I try to make my voice as commanding and in control as possible.

A corner of Elias's mouth quirks up. "You don't remember what happened?"

I try to think back to my most recent memory before waking up to the ever-lively Peony inches from my face. With crisp clarity, I recall the three hunter thugs who jumped me—four if I count the tall dude who practically ran screaming down the hallway.

I can almost remember the entire fight—every one of my strikes, counterstrikes, and jabs with my knuckle-duster— right up until the pressurized blast from my pneumatic dart gun and the moment the leader snapped my arm back.

From there things are a little fuzzy, but desperation and rage flutter through me like an echo when I sift through the scattered memories. The pain in my arm wasn't what caused me to black out, but I remember agony exploding through my body when someone kicked their heavy boot into me over and over again. In my last remaining seconds of consciousness, I swear I saw the tall guy running back down the hall toward us with Elias in tow.

The dull ache in my elbow brings me back to the present, and I cast my best accusatory glare at Elias.

He grins at me. "Good, you do remember." Gesturing to my sling, he adds, "You earned yourself a dislocated elbow and a few torn tendons, along with a new collection of bruises, fractured ribs, and a few minor cuts and scrapes, but it looks like the Ylixium has already taken care of a lot of the wounds over your face, at least. How's the rest of you feeling?"

I frown when I register no pain from the apparently fractured ribs; it must've been a few hours since I took the Ylixium. That's a relief, at least. Other than a slight case of dizziness, there's nothing hindering me from getting out of here—which reminds me...

"Why did you bring me here?" I demand. And exactly how long have I been in Elias Ragefire's room, of all places—especially considering that last time I saw him, I attempted to pound his jaw into dust and threatened to gut him with my Diamantium-tipped knuckle-duster in front of the whole cafeteria?

Elias gestures to my arm. "You were hurt."

"So were your friends." I make a point of looking around the nondescript bedroom with a double bed, two bedside tables, and a small wardrobe in the corner. "But I don't see any of your buddies here, unless you've got them bunking in the wardrobe."

Elias shakes his head; a ghost of a smile plays on his lips. "No, no one's in the wardrobe. Our medic is taking care of those four you had a tussle with. Thanks to you, between the four of them, there were several broken ribs, punctured lungs, a few concussions, a broken nose, a broken collarbone, sprained wrists and ankles, countless lacerations, and shallow puncture wounds, and that's just what I can remember off the top of my head. And by the way, was a pneumatic dart gun really necessary?"

I shrug my good shoulder. "I didn't have any Myst handy."

Elias arches a brow at my dig. Regardless of his lack of smile, I definitely pick up a twinkle of amusement. "Myst or not, Danika's lucky she dodged in time. The dart missed her eye by inches, but it managed to slice through her ear."

I huff a noncommittal noise. During the "tussle," as Elias called it, I didn't actually see where my dart landed. I did figure it ended up somewhere nonlethal, as the chick, Danika, managed to continue kicking me in the ribs as if I were a cheating ex-boyfriend. To an extent, I'm kinda relieved my dart missed her eye, considering I planned to only maim and not kill. Sometimes it gets a little difficult for me to control my inner mongrel once I set her free.

Ignoring Elias's disapproval of my weapon choice, I state, "You still haven't told me why you brought me here."

He shrugs. "With the damage you caused, no one from my barracks was interested in giving you aid, especially when they realized you were a Branstone. Your brothers and almost everyone else from your barracks had already left to hunt by the time I found you. Plus, my room was closer than the infirmary. I also figured it would be easier to use my own stash of Ylixium than rely on someone from your barracks to give me some."

I take a moment to analyze Elias's reasoning. It almost sounds like a bunch of half-assed excuses.

An edge of seriousness clouds Elias's amusement. "There was also the fact that when Mario came to me and said there was some crazy chick beating the crap out of Bandit and his friends, I didn't have anyone to look after Peony."

"Oh." I glance at the open doorway, in the direction of the cartoon music. "Peony was left by herself?" I picture a darkened lounge room illuminated by the technicolor strobing of a TV screen, and a tiny Peony huddled under a tattered blanket, whispering to her dolls that everything is okay and Elias will come back soon. The thought sends an unexpected stab of concern through my stomach.

"She wasn't alone for long," Elias assures me. "I promised Peony I'd stay with her tonight and watch a few cartoons instead of going hunting. Your timing was pretty bad, I might add. You have no idea how gutted I was to miss out on the princess sisters singing about building a snowman for what has to be the hundredth time. But when

Mario was freaking out over 'the crazy chick,' it didn't take me long to figure out who he meant."

I decide not to read too much into Elias's obvious merriment, nor do I feel like challenging the "crazy chick" title shoved on me by Mario, who I assume was the tall coward who took off halfway through my butt-whooping. Instead, my annoyance latches on to the fact that the rest of the hunters have left for the night without me. Not only did I miss out on this afternoon's training; I'm missing out on yet another hunting trip. My stupid brothers didn't even bother to come find me. Those jerks! I'll have to think up some decent payback for them later.

"So, no hunting for you tonight either?" I ask.

Elias shakes his head. A dark expression clouds his features, and for a second, I swear I glimpse a hint of severity behind his eyes, but it clears before I can consider it further. "Nah, I've been out a few too many nights this week."

I incline my chin in the direction of the cartoon music. "How old is she?"

"Five, going on fifteen." Elias casts a small smile toward the sound of a giggle now joining in with the energetic song.

"And Peony's your..." I trail off, trying to piece together my foggy knowledge of Elias's family.

"She's my sister," he confirms.

I can almost feel the weight behind his use of the word *sister*, as if he just announced he's in possession of a prized relic. For a moment, Elias's eyes glaze over as he focuses on some faraway thought. Then with a blink and a half smile, he's back in the present. "Peony was born not long before our mother died."

Yes, I recall him cuddling a small bundle at his mother's funeral. I struggle to keep my own grief at bay as I think about the little girl who, like me, is also growing up without a mother. At least I have my memories. Peony was a baby. What are the chances she remembers anything about her mother?

"Anyway"—Elias pushes himself to his feet—"I'm hungry. What about you?"

"Uh..." I almost say I'm fine, but a pang in my stomach tells me otherwise.

Before I can say anything further, Peony explodes back into the room with a flurry of vibrancy, throws her arms in the air, and declares, "I've finished my chicken nuggets!"

"Good work," says Elias with a snigger.

Peony frowns at me as her brother reaches down to pick her up. "How come you're still sitting on the floor?"

"Good question," I eventually say. "Maybe I think it's a little comfier than the bed."

Peony giggles at me. "You're such a weirdo."

"Peony," Elias hisses, "what have we said about calling people a weirdo?"

His gentle scolding earns him a groan and an eye roll from the small girl in his arms. "Don't call people a weirdo to their face, even if they are a weirdo," Peony says in a robotic voice.

"What? No, that's not what I said—ugh! Never mind, we'll talk about this later." Elias sighs and pinches the bridge of his nose before giving me an apologetic smile. "We're still learning the basics in manners."

I wave my hand that isn't trapped in the sling. "It's not like I haven't been called worse."

I half expect Elias to chuckle at that statement, but he regards me with a thoughtful look that holds an edge of regret... or perhaps some kind of... resentment?

"Can we get ice cream?" Peony blurts.

Elias purses his lips and begins to shake his head just as Peony starts to whine.

"Aww, you promised! You said next time you stayed back from hunting, you'd take me for ice cream."

"Seriously, Peony. I said *maybe* I would take you for ice cream. Besides, the closest ice creamery is in the city—"

"Pleeeeeease, Elias." Peony bounces in his arms and swings her legs in the air. "I've eaten all my dinner."

"Chicken nuggets and ice cream is hardly a substantial meal."

"I promise I'll eat all the veggies you give me for dinner tomorrow. You can give me any veggies you want, but only if we get ice cream now."

Elias shakes his head, but after a few more pretty-pleases and a substantial amount of promises only a five-year-old could believe themselves capable of fulfilling, he finally relents.

Peony celebrates her victory with a high-pitched squeal. "Yes, ice cream!"

I fight a smirk. It's unbelievable how much this petite little tyke has the infamous Elias Ragefire wrapped around her itty-bitty pinky.

Peony jumps down from Elias's hold and bounds over to me. "I'm going to get rainbow flavor and sprinkles. What flavor are you going to get, Nika?"

"Whoa, wait a sec." I hold up a hand. "I'm not coming."

"You're not?" All joy evaporates from Peony's little face. From the shock in her eyes, it's as if I announced I'm going to hacksaw her dolls into pieces. "But why? Don't you want to come? You don't have to have rainbow ice cream like me. You can have cherry flavor or caramel or chocolate or what-ever flavor you want. Don't you like ice cream?"

"It's not that I don't like ice cream, it's just... that you don't... need me to come along." Before I can flounder further in trying to explain how odd it would be for the likes of me to crash her ice cream outing, Peony's bottom lip droops and her shoulders slump.

My jaw hangs open as I lose all words. Give me a vicious shifter any day. Give me a grizzly bear to deal with. Heck, I'd even prefer walking down a catwalk in nine-inch stilettos and a string bikini in front of a bunch of fashion-snob strangers. I'm self-aware enough to realize I am in no way equipped to handle a distressed child.

I grimace further. *Good grief*, are her eyes starting to well up with tears?

"Uh, Elias? A little help?"

Elias's smirk is a little too similar to the one I was fighting earlier when Peony trumped him with all her best manipulation tactics.

"You know, you could come," he finally says.

"What?" Now it's my turn to look at him as if he just announced he's going to hack up Peony's dolls.

"Other than waiting for your arm to heal, what other plans did you have for tonight while everyone else is out hunting?"

I narrow my eyes. He had to rub it in that I'm once again missing out.

"I know you haven't eaten in a while," he adds, "so how about we swing by the cafeteria for a dinner-to-go, and you can join us for dessert in the city?"

"Yes, join us for dessert," Peony echoes.

I stare at Elias and give him a slight shake of my head, willing him to receive my telepathic message.

By the glimmer in his eye, he knows all too well what I'm trying not to say out loud. "Come on," he coaxes. "Do you really want to mope around here, waiting for the others to come back to gloat about all the hunting you missed out on?"

Peony clasps her hands in front of her bedazzled "I'm a mermaid in disguise" T-shirt. "Please come with us, Nika."

I purse my lips in resistance.

"It's just ice cream. How bad can it be?" says Elias. With a winning smile, he adds, "I'll even promise to leave my Myst here."

I let out a sigh. It's one thing to be on the receiving end of Peony's adorable beseeching, but to have her big brother join in on the negotiations is just plain cheating.

Chapter Twelve

"HERE'S one rainbow unicorn sundae, one choc-dipped cotton candy swirl, and a sherbet fizz waffle delight," says the ice cream guy, placing each cone in a holder on the countertop.

While Elias sorts out the payment, I hand Peony her vibrant color-infused treat.

"Careful, don't drop it," I warn as Peony reaches up to snatch the dessert from me, all the while bouncing on her feet. She squeals in delight at the first taste of her sugar rush.

"This is the best ice cream ever!" she declares, throwing a fist into the air.

I don't even have a chance to cringe at Peony's public outburst before the two ladies behind us giggle.

"Your daughter is so adorable," says the blonde while the brunette nods her agreement with a big smile.

"No, no, she's not my daughter." My arms flail pathetically toward Elias. "She belongs to him."

Both the ladies' eyes grow wide, and their grins become dreamy as they look Elias up and down. The brunette sidles up to me and whispers conspiratorially in my ear, "You lucky thing. Single dads are all the rage these days."

I blink, taken aback. What the heck did that chick just say to me?

As if it has a mind of its own, my lip curls in disgust as the brunette and her blonde bestie continue to eyeball Elias like a choice rack of barbecued ribs. Before I can manage a rebuttal—or better yet, a fist to the throat to set her straight —a chocolate-dipped ice cream appears in front of my face.

"Here's your ice cream," says Elias. "Shall we take the scenic way back to the car and hope all this sugar sends Peony to sleep when we get back to the barracks?"

"Sure, why not?" Following Elias and the still bouncing Peony out of the ice creamery, I shoot a glance over my shoulder to find Brunette and Blondie gleefully giving me the thumbs-up.

In the end, I roll my eyes and shake my head. Those chicks have no idea what they're on about.

Once we're back out on the sidewalk, Elias's phone buzzes. He takes it out of his top jacket pocket, taps the screen for a few seconds, and then returns it.

As we walk, I bite into my ice cream. The crisp chocolate coating crunches perfectly, a winning combination with the velvety ice cream inside. The cotton candy flavor manages just the right amount of sweetness without being sickening, and the texture is unbelievably fluffy and delectable, like its namesake. *Wowzers*, no denying this was definitely worth the hour-long drive to the city.

"It's that good, huh?"

Dragging my attention away from my ice cream, I look up to find Elias grinning down at me.

"I've never seen you look at anything with such fondness before," he adds.

I shrug a shoulder and flash a grin. "It's not too bad," I say after a heartbeat.

Elias chuckles and shakes his head, then bites into his own ice cream. "You know, you don't really strike me as a cotton candy ice cream kinda gal."

"Why? What did you expect?"

"I don't know." He shrugs. "Maybe something a little more hardcore, like a brandy nougat ice cream with a swirl of shrapnel and topped with gunpowder."

I let out a huff of amusement. "Oh really? And what about you? Who knew the badass Elias Ragefire had an affinity for sherbet fizz and not a chloroform-creme delight in a black-licorice-flavored cone topped off with a drizzle of gasoline?"

Elias throws his head back and laughs. "I'm never going to live down that Myst incident, am I?"

I shake my head, and after a few moments, I can't help but add my own laughter. Peony peeks at us over her shoulder, her brow furrowed in curiosity. Then with a shrug, she continues to skip ahead down the street.

"Wow, would you look at that. The 'Branstone Iron Maiden' knows how to smile after all."

I groan. "Not you too."

"What's wrong?"

I let out a breath through my nose. "Look, I get it. 'Iron Maiden' as in I'm hard on the outside but much more prickly on the inside. But then if it's not the 'Branstone Iron Maiden,' I get called 'dollface' or some other names I can't say out loud in front of Peony. It's just... I don't know. No one ever calls me 'The Branstone Warrior' or something else that highlights my skills as a hunter. They just focus on how I look or how I act."

I take a breath and look up at Elias. "Sorry. I didn't realize I was in the mood for a rant."

Elias frowns. "Don't apologize for that. What you're saying is valid. Don't take any of it to heart. People can be stupid... You know what? I take it back. Forget I said anything about the Iron Maiden."

A minute or so passes in contemplative silence—at least, I'm pretty sure I'm not the only one contemplating. Elias is punishing his lip with a hard bite.

"What happened to you?" I blurt.

Elias glances at me, brows slightly furrowed in confusion. "What do you mean?"

"I remember you as this crazy boy with a whirlwind fury, like your name. You fought without fear or remorse, and you never once worried about something asinine like name calling. I mean, come on, Peony calling people 'weirdo'? The 'Branstone Iron Maiden'? Since when do you care how that affects others?"

Elias looks at me long and hard, as if I'm the one who needs to answer my own question.

Or maybe I have ice cream smeared on my face, and he's wondering whether to tell me or not.

"You know, it's been a while since I thought about my childhood," he finally says. "I think you're right though. Things have changed—I've definitely changed—especially since Peony was born. When Mom died, Dad just... spaced. He practically turned his back on everything to do with parenting. He didn't go near Peony for months. He still doesn't have anything to do with her. His lame-ass excuse is 'She reminds me too much of your mother.'"

Elias scoffs with disgust. "What a moron. When he checked out, I stepped up. I had to be there for Peony. So now, I'm doing my best to raise her the way Mom would have wanted. And believe it or not, name calling was something she used to always call me out on."

Despite the small smile on Elias's face, the depth of his sorrow is unmistakable. It mirrors the grief I have over my own mother. Maybe that's how I recognize what he's feeling. But I can't pity him, not when in the midst of losing his mother, he took it upon himself to step into the role of caretaker for his infant sister.

What have I done since my mother died? Definitely nothing admirable like Elias.

You've earned four colors for your amulet so far, the slightly optimistic side of myself reminds me. I tune in to the familiar weight hidden under my shirt, which bumps against my sternum as I walk. I've been channeling so much of myself into filling each vial in the last few years. With four colors in my amulet, I'm now entitled to a notable level of respect in the hunter community.

Hunting shifters and claiming their blood has been all I've ever known—it's all I ever wanted. I always figured once I filled all my vials, I'd have plenty of time to complete my other dreams.

But now that my other dreams have been dashed to oblivion, the achievement of four colors in my amulet feels empty—even more so compared to Elias's priorities.

My focus shifts to the bouncing Peony still a few paces ahead. Her light brown hair springs up and down behind her and is in dire need of a good brush. The mermaid-themed T-shirt and matching scale-print skirt fit surprisingly well into the vibrant and colorful nightlife we're walking through, especially with the flickering lights in her sequined sneakers strobing to life with each step.

In a world of cutthroat and bloodthirsty hunters, Elias has gone against all odds in raising a confident, carefree, and remarkable little girl. For the first time in my existence, I begin to wonder how my life would have turned out if I hadn't been raised in a hunting family.

Peony comes to a halt, does a one-eighty, and holds her hands up to Elias.

"Yikes," he says, assessing the drippy, sticky mess.

He pulls out a stack of napkins and expertly cleans up the rainbow rivulets streaming down her hands and forearms, then wipes another clean napkin over the multicolored remnants of ice cream on her face. Within a minute, Peony once again takes the lead and weaves us through the city streets—thankfully the ones geared toward family-friendly restaurants and retail shopfronts rather than the pill-poppin', club-hoppin' kind of establishments I'm more familiar with.

"Does Peony know which way the car is?" I ask after about five minutes of meandering.

Elias grins. "Maybe she does, and maybe she doesn't."

I raise an eyebrow.

Not for the first time this evening, I question my sanity for allowing myself to be dragged along on this little adventure for dessert. But also, not for the first time, I'm surprised by how comfortable I find myself with these two Ragefires, of all the hunters I could have spent my time with. If I'm being honest, I'm even more surprised by how little I miss being out on the hunt tonight.

As we walk along, Elias and I fall into a companionable silence, much like the few times in the car ride over when Peony wasn't chatting away at warp speed.

"How's your arm?" Elias asks.

"Fine."

Thankfully, eating ice cream is a one-handed job. Much to Elias's disapproval, I tossed the sling into a trash can as soon as I got out of the car. My elbow is still a little tender—soft tissue always takes longer to heal than broken bones—but the Ylixium is doing its job. Another hour or so and my arm will be as good as new. I'll just have to remember not to favor it too much in the meantime. Elias doesn't need to know how much it still hurts.

I point to Peony with my ice cream. "You know if you keep letting her wander around like this, she's going to get us all lost."

"Come on, Branstone, where's your sense of adventure? You've got to admit this is much better than moping around the barracks all night." Elias gently nudges me with his elbow when I don't answer straightaway. "Go on, you can say it. 'You're right, Elias. This was a great idea.'"

At his soprano impression of me, I regard him with a deadpan gaze. But I can't hold eye contact for long and maintain a straight face, so I quickly return my attention to my half-eaten ice cream. "Okay, fine. This wasn't the worst idea in the world."

"You're right. The worst idea was probably letting Peony take the lead." Elias throws his head back and guffaws when I cast him an "I knew it" look. "Relax, Nika. You'll get home safe and sound, I'll make sure of it. Don't worry about Peony. It's not often she gets to roam free and explore without the risk of coming across weapons, explosives, half-mutilated shifter carcasses, and, you know... all the other child-friendly stuff found in a barracks." He chuckles with dark humor. "A barracks isn't the best place for a kid to grow up."

I humph. The "child-friendly" stuff in our barracks is all I've ever known. "Growing up in a barracks isn't that bad."

"Oh, yeah? How has it ever benefitted you?"

Instantly, half a dozen advantages come to my mind, but

after a second I realize they're all the things I'd be expected to say, the things I've been conditioned to believe all my life.

Elias takes my silence as an answer. "See? Children shouldn't be subjected to the life that you and I have." He juts his chin at Peony. "I'm trying to shield her from the horrors of our reality. Poor Peony's confined to our rooms most of the time back home, and I'm the only person she sees most of the time."

"If you hate it so much, what's stopping you from leaving?"

Elias is silent for a long moment. I start to wonder if he's going to scold me for bringing up a topic hunters never speak about.

"I think you already know why we can't leave," he finally says. "A life on the run from her own people isn't what I want for Peony. Besides, my father has been arrogant and stupid enough to make himself many enemies—some who wouldn't hesitate to seek revenge if given the chance. For now, the Ragefire name and the protection of the barracks ensure Peony's safety from outsiders."

"And as for the insiders?"

Elias studies me with the intensity I'm becoming familiar with, his honey-brown eyes boring into mine. He's just opened his mouth to say something when his phone buzzes. Giving me an apologetic smile, he once again retrieves it from his top jacket pocket.

I crunch through the rest of my ice cream cone while Elias tap-taps on the screen.

Peony turns the corner at an intersection, then squeals and pumps her fists in the air. "I see a jumping castle!"

The street beyond has been closed off to traffic, making way for a street market. Artisans, food trucks, bespoke clothing, balloon vendors, knock-off handbags and sunglasses stalls, and many other small businesses line each side of the street as far as I can see through the crowd. And of course, as Peony exclaimed, right in the middle of the marketplace is a giant jumping castle.

"Can I go on the jumping castle? Pleeeeeeeeease, Elias. I promise I'll eat all my veggies for the next *two* nights."

"I don't know." Elias strokes his make-believe goatee. "An ice cream and a jumping castle all in one night is worth at least five nights of veggies."

"Five!" Peony's eyes bug, as if he suggested she eat squid guts instead.

I lean against the brick wall, looking on in amusement as the negotiations go back and forth; eventually they land on three nights of veggies and one night where Elias gets to choose the Disney movie before bed.

Overflowing with enthusiasm, Peony guides us to the inflated castle. Elias pays for a ten-minute session, and within seconds, Peony's sequined LED shoes are off and she's jumping, squealing, and giggling with about twenty other children.

Elias nudges me and points to a coffee van parked on the other side of the castle near a side street. "Want a coffee or something while we wait?"

"Sure, why not?"

We place an order for two caramel lattes. When Elias goes to pay, I nudge him to the side and try to hand the vendor some cash.

"No you don't." Elias gently moves my extended arm away. "I've got this."

"You already paid for the ice creams," I counter. "I've got this."

"No, Peony and I dragged you out tonight. My treat."

I narrow my eyes, ready to argue, but something in

Elias's face gives me pause. He takes my hesitation as acceptance and hands his own cash to the coffee vendor. When we step to the side to wait for our beverages, that piercing look remains as he turns his attention back to me.

What is with this guy? He's much harder to decipher than the rest of the hunters I grew up with. Most of them have the emotional depth of a shot glass, and all have a simple, predictable routine: eat, sleep, train, hunt, find someone to humiliate, then repeat. If the conversation doesn't revolve around hunting, then it isn't worth their time. There are none of these deep expressions I have to interpret, no discussions that wander around the edges of the painful past.

Something about the look Elias is giving me—even if I can't quite grasp its meaning—makes my stomach flutter and heat rise in my cheeks.

"I still don't get it. Why are you being nice to me?" I ask, fighting the rising shame of how I reacted after the Myst incident. "I didn't exactly give you any reason to be nice with the way I treated you in the cafeteria."

My shame increases when I recall how he also gave me a dose of Ylixium from his own personal supply. Absolutely no one I know would share even a drop of their Ylixium without asking a hefty price—not with the noticeable decline in the Yranum shifter population and, by extension, their pearl-white healing blood. Ylixium hasn't reached rationing levels yet, but hunters are becoming mindful of protecting their stores.

Elias takes a step toward me, the gap between us reduced to millimeters. I'm so surprised by his brazen move I actually freeze. This is the closest someone's ever come to me without delivering a sucker punch or a threat of bloody murder.

My curls dance around my cheeks in a gentle breeze, and Elias catches hold of one sweeping over my face. I expect him to do the cliché move of tucking it behind my ear. Instead he twists the lock into a coil around his fingers. The odd, simple action feels somehow symbolic, and the significance of the rising butterflies in my stomach starts to become clear.

"If I tell you something, do you promise not to freak out?" Elias says in a soft voice.

A light panic lances through me, along with the searing memories of being vulnerable with my feelings toward another hunter.

Elias must see my expression shift. "It's nothing bad," he rushes to say. "At least... I hope you don't think it's bad." His knuckles, still wrapped in a curl of my hair, brush over my jawline with a feather touch, as if to soothe my rising doubts.

With the next breath I take, I draw in his earthy essence, along with the scent of sherbet and buttery waffles with a hint of maple, setting my mind into a spin. "What do you want to tell me?"

He tilts his head down, closer to mine. His honey-brown eyes search my gaze—for what, I'm not quite sure. But several pounding heartbeats later, his pupils dilate, and the corners of his mouth rise in a smile.

"Nika, I want to say—"

Elias's phone buzzes again. This time the buzz is continual.

He blinks, and the potency in his gaze wanes. The enchanting moment shatters.

"Uh, sorry. I think I'd better take this call."

"Sure." I take a step back, silently cursing whoever's on

the other end of his phone call. I point my thumb over my shoulder. "I'll grab the lattes."

He gives me an apologetic smile, then glances at the jumping castle.

"I'll keep an eye on Peony," I assure him.

He nods his thanks, then disappears down a side street.

A minute goes by and the two lattes are ready, but Elias still hasn't returned.

Eight minutes and half a caramel latte later, Peony's time on the castle is up, and Elias still hasn't come back. I prepare to fumble my way through helping Peony back into her blingy sneakers, but before I can, she's already laced them up like a pro.

"Great work." I give her a relieved smile as she beams up at me with pride. "Now let's go find your brother."

I wedge both latte cups into the crook of one arm, and much to my amazement, this little girl places her hand in mine. My heart skips a beat—but not in the about-to-have-a-panic-attack kind of way. I'm not sure I even understand what I'm feeling. Still, it's not lost on me that this sweet, vulnerable child has symbolically put her trust and safety in my hand. The enormity of that realization is inde-scribable.

Still a little awestruck, I lead Peony into the side street where Elias went. It grows darker and quieter the farther we walk.

"Where's Elias?" Peony's small voice feels abnormally loud over the fading hubbub of the market.

I give her a little squeeze. "We'll find him."

But just as I'm starting to think no one's here, a voice drifts over to us on the wind.

"Who was that?" Peony asks. "Was that Elias?"

I shake my head. "No, I think it was a woman."

The voice grows a little louder, coming from an alley farther down.

"I don't like it down here," says Peony in a whisper. She huddles closer to my side. "It's a bit scary."

"Don't be scared." I smile down at her. "I'm here, and I won't let anything happen to you."

"But are you sure Elias is this way, Nika?"

"Maybe. We'll just have to check." I force as much light-heartedness into my voice as possible but, at the same time, note the locations of my crystal dagger and a few other weapons, just in case.

Another voice becomes clear as we draw closer to the alley. When we turn the corner, I stop dead in my tracks.

"Oh, Elias is here," says Peony. "But... who's that?"

Who indeed? The most stunning woman I've ever seen is speaking with Elias. Her black dress is covered in pearls and rhinestones that perfectly accent her mid-shin silver holographic boots.

Just as Peony finishes speaking, the woman throws herself at Elias and kisses him on the cheek.

I suck in a sharp breath, taking a moment to process that this woman has her arms wrapped around Elias's neck, and his are circling her waist. Only when I spot the woman's lipstick branded on Elias's cheek does my nausea kick in, and bile sears the back of my throat.

Elias spots Peony and me at that moment, and the woman, still clinging to Elias like a spider monkey, also turns her attention to us.

Fierce hate pollutes the woman's beautiful face when her eyes lock on to me. At any other time, I'd likely be indifferent toward this stranger's hostile expression, but when I look at the lipstick mark on Elias's cheek again, something hitches deep in my core, causing me to take a step back.

I need to get out of here.

I release Peony's hand—barely registering the clatter and splatter of the coffee cups I drop—spin on my heel, and take off. I bolt back down the side street, and a moment later, market stalls fly past me as I run.

My heartbeat hammers in my ears, in sync with the phrase I repeat over and over in my mind.

How could I be so stupid? How could I be so stupid?

Chapter Thirteen

I sɪɢʜ for what must be the hundredth time.

Come on, Nika! Get some sleep!

Refusing to check the time—again!—I roll onto my belly. After a few seconds, I punch the pillow before dropping my face back into it with another sigh.

There's no reason for me to struggle to fall asleep. I showered, dressed in fresh sleeping clothes, dimmed the daylights in my room, and jumped into bed what feels like hours ago. My circadian rhythm has long since synced with the hunting schedule: sleep in the morning, train in the afternoon, hunt at night. Even when I'm not on-site at the barracks, I don't deviate much from the hunting routine.

Sleep, damn it!

Training will start in a few hours. Since Francine reduced all my training during my recovery to a strict physical therapy regime, I'm determined to get back to my normal training this time, especially after missing out on the last few sessions.

After ditching Elias and poor Peony, I found my own way home from the city. The owner of a race-red convertible Ford Mustang is likely pissed their car is no longer where they parked it, but the gearhead hunters who hang out in the garage will likely love the new addition to the barracks' vehicle collection.

The moment I got back, I went straight to the private gym exclusive to our barracks' legacy families. The rest of the hunters were still out, so I killed a few hours testing my healed arm with some light weights, doing a little cardio on the stair climber, then finishing up with some boxing drills on the bag. At last, drenched with sweat and ready for a shower, I headed to my room.

But as I approached the intersection to my hallway, I started getting slight heart palpitations, the kind that flare to life when I know I'm not alone. Sure enough, when I peeked around the corner, Elias was leaning against the wall by my door.

He looked as if he'd been there for a while already: stooped posture, hands in his jeans pockets, head resting against the wall, eyes closed. He stood still as a statue, and for a second I thought maybe he was asleep.

But then his chest heaved with a deep breath, and his eyes opened.

I ducked back out of sight, my rapid heartbeat booming in my ears as I waited. When it became clear my flicker of movement hadn't gained his attention, I skulked back to the gym like the coward I was.

I made my way to the indoor pool this time, losing count of the number of laps I swam and wasting at least another half hour in the sauna. When I finally chanced going back to my room, thankfully there was no sign of Elias.

By then it was the early hours of the morning, based on the shouts and banter of hunters returning from their night-time adventures. For the first time in a long time, instead of joining them to hear about their exploits, I decided to dodge them all and continue to hide in my room.

When I show up to training, though, no doubt I'll get amulets shoved in my face by each hunter brandishing the new bloods they acquired. I can handle that. My only hope is that Elias will be too busy looking after Peony to bother showing up to training.

I grit my teeth. What the heck is wrong with me? Why does this guy bother me so much? I've never, *ever* avoided anyone like that before. I should have just booted him out of the way when he was lurking by my room, then slammed the door in his face.

I release a strangled groan and flick over to my back. Who am I kidding? I turned and fled back to the gym, just like I turned and fled back to the barracks.

The image of that beautiful woman in the street with her arms locked around Elias's neck flashes in my mind, making my stomach turn, just as it does every time I think about her kissing him.

I couldn't face Elias last night—wouldn't face him. *And all because I'm a stupid, stupid girl with a stupid, stupid crush.*

My eyes ping open. Stunned, I take a moment to wrap my head around that last thought. Familiar anxiety slams into me as I remember what happened the last time I—

No! I can't like Elias. Not like *that*.

When I was about fifteen, I made the mistake of letting it slip in front of my brothers how much I liked a particular hunter. My brothers considered the concept of me being fond of anyone beyond hilarious. Before I knew it, they'd humiliated me in front of everyone one day during a training session. The guy I liked laughed his ass off along with everyone else.

I can't risk that kind of humiliation. Not again. Besides, a lovesick chick doesn't belong in the hunting world.

And yet... as I think of Elias and the small amount of time I've had with him and his sister, a thought strikes me. Maybe the possibility of liking him, or even caring for him, isn't the worst part.

I stare at the outline of my ten-by-ten-foot ceiling under the dim lights, my mind abuzz as I recount the events in the city.

A few ice creams, a casual stroll through the illuminated streets.

Lighthearted yet meaningful conversation.

A carefree girl skipping and squealing with no concern about the darkness within this world. Her small hand, reaching out to take mine.

That simplicity is an almost startling contrast to the grueling normality of my life in the barracks. It feels so foreign, yet I can't help but yearn for it. Being with Elias and Peony is exactly what I imagine it's like to be part of a normal, happy, non-carnage-wreaking family.

Of course, Quill and Hestus are my brothers—I won't diminish that—but even with them, I sometimes feel like an outsider. The two of them stick together. Through thick and thin, they've had each other's backs. Sure, they'll have mine as well, but only when it suits them or they feel the Branstone name is being threatened.

There's no way I'd tell them my secrets, the way they tell each other theirs. I can't trust them to always be available when I need them. In fact, since our mother died, I can't think of anyone in my family I can rely on. Dad's hardly ever around, and when he is, he only checks in when it's convenient. At one time, I felt most at home with my cousins Lyla-Rose and Sagan. But then Lyla-Rose died tragically, and Sagan disappeared without a trace.

So I've learned to protect myself with barbed words and my Diamantium-tipped knuckle-duster. There is no one I can depend on, except myself.

But in that meager couple of hours I spent with Elias and Peony, it was so easy to get swept up in their world. A world where shifters and hunting aren't important. Amulets don't dictate someone's worth. Grudges aren't clung to, and forgiveness is freely given.

Elias and Peony are a unit.

And you were beginning to see yourself as part of that unit, sneers the sardonic side of me.

Of course, my ever-reliable insecurities rise to dismiss that thought. But another side of me begins to poke at my shallow excuses: the exhausted, long-suffering side that's tired of all the lies I tell myself. Of all my vulnerabilities, this one seems the easiest to face.

Yes, I admit. For a moment there, I felt as if someone saw me for who I was, that there was no need to fight to prove my worth. I began to believe I could find a place to belong in this gloomy world.

But that was before I saw that chick wrapped around Elias's neck and kissing him.

Right there in that alley, the very same humiliation I'd experienced in a training room full of laughing hunters engulfed me. Only when I sprinted back through the street market did it become obvious my feelings for Elias had shifted from indifference to something more.

In the end, I only have myself to blame for thinking Elias might see me as anything more than just another hunter from another barracks. Someone more than just

Nika, the smallest and most insignificant of the Branstone legacy.

He's Elias freaking Ragefire, after all. He has a reputation that precedes him and a charm unlike any I've encountered. Even Blondie and her brunette friend back at the ice cream parlor practically committed their ovaries to Elias, and they weren't even hunters. Hunters of his caliber do not pay attention to the likes of me, definitely not in the cuddly, dateable kind of way.

"Who cares!" I hiss into the darkness.

With a burst of frustration, I kick off my blankets.

This self-pitying mode is starting to get on my nerves. I need to set my over-analyzing mind on something else.

Reaching for the chain around my neck, I fish around for the amulet and hold it up in front of my face. With the lights off, it's difficult to make out the black metal design the blood vials are embedded in; however, the shifter blood glows in the darkness—silver, teal, magenta, and bright orange.

I focus in on the bright orange sample, my feelings mixed. The pride, elation, and validation still haven't come over me as they did the previous times I filled a vial. What is wrong with me? I used to have such passion. I lived for the hunt, perhaps even obsessed over it. But now...

...*having children is no longer possible.*

No, no, no. Didn't I, just a minute ago, decide not to wallow in self-pity? Covering my face with my hands, I draw in several deep breaths to try and clear my head.

Maybe I need to switch up distraction tactics. I reach for my holstered dagger under my pillow and remove the crystal blade from its protective pouch. I still haven't cleaned it since my failure in hunting down the Meruvo shifter. Just as I suspected, the black blood of the Meruvo still coats the tip from when I nicked her.

As I slowly twirl the crystal dagger, the blade catches the gleam of the dim nightlight and scatters rainbow flecks across the walls. As stunning as the tiny rainbows are, the dried black blood enthralls me even more. The ethereal Meruvo blood still holds its paradoxical glow in the darkness. *Beautiful.* Maybe the most beautiful of all the shifter bloods.

The silver blood came from a Lycan, one of the werewolf shifters associated with the moon.

The teal blood is from a Veniri, a reptilian shifter with crystalline spikes, associated with Venus.

The magenta came from a Magneii, a member of the shifter species that draws its magma and fire abilities from the light of Mars.

And then there is the vial of orange blood, the newest addition to my amulet. That blood sample came from a Jiovis, a metalloid shifter like a walking, talking statue made of precious metal, associated with Jupiter.

Running my fingers over the empty glass vials in my amulet, I try to picture what a sample of black would look like alongside the teal, magenta, orange, and silver.

The longer I look at the glistening black blood on the tip of my crystal dagger, the more my annoyance resurfaces. I was *so close* to filling my black vial. I would have reveled in all the envious looks from the other hunters, and I bet the novelty of my Meruvo blood would have lasted for a couple of weeks, perhaps even a month.

But thanks to Elias—

Oh, for crying out loud! Can't I go a minute without thinking about that guy?

I huff out an agitated breath, resheathe my dagger, and

toss it back onto the bedside table. I need to stop pining over that guy. I need to refocus.

Actually, I need to get some sleep, go straight into training, and get my butt back out hunting.

Chewing on the inside of my bottom lip, I can't help but notice my enthusiasm for the hunt dwindling. For the first time since coming of age and receiving my amulet, I'm having some doubts.

Yranum blood, Meruvo blood, all the rest of the shifter bloods... say I get them all... then what?

Sure, I'd be a legend and my name would go down in history. No one would dare cross me. Not to mention the political and financial gain... But all those benefits would exist only in the hunting community. To everybody else on this planet, I'd still be a petite little lady with bouncy curls and Shirley Temple–blue eyes—someone they'd assume was just asking to be hit on or treated like a submissive doormat.

If that's all the payment I get for my lifelong work hunting down shifters, then how much do I actually want my life to revolve around a set of blood vials hanging from my neck?

I look over at the photo frame on my bedside table. Grief once again rears its freaking head and gnaws at my insides, but after a few moments of hesitation, I reach out to take hold of the frame.

The photo depicts my beautiful mother, with eight-year-old me sitting on her lap. She's an older version of what I look like now, only her hair and skin tones are a little darker and richer. Her long chestnut hair drapes over my shoulder and mixes with my curly tangle of locks. Both of us are smiling, our teeth flashing in mid-laugh. Mother looks tenderly down at me, and I'm looking up at her as though she's my whole world.

As I look at the photo, the prospect of never having my own children guts me all over again, more brutally than ever. My mother was pivotal in making me the person I claim to be—all my sentiments, emotions, memories. Her unequivocal love for me, her unapologetic strength, and her fervor in her purpose as a mother are just as clear to me today as they were ten years ago when she was alive.

For the first time since she died, I can admit I've lost my own sense of purpose without her here to guide me. After she passed, I channeled my sorrow, my anger, and the pure hatred of the void she left in my soul all into hunting.

I may have been able to convince myself for a while that hunting shifters and filling vials would have made my mother proud. But not until my time in the infirmary after the grenade blast did I realize I have a much deeper dream —one that resonates more with my memories of her.

I want to be just like her. I want to be the woman she always hoped I would be. And what better way to pay tribute to my mother than to pass on all she taught me to my own children?

My hand presses against my mutilated and infertile abdomen, and an overwhelming grief thrashes at the mental barricade I've kept in place since my mother's funeral. Finally, after all these years, I no longer have the strength to maintain it—or maybe I now have the courage to let all these emotions in.

Tears prickle at my eyes, and this time, instead of holding them back, I let the tears fall.

Chapter Fourteen

"WOULD YOU LOOK AT THAT." Quill holds up a Diamantium shard under his flashlight. It reflects speckles of rainbow light over his face as he whistles with genuine appreciation. "It's like printing money."

"It would have been a pretty decent shard," Hestus agrees, "but it's a pity it wasn't a clean break when the Veniri slammed into the cliff face. Look how splintered the end is."

"It'll still be worth enough to place a few bets at Tempecrest." Quill jabs me in the ribs with his elbow. "How about it, Nika? Wanna join us at Tempecrest for the weekend? I'm sure even you could find a worthy mongrel worth placing some bets on."

"Or we could help you catch a mongrel tonight to take as your champion if you'd prefer," offers Hestus.

Screwing up my nose, I shake my head. "No thanks, I'm not interested in keeping a Lycan as a pet and carting him over to Tempecrest Island. And I don't give a crap about that gladiator garbage."

Quill shrugs a shoulder. "Suit yourself." He strides over

to a net-bound shifter, the previous owner of the crystal shard. "Hestus, do me a favor and hold down the slith."

Hestus raises an unimpressed eyebrow. "Really, Quill? Now?"

"Yes, now." Quill points to the Veniri on the ground at his feet. "Those elbow blades are the biggest chunks of Diamantium I've seen in ages, and I want to claim them now before anyone else does."

Hestus's brow furrows. "You've already got your chunk of Diamantium. You can wait until we get back to the barracks for the harvesters to extract the shards."

"Nah. I don't trust the harvesters not to claim the shards for themselves."

Hestus *tsks* and mumbles something about an impatient moron.

"You got something to say, Hess?" Quill stabs a finger into Hestus's chest.

"Jab me again, and my boot is going straight up your clacker."

"Sheesh, bro. What's your problem?"

"I'll tell you what the problem is!"

I roll my eyes as my brothers pitch themselves whole-heartedly into a bickering match. Instead of letting their immature disputes get to me, I busy myself with cleaning my Diamantium dagger in a clump of long grass on the forest floor. Teal Veniri blood smears over the lush greenery with each swipe. As always, the luminous liquid glows vibrantly in the night, even without the aid of our Luxium-powered flashlights.

Upon standing, I raise my face to the heavens and inhale an earthy breath of air. My gaze roams over the star-scattered sky. It's great to finally be away from the barracks and away from civilization.

Even though I've been out of action for so long, getting back into hunting feels like sliding into a second skin. My body might be a little rusty around the edges, but regaining my agility hasn't taken too much effort.

Tonight's selected hunting ground falls within the Thunder-Rock Hinterlands. Hunting out in the wilderness requires a few different skills and equipment as compared to the urban jungle of a city. Tracking our prey in this landscape usually involves a bit of hiking, scaling ravines, and crossing over creeks.

Yet within two hours of leaving the Defender cars behind and peeling off from the rest of the hunters, Quill, Hestus, and I have already managed to track down a Veniri. That's a record for us; those scaly shifters can be pretty slippery, considering they're also expert trackers themselves. Nothing a bit of experience and finesse can't handle, although a Diamantium-tipped harpoon gun and electrified net launcher are also a big help in getting the job done.

Catching the Veniri tonight is an unexpected bonus, considering we came out to the hinterlands to track down a pack of Lycans.

"Fine!" Hestus blasts, his voice ringing out into the night. "I'll hold him down just to make you shut up. But *only* if one of those elbow shards is for me."

"Forget it, Hess. I'm already picturing the twin blade set I can get one of the weaponsmiths to forge for me."

"In that case, get your own damn shards." Hestus crosses his arms in a huff and leans against a nearby tree.

The two launch back into their incessant arguing. With my own Diamantium dagger now cleaned, I return the blade to its holster and place my hands on my hips. While I wait for idiot one and idiot two to finish their squabble, my eyes fall on the captured shifter lying deathly still on the ground between us.

For a moment, I wonder if my dagger nicked something vital, or perhaps Quill got a little overzealous with his crystal throwing blades. If the Veniri is, in fact, dead, then Quill is going to be pissed, because shifters turn back into their human form a few minutes after death. If that happens, Quill can kiss his fancy twin blades goodbye.

I scan the shifter, looking for signs of human features. The metal launch net is still wrapped snugly around the captive. Iridescent scales in complex patterns gleam from the shifter's head right down to his raptorlike feet, where three toes on each foot glisten with crystal talons. The clusters of scales around each spike glow with their own inner light.

The Veniri's crystal spikes jut out from the metal net. The largest adorn the creature's knees, elbows, and collarbones; however, the most lethal are located at the Veniri's elbows. The foot-long crystal blades run parallel to his forearms.

After surveying the creature for a few seconds, I still don't see any sign of scales smoothing back into human flesh. Still, I would gauge there's at least another minute or two to go before we'll know for sure if the shifter died.

A little flicker of movement draws my attention, and I catch the shifter's open eyes staring straight at me. He blinks. The fear in his gaze is obvious, but so is his severe hate. His top lip curls into a silent sneer, further revealing the set of triple fangs made of the same Diamantium crystal as the rest of his shards.

Usually I don't pay much heed to the prey we catch, but this time, I can't bring myself to break eye contact. The longer I stare back, the more the hate in his eyes wanes;

soon, I see what might even be a flicker of hope. But the fear remains paramount as the Veniri quickly glances at Quill and Hestus, who haven't stopped fighting over how the shards will be harvested and distributed.

"Damn it, Hestus. You wanna play pain in the ass, then go right ahead," growls Quill.

"I'm not playing anything. All the harvesting tools are back at the barracks. If you want my help now, you already know my terms. Take it or leave it, bro."

Quill grunts with frustration and kicks a rock. It bounces a few feet before disappearing over the edge of a steep ravine that leads to a freshwater creek far below. "Fine! You help me get these elbow shards now, and one is yours."

A triumphant smile lights up Hestus's face. "I knew you'd come to your senses, bro."

"Yeah, yeah. Whatever." Quill waves a hand of indifference, but there's no mistaking the greed twinkling in his eyes.

Hestus kneels down by the bound Veniri shifter, who bucks like a caterpillar trapped in a spiderweb.

"Quit it," Quill snarls at the Veniri.

"You know it's going to be much easier to harvest the shards if the slith is unconscious," says Hestus.

"Thank you, Captain Obvious. This isn't my first time harvesting shards." Quill punches a button on his net launcher, and a network of electrical sparks crackle through the weave of the wire net around the shifter.

The Veniri convulses with a shrill scream.

After a few seconds, Quill switches the electrical shock off with another press of a button. The creature becomes silent and still, the rise and fall of his chest the only indicator he's even still alive.

Quill kicks the Veniri for good measure. "That's more like it," he says when the shifter doesn't react. To Hestus, he says, "Now that wasn't that hard, was it?"

"Says the guy who's always gotta make things harder than they need to be." Hestus shares a knowing look with me.

Usually I'd respond with a chuckle, but for some reason I can't bring myself to smile or laugh. Something is feeling really... off. I can't deny I've had a blast with the hunting so far, but the prospect of what's about to happen to the Veniri isn't sitting well with me.

Hestus rolls the lifeless Veniri onto its back.

"Nika, help us out," Quill calls over.

"Nope." I give a sharp shake of my head. "I'm not getting involved in another one of your stupid schemes. It's bad enough you convinced Hestus to help you. Both of you should know better."

Hestus grumbles a few choice words as he wipes his hands on his pants. A few smears of viscous teal smear down his hunter-black jeans. "It's times like these I miss having Sagan around. He was much better at explaining how stupid your ideas are, Quill."

"Hey, you agreed to help me," says Quill.

"Yes, but I never agreed it was a great idea."

"Well, Sagan's not here, is he?" Quill elbows Hestus in the ribs. "So quit your whining and hold out the slith's arm."

As soon as my brothers wrestle one of the Veniri's arms out from the net, a deep drum-like beat resonates from within the creature's chest.

"The stupid thing's still awake," groans Hestus.

"Shut it!" Quill barks with another kick at the shifter. "You sliths need to learn when you've been defeated."

But the drumming war cry only continues.

"Hestus, hold his arm down," Quill says over the drumming.

"What? You're still going through with this?" Hestus asks.

"Yeah. Why not?"

"Because," I interject, "for one, you're only going to achieve breaking the shards without the right tools. And two, the thing is still awake, you sadist."

"Shut up, Nika." Quill turns his back on me. "Hestus, quit being a baby and hold the sucker down."

With a groan, Hestus resentfully obliges. "Why don't we just get out a Myst atomizer?"

Quill scoffs. "No need to waste Myst on this thing. Now hold him still."

I've already visualized what's about to happen, and I'm not keen on sticking around for Quill's temper tantrum when things don't work out for him, which they clearly won't. I decide to wander off and take advantage of not being stuck in the barracks.

Just as I'm about to turn away, I catch the Veniri's gaze again. This time, there's no hate in his eyes, only pure, unadulterated panic.

A pang of... *something* hits me in the chest. It almost feels like... shame?

I finally break eye contact with the Veniri and manage to stroll away, trying to shake the afterimage of that cutting look, along with whatever emotions it stirred up. My Luxium-core flashlight illuminates the way ahead as I sweep the magenta-tinged beam over the trees.

The dense scent of foliage engulfs me, bringing with it a flood of nostalgia for the annual family camping trips we used to take when we were kids. Running through the forest and exploring caves with my brothers and cousins, Lyla-

Rose and Sagan, are some of my greatest memories. One year we came across a cave that had its own underground lake about the size of a tennis court, complete with hanging stalactites that continuously dripped mineral-rich water. Every camping trip after that, we would escape our parents and spend hours in that cave, gradually filling it with toys, snacks, games, camping equipment, and anything else to make our secret hideout a little more cozy.

A rustle of grass snatches me out of my reverie. My instincts flare, my senses on high alert, but for the next few seconds, nothing stirs but the trees swishing gently in the breeze. I pan my flashlight across the forest in front of me, homing in on every little movement, searching for anything that may be out of place.

Nothing becomes apparent. But the tingle of my instincts hasn't receded.

I'm not alone.

Adrenaline begins to pound through my veins as I reach for my crystal dagger. I ready my stance, preparing to spring into action if I need to, and then I hold my breath and listen.

My head whips to a clump of tall grass and tangle of waist-high weeds on my right. I swear I heard a small whimper—whether animal, shifter, or something else, I can't quite tell.

Even if it's nothing, I won't allow myself to be blind-sided. I dart forward and part a section of grass with my dagger hand.

And my jaw drops.

Chapter Fifteen

Huddled together in the scratchy grass are three women—*human* women. They cower back from me, shielding their eyes from the magenta-tinged light I shine over their gaunt faces. Their hair, clothes, and general appearances are dirty and worn, as if they've been really roughing it for the last few days.

For a second I stare, speechless. Of all the things I imagined might be hiding in the grass, this definitely didn't come to mind.

Perhaps because I make no further sign of advancing on them, the woman with wavy auburn hair tilts her head, her expression timid but curious. "Are you the one who's meant to help us?"

"Shh, Genevieve," says one of the other women, laying a hand on her shoulder in warning. "We don't know if we can trust her."

"That's why I asked," replies Genevieve.

I frown. *The one meant to help them?* What did she mean by that?

All three women stare up at me. Their eyes are dull

with weariness, but a slight spark of hope burns in them as they wait for my answer.

"So, are you?" asks the third woman.

"Oh... I'm—" My mouth hangs open as I flounder for words. What if I say no? Who *is* meant to be helping them? What if I say yes? *How* am I meant to help them? I doubt Quill would appreciate three hitchhikers in his Defender and a detour on the way back to the barracks.

A small whimper, much like the one I heard earlier, interrupts my thoughts. The three women cast nervous glances at the wad of fabric Genevieve clutches to her chest.

No, it isn't *just* a bundle of fabric.

My eyebrows fly up with the realization.

She's holding a baby. Actually, now that I look at the others more closely, each woman is holding a baby. The little bundle in Genevieve's arms begins to writhe and fuss, and my shock kicks up a notch when the chubby infant's smooth skin ripples for a split second, then acquires a thick coat of downy teal fur.

No. Freaking. Way.

The baby is a shifter. A Veniri shifter. And based on the sheer terror the three women now regard me with, I can only assume the other two babies are Veniri shifters too.

"Heavens above," I whisper, resting my dagger hand over my belly as my mind races to put the pieces together.

In all likelihood, these wraithlike women are Veniri breeding slaves, kidnapped and forced to procreate with the Veniri scum. Rumor has it the Veniri population is on the decline, so the reptilian shifters have taken the extreme measure of kidnapping human females. I don't know why humans are their species of choice for incubating their young, but the Veniri snatched my cousin Lyla-Rose when she was sixteen, and she died trying to escape the same fate these women endured.

Suddenly it makes sense why my brothers and I lucked out on finding a Veniri shifter tonight. I'd bet my amulet these women are on the run, and the Veniri we caught was sent out to either recapture the slaves or execute them.

As the baby's cries grow a little louder, my own fear spikes.

I shoot a glance over my shoulder, relieved to find neither Quill nor Hestus in sight. What would they do if they happened to catch sight of these women? I can just picture it: The three shifter babies would be "dealt with" first, then Quill and Hestus would claim it would be a mercy to have all three women "dealt with," regardless of the hunter code. After all, we couldn't bring them back to the barracks, not after they'd been tainted by the Veniri. And no way would we give the Veniri the satisfaction of retrieving what they'd lost.

Perhaps at one stage, I would have agreed with the hunter way of showing these women "mercy." But now, looking at these scared, helpless mothers as they hold their precious bundles tight, I can see the determination in their eyes to find a safe place for the babies they love.

What I wouldn't give...

Genevieve expertly consoles her baby, like someone who's been forced to learn the best ways to keep an infant as quiet as possible.

My heart starts to break as I see each malnourished, ragged, sunburned, and wind-chapped woman in a new light. I can't begin to imagine what they've been through to get where they are now, huddled in the grass and weeds.

One thing I know for certain: I can't let my brothers see them.

"You have to go," I say in a low voice. "You need to get out of here as fast as you can." I point in the direction I think will be safest for them, hoping with all my might that no other hunter has bothered to go that way tonight.

"But..." Genevieve blinks a few times, her eyes now glistening with tears. "We need help. We've walked nonstop for three days. We ran out of food a day and a half ago. We're out of water as of this morning. And our children—" She chokes on a sob, but I don't need her to finish her sentence to understand how dire their circumstances are.

Without any hesitation, I slip my small survival backpack off.

When hunting out in the wilderness, it's become protocol for each hunter to always carry a survival pack stocked with emergency supplies. All the items are light, vacuum formed or super compact so as not to hinder our hunting: a first aid kit, extra water and hydration gel sachets, several ration packs, an ultralight one-person hiking tent, a foil thermal blanket, a fire-starting kit, flares, another Luxium flashlight, and a burner cell phone, just to name a few.

"Take this." I hand the pack to Genevieve. "It may have enough supplies to last you another day or so." I'm now kicking myself for discarding a few extra items I figured I wouldn't need, just to lighten the pack a bit.

"But we don't know how to get to the safe house," says Genevieve. "Someone was supposed to meet us to tell us how to get to a compound, or a shire of some sort—"

I wave my hands in the air to cut her off. "I don't know anything about a safe house or a compound." For the sake of giving them a fighting chance, I also hand over the Diamantium dagger and hiss with more urgency, "You need to take this, and you all need to go, *now*. Get your babies out of here before—"

"Nika?"

An icy chill rushes through my veins.

I slide my hand into my jacket pocket, threading my fingers into my knuckle-duster as I turn.

Elias Ragefire approaches from the opposite direction I came from. He halts about ten feet away; as far as I can tell, he hasn't yet seen the women. He eyes me with suspicion, but I don't miss his darting glances at the foliage around us. "Nika, what are you doing here?"

A toxic mix of emotions floods through me. I've managed to avoid Elias since I found him waiting by my bedroom door two nights ago. Thankfully he didn't show up to training earlier this afternoon; perhaps he couldn't find someone to look after Peony. Up until now, I assumed he also didn't come along for the hunt.

"I'm... hunting." I'd usually retort with a smart-ass comment, but my anxiety over the women and their babies quenches my sass.

"Oh." Elias takes a small step closer, his eyes scanning our small clearing again. "Are you with anyone?"

"Nope, no one."

He frowns. "What happened to your brothers? Did they ditch you?"

"My brothers? Right, them." Slight relief washes over me—but it's ever so slight. I point in the direction I left them. "They're back there somewhere fighting over... the *prey* we hunted down."

I've never downplayed a hunt before, but Elias is smart. I can't trust he wouldn't have a few suspicions if I mentioned we'd caught a Veniri instead of a Lycan.

Elias slowly nods.

A few tension-filled heartbeats pass.

I don't move. I can't.

But Elias doesn't move either.

I'm not exactly one for smooth talking and duplicity, not when I let my fists do most of the convincing. How on earth am I going to get this guy to leave and ensure the safety of those hiding behind me?

"So, um... how've you been, Nika?"

"Great." An internal cringe ripples through me; I don't like how dismissive my tone is. At least it might help Elias get the hint that I need him to leave.

"I've been meaning to talk to you."

Damn. So much for him getting the hint.

Elias rakes a hand through his dark curls, and his eyes dart around nervously before landing back on me.

My stomach drops. Not because of his ever-perceptive gaze or because he's trying to start a conversation I'm not ready to have, but because I spot something stalking through the dark foliage behind him.

I almost curse out loud.

It's another Veniri.

The scaled shifter crouches low, getting ready to spring.

Without a single thought to the consequences, I launch myself forward. Elias has only enough time for his eyes to grow wide before I barrel into him, and with a teeth-jarring *ooph*, we slam into the ground together.

Almost in the same instant, the Veniri lands right where Elias was standing.

But the shifter doesn't whip around to attack us. *He isn't after Elias.*

Horror tears through me as I realize my mistake.

I have a split second to do something. Quill and Hestus still have the net launcher, and I don't have my pneumatic dart gun with me. But when I tackled Elias, I spotted a familiar object in the bandolier over his chest.

With sheer determination, I push aside the memories of blinding magenta light and agonizing hellfire. I snatch Elias's Luxium grenade off his bandolier, yank out the linchpin, and hurl it at the Veniri.

Before the scaled shifter is eight feet from the clump of tall grass and weeds, an almighty boom rattles through me, and a flash of brilliant magenta light bursts across my vision. The Veniri's shrill cry of agony lasts a second before it collapses to the ground. Teal blood, gore, and chunks of hide litter the forest floor all around him, and a mutilated stump is all that remains where the Luxium grenade struck below his knee.

The Veniri lies deathly still.

However, a trifecta of baby cries ring out into the night.

Elias scrambles to get up.

"Oh no you don't," I growl, kicking a leg out. My boot clips his shin, and Elias stumbles, giving me the opportunity to hop up and put myself between him and the vulnerable mothers. I move to unholster my Diamantium dagger, only to remember I gave it to Genevieve. The knuckle-duster will just have to do.

I enter a defensive stance. White dots dance over my vision every time I blink, and my ears are still ringing from the grenade, along with the shrill pitch of hysterical babies.

Elias is now up and facing me, his severe expression unreadable.

"Back off, Ragefire." I raise my fist; the crystal tips of my knuckle-duster glint with a warning. "You come any closer and I'll gut you." Tossing a glance over my shoulder, I tell the mothers, "Get those babies out of here. The other hunters will have heard the blast and will be here any second to investigate."

Tentatively, the three women rise out of the grass. I set my sights back on Elias.

"Wait," he calls out. "Yumiko? Pradhi? Genevieve?"

It's my turn to be startled as all three women halt.

"Yes, yes! That's us," says Genevieve.

Elias points to a green camo bag near where he'd been standing before I tackled him. "Take that bag. It has supplies and the directions for the compound. Ask for Skye or Dawn. They can help you get to the safe house."

"Thank you." Genevieve's voice is thick with emotion and gratitude.

"Go. *Now*," Elias demands.

Without any further hesitation, one of the women scoops up the bag. The three ladies pause long enough to nod at me in thanks, and Genevieve gives me a small sad smile before turning to flee into the night.

Elias and I stare each other down as the crying fades into the hinterlands. As the seconds tick by and no other hunters show up—not even my brothers—my posture gradually begins to relax.

Yet my mind continues to whirl with the revelation that Genevieve and the others were waiting for *Elias*—that *he* was the one meant to help them. How is that even possible? I've never, ever heard of a hunter *helping* shifters. Trying to eradicate them, definitely. But helping them?

Elias's stance also becomes less rigid, but his intense expression remains. He doesn't seem angry, or even annoyed that I crash-tackled him to the ground—not for the first time. Still, I fight not to fidget under his scrutiny.

"What?" I finally say. "Why are you looking at me like that?"

"How did you find out about those women?" he asks after a slight hesitation. "Who told you about them?"

I raise an eyebrow. I'm not quite sure how I want to answer that. Should I make out I know more than I do and try to glean information about why Elias is helping breeding-slave runaways, or should I be honest and hope he tells me anyway?

Before I can decide, a flash of movement in my periphery grabs my attention.

"You let the slaves get away, you impudent fools!" Even with a missing leg, the Veniri launches up from the ground with incredible speed.

The shifter charges, but Elias reaches me first, wrapping one arm around me as he roars my name. There's a flash of a crystal blade, a spray of teal, and then the Veniri's guttural shriek cuts off with a liquified gurgle.

My stomach flips as Elias and I go airborne, but just as suddenly we're crashing to the ground. Elias grips me tighter. My world spins when the momentum of our fall drags us into a few painful rotations along the rough ground.

And then my stomach flips again.

Because in the next heart-stopping moment, Elias and I have rolled off the edge of a cliff and are falling into the ravine below.

Chapter Sixteen

Rocks and shrubs hammer my body on all sides—at least they would if Elias didn't cocoon me with his arms and legs, taking the brunt of most of the collisions as we tumble down the seriously steep ravine.

Elias's face is buried in my neck, and mine in his. A few times he lets out a grunt of agony. Once I swear I hear something go *crack*, whether a twig snapping, a bone breaking, or some of the loose rocks smashing into each other, I'm not sure.

A final slam into the ground brings us to an agonizing stop, with me on top of Elias. I take a moment to heave in a few breaths. Even with my body no longer rolling, my head still spins wildly.

"Elias, are you okay?"

My breath hitches when he doesn't answer. His eyes are closed, his head lying back on a patch of dirt and grass.

I gently pat his cheek. "Elias?"

Again, no response.

My blood runs cold. *Oh, no! Please, no! This can't be happening.*

I try to recall all my basic emergency training, furiously kicking myself for not paying better attention in those sessions. I was way more interested in killing things than in keeping them alive. When I place two fingers on Elias's neck, the relief at feeling his pulse still ticking almost overwhelms me. At least that's something. Now, what else did I learn in my first aid training?

Being extra cautious not to jostle him too much, I try to disentangle us. It's a bit of a challenge and takes some wriggling, given his arms are still slung around me. I've almost managed to free myself when Elias's arms snap tight around me again.

"Whoa. Elias? Elias, can you hear me?"

This time he answers with a groan. His face screws up in a grimace, and then his eyes slowly flicker open. They roam about before landing on me. "Nika?"

"Yeah," I wheeze. "Do you mind... can't breathe..."

It takes a moment for Elias to comprehend what I'm saying. "Oh, sorry." He relaxes his grip a little but doesn't remove his arms completely. "What happened?"

I've just opened my mouth to answer when Elias bolts up. Immediately he cries out, then slumps back on the ground with me still encased in his arms.

"Careful," I warn. "We've just—"

"Taken a dive into a ravine. I remember. Are you okay, Nika?"

"Yeah. A little bit battered, but I'm fine."

"Great." Elias's hold relaxes a little. "What happened to the Veniri?"

With a start, I squint into the darkness and tune my ears in to the night. I'd completely forgotten about the slith. Running water burbles close by, close enough that if we hadn't stopped where we are, we would have ended up in an ice-cold creek. A few crickets chirp, a night owl hoots in the far distance, and the indecipherable skitters of creatures move through the nearby grass and leaf litter.

Several heartbeats pass. Nothing makes me think we're in any immediate danger, although as I look around, I catch sight of a dark oblong mound with perhaps a few faintly glowing patches of teal.

"I think he's over there," I whisper. "I'll go check."

"Wait—"

But I slip out of Elias's arms. With as much stealth as I can muster in my post-rolled-down-a-ravine state, I make my way over to the suspicious mound. Thankfully I didn't lose my knuckle-duster in the fall. Although a little shaky, my fingers are still laced in the familiar comfort of the weapon.

After a few more steps, the distinct Veniri features become clear. Several of his crystal spikes snapped or shattered in the fall, and all his limbs, minus half a leg, are twisted into unnatural angles. As I approach, the Veniri remains still. He doesn't even flinch when I nudge him with my boot. Knuckle-duster at the ready, I press two fingers against his neck, but this time there's no pulse.

I recall the flash of a crystal dagger—Elias's dagger—just before we dove over the edge of the ravine. Then I spot the patch of teal on the Veniri's torso. Elias stabbed him in the ribs with expert precision, in the exact location necessary to not only puncture the shifter's heart but rupture the poison glands. The poison in those glands burns like acid.

Yikes. That would have been an excruciating, yet near instant, death for the Veniri.

"Nika? Is that our slith?"

"Yeah. He's dead though." Before I even finish speaking, the Veniri's scales begin to ripple. I gape, mesmerized, as the triple set of crystal fangs glide back beneath his top lip. Each Diamantium shard retracts into the scales, which then smooth out into human flesh.

The transformation finishes within seconds. The contorted figure on the ground is now an average-built man somewhere in his midtwenties, with a round face that belies the much more severe features of his reptilian form. A cool breeze tugs at several strands of his shaggy hair. He could be anyone's neighbor, or the local handyman, or even a dude who would hold the elevator door open for you while you fumbled in with half a dozen bags of groceries. Hard to believe this is the same vicious creature who, only minutes ago, tried to attack three mothers and inadvertently launched himself, Elias, and me over a steep ravine.

I don't know why, but somehow the idea of lugging this Veniri back to the barracks for his crystal skeleton repels me. But if I don't dispose of the body, someone—or something—is bound to find him. It's best not to leave him just lying around.

After a moment's indecision, I gently take hold of the Veniri's arms and drag him over to the water's edge. The creek is about the width of a two-lane road and appears to be several feet deep. Moonlight glints off the ripples and eddies, casting flickers of silver over the creek's surface.

When I push the corpse into the water, the current latches on to the Veniri and gently carries him downstream until he disappears around a bend.

I say a silent prayer for him, and also for the three mothers to find the refuge they're seeking. Hopefully—with this Veniri gone, along with the one my brothers and I captured earlier—there aren't any more shifters hunting them tonight.

I make my way back to Elias, who is on his feet but leaning heavily against an outcrop of boulders.

"What was that about?" Elias asks. "You're not interested in cashing in on that slith's Diamantium?"

"Nah." I make a point of looking back up the way we came. "It's already going to be a pain in the ass getting back up to the top without dragging a literal deadweight behind me. Speaking of which, should we get going?" I check my watch; we still have about five hours until sunrise.

I do a quick study of the ravine wall. It may have taken less than a minute to tumble down, but it will take much longer to find a way back up. "I reckon it'll be about a two-hour climb."

Elias lets out a low groan.

"Or if you want to be a crybaby about it, we can walk around to try to find a less steep path."

"Yeah, about that." Elias's face scrunches up into a wince. "I think I must have twisted my ankle, or maybe broken something on the way down."

"You're joking, right?"

"Wish I was."

I put my hands on my hips. "Are you sure it's not just in your head?"

Elias takes a few steps, walking as normally as he can while maintaining an impassive expression. I may not be a medical expert, but it's clear he can't put weight on his ankle.

I let out a frustrated huff and quickly assess my options. Firstly, Elias is half a head taller than me, and bulkier too, so there's no way I could drag his sorry ass up the ravine.

A second option would be to make the trip myself and bring someone to help carry Elias back up, although I'd have to get to the cars in time before everyone started heading back to the barracks. As much as we're an amicable bunch of hunters, we're not exactly the "roll call" type. You learn early to look out for yourself. If you get left behind, it's up to you to find your way back home.

With a sigh of annoyance, I think of a few more scenarios to get Elias and me back up the ravine, but each one seems more troublesome than the last. The fact that I gave away my survival pack complicates things further, although Elias does still have his strapped to his back.

I chew on my lip for a few seconds, deciding what to do. *Screw it.* I'm not in the mood to drag this predicament out any longer than necessary. I'll deal with the hit to my reputation later.

I hold out my hand. "Give me your burner phone. I'll call my brothers to come get us."

Elias hesitates.

"What?" I ask.

He sheepishly rubs the back of his neck. "I gave my burner phone to the women. To be honest, I didn't think I'd need one so soon after giving it away. Can we use yours?"

"I... um, also gave my phone to the women"—I try not to shuffle from one foot to the other—"as well as the rest of my survival pack."

Elias's brows hit his hairline, and enough warmth fills his eyes to melt the coldest of hearts. I don't know if anyone's ever looked at me the way he's looking at me now. "You never cease to surprise me, Nika."

I frown. Is that a good thing or a bad thing?

"Sit down and show me your leg," I blurt when I can't hold his gaze any longer.

When Elias is perched on a nearby boulder, I help him wrangle his boot off. Sure enough, his foot and ankle are swollen. He winces as I prod here and there.

"Do you still have your first aid kit?" I ask.

Elias nods.

"Then I don't see what else there is to do except take a dose of Ylixium," I say.

Elias purses his lips. "It'll take a few hours for the Ylixium to work enough for me to try walking again. Besides, I'm not a huge fan of... taking that stuff."

I throw my hands up. "What choice do you have? Do you see a helicopter on the way to airlift your ass out of here? A magic carpet, perhaps? And what do you mean you're 'not a huge fan' of Ylixium? You didn't hesitate to give me a dose the other day."

"You were in pain, and in desperate need of healing."

"Newsflash, Ragefire, so are you. If you want to get out of here anytime soon, you're going to put your big boy pants on and swig away."

Elias gruffs something I can't quite catch. Then, after a moment, he looks up to the heavens, almost as if he's preparing himself to do something heinous. "Fine, if that's the only choice I have to work with."

He shrugs off his pack. Both of us lost our flashlights in the fall, so he cracks one of the glow sticks, which casts a bright orange light over the contents of his bag.

I snag the first aid pouch, fish out the vial of pearl-white liquid, then unscrew the lid and hand it to him. "Here, toss this back."

He takes a mouthful of the Ylixium and half gags it down. There isn't anyone I know whose gag reflexes don't kick in when taking Ylixium. That stuff is foul.

"Better take another swig, just for good measure," I tell him as he coughs and splutters.

Elias half narrows his eyes at me. "For my benefit or yours?"

I just grin.

He barks a humorless laugh and, with a shake of his head, chugs down another gagging gulp. The vial is half-empty by the time I return it to the first aid kit.

"Now I suppose we wait."

Just as I speak, raindrops begin sprinkling down.

Chapter Seventeen

"Ugh, of course," I groan.

"It's only a bit of rain," says Elias.

Within seconds, Elias's "bit of rain" turns into a raging downpour with fat and heavy drops.

"Come on." I snatch up Elias's backpack. "Earlier, I thought I saw a little cave over there."

I sling Elias's arm over my shoulders, and we stumble through the heavy deluge to a stony outcropping near the base of the ravine wall. The overhanging rocks create a small nook just deep enough for Elias and me to squeeze into, although not high enough for us to stand.

I help Elias settle onto the soft earth, then run back out into the rain.

"What are you doing?" he calls after me.

I pick up a couple of big rocks, then return and assemble them in a formation that allows Elias to rest with his leg slightly elevated. Only after I pull an instant ice pack out of the first aid kit and strap it onto his ankle do I take a seat on the ground next to him. With our backs pressed against the innermost wall of the nook, there's just enough room to stretch our legs out without getting rained on.

"Thank you," Elias says after a few moments. He gestures to his elevated foot. "You didn't have to put in that much effort. I'm sure the Ylixium will do its job sooner or later."

I shrug. "It won't hurt to try and speed up the healing process, and the ice pack will help with the swelling in the meantime."

We fall into rain-filled silence. The bright light of the glow stick casts an almost cheery shade of fluorescent orange around our little cave.

"You know, I wouldn't blame you for leaving me here and going on ahead, Nika. There's no reason for you to stay."

I give a shrug. "I suppose I don't fancy wallowing in the mud at the moment."

"What about your brothers? Won't they start to worry?"

"Not unless they've got a bet on who can find me first, or something stupid like that."

Elias's brows draw together. "If Peony went missing, I'd be freaking out and drop everything to go looking for her."

A surge of emotions roll through my chest. I can't tell which I feel the strongest—resentful toward my brothers for not caring more or super envious of the sibling relationship Peony and Elias have. "My brothers know I'm a big girl and can look after myself," I finally say.

I readjust on the ground, but I can't help wincing when some tender spots over my legs, backside, and torso twinge. Even though Elias shielded me from the worst of our fall, apparently I'm not completely without injury—and Elias must have way more injuries than just his ankle. I wonder, if it wasn't for the fact that he can't walk, would he have said anything about his ankle at all?

If I were in his shoes, I wouldn't have said anything. Maybe it's better not to ask what other injuries he might have. At least the Ylixium will also be taking care of those.

"You should take some Ylixium too," Elias says, holding out the half-full vial.

I shake my head. "I've taken a little too much over the past few months. If I take another dose, I think I'd be coming precariously close to my Ylixium limit."

"Okay. At least take these then." He offers me a tray of painkillers and a flask of water. "Please," he says when I don't move to take it. "It's the least I can do after what you've done for me."

I oblige with a sigh that's a bit more dramatic than necessary. After I'm done, we sit in silence for a bit, watching the rain streak down through the mouth of our makeshift shelter.

"I love the smell of rain." With a grimace, I almost bite my tongue. Since when am I the chick who suddenly babbles on about stuff like that? I may as well have added that I like poetic literature and long walks on the beach.

"Me too," Elias states. "There's something about it that just seems to enliven your soul."

I turn to look at Elias.

He raises an eyebrow. "What?"

"Do you like poetic literature and long walks on the beach too?"

He snorts. "Of course not. I'm more of a paperback-romance type and prefer casual strolls over a carpet of fragrant flower petals."

After a moment or two, I grin.

"There's that smile." Elias's expression radiates warmth.

"I've missed it these last few days."

My face falls as it all comes rushing back to me—that girl in the city with Elias, me running away, then avoiding him like a wuss.

The look on Elias's face changes, just as mine did. Eventually he clears his throat. "You never said who told you about the three women and their babies back there."

Several sassy remarks come to mind, as well as a few misdirecting comments. In the end, I figure there's nothing wrong with stating the truth. "No one told me."

"What? I don't understand."

"It was a fluke I found them. I just stumbled upon them."

"You did, huh?" He pauses for a moment. "So no one told you about them. You happen to find them, and yet... and yet you put yourself between me and them and told me not to come any closer."

"Pretty sure I said I'd gut you if you came any closer."

"Why though?"

"Because their babies are shifters, and you're a hunter."

Elias's brow shoots up in surprise. "You knew the babies were shifters?" His lips press into a tight line. "But *you're* a hunter. And yet you gave them your survival pack. Why?"

"Because I've already got my teal vial filled, and it wasn't worth the bother in hunting them down."

"No." Elias shakes his head. "I don't believe that's the real reason. You protected them from the Veniri. And from me when you thought I was a threat. As far as I know, hunters don't protect shifters."

My teeth clamp down on the inside of my cheek. Of course I was trying to protect them. They were just babies, innocent and defenseless. Their mothers may have been gaunt and terrified, but I couldn't help but admire those women's courage in trying to flee and find a safe place for their children.

Compassion and mercy aren't things we're ever taught as hunters. Yet those who harm the defenseless, whether shifters or not, sicken me and should be strung up by their entrails. I absolutely would have gutted Elias and blamed it on a Lycan if it turned out he was there to harm them, no matter how much he makes my stomach all fluttery.

But as for the main reason why I did it... I inadvertently put my hand on my abdomen.

The frequent echoes of Francine's voice have become more distorted in my mind, but her words lacerate just as viciously as they did the first time she said them.

...having children is no longer possible...

With a start, I realize I got caught up in my own thoughts. I look up to find Elias watching me, calmly observing my reaction. Clearly he's been waiting for me to respond, but—whether it's with the honest truth or a blatant lie—I can't bring myself to clarify anything.

Unable to hold his gaze, I turn my attention to the knuckle-duster still in my hand. I flip and twist the weapon, trailing my fingers over the smooth metal, careful to keep clear of the Diamantium tips. "Are *you* going to tell me about how your little rendezvous came about and how you got involved in helping shifters?" I eventually say.

A beat of silence passes. I begin to think Elias isn't going to say anything, and I glance at him out of the corner of my eye. It's obvious he knows full well I'm trying to deflect, yet he surprises me by letting his interrogation drop.

"Did you hear how my mother died?" he asks.

"Uh, yeah..." I squint at him in confusion. What does his mother have to do with what I asked him? "I heard there was an unfortunate hunting accident about five years ago."

Elias chuckles, but it holds an edge of darkness. "If only that were true."

"What happened?"

He heaves in a deep breath, as if he's about to release a heavy burden. "My mother was a shifter sympathizer."

My eyebrows shoot up. I've heard of humans being sympathizers—those who are in the know regarding shifters, at least. Almost every human is ignorant. Most have likely had multiple encounters with a shifter of one kind or another, perhaps even invited them into their homes, establishing a life and family with them without being any wiser.

But I've never heard of a hunter being a shifter sympathizer, at least none who dared to admit it.

"Well," continues Elias, "when my father found out she was helping shifters and going so far as to sabotage hunting trips, he was the one who killed her."

"Whoa, that's... brutal. How did you know it was him?"

"I walked in after it happened. He didn't see me though. We were out hunting—that part of the story is true. And it's also true my mother was stabbed in the heart with a Diamantium shard. Of course, my father neglected to tell anyone it was *his* Diamantium blade that killed her, not a Veniri shifter's. He still doesn't know that I know. I've never told anyone."

I shake my head, trying to picture Stellan Ragefire turning on his own wife. "Stellan would have been imprisoned or executed for attacking another hunter, even if it was his wife. How come you didn't tell anyone?"

"Because it didn't make any sense. My father loved my mother. I couldn't understand why he would do such a thing. For a while I thought maybe I was fatigued from hunting and had somehow hallucinated things. Perhaps I didn't actually see him yanking his own blade out of her chest. But then one day, about four months after my mother's funeral, I was out hunting down a Sathoi."

I crinkle my nose. Hunting down a Sathoi would have been messy. Those shifters derive their shifter abilities from the light of Saturn. Sathoi spit Viscid, a gelatinous goo that can be venom or acid or some kind of super-sticky glue, depending on the variety of Sathoi you encounter—either insectoid or funguslike. If you're really unlucky, it's possible to find a rare Sathoi that spits all three types of weaponized goopy Viscid.

"It turns out the Sathoi knew my mother," Elias continues, "and I wasn't the one to track him down. He tracked me down. My mother had given him strict instructions to find me if anything happened to her and to give me a parcel that would explain everything to me."

Elias falls silent for a few moments, and the mood within our little cave grows somber. When he does go on, his voice is thick with emotion.

"Within the parcel the Sathoi gave me were several of my mother's journals. Each journal entry was a letter, all addressed to me. She described in detail her challenges, joys, and heartaches over not just raising me in a barracks but also doing the work she'd dedicated her life to.

"My father's a legacy hunter. A renowned Ragefire. My mother was a new recruit to our barracks when they met. At least, that was the story I'd been told my whole life. In actual fact, my mother was a shifter sympathizer well before she was initiated into our barracks and married my father. In my mother's written words, she had gone behind enemy lines to save as many shifters as possible from being hunted down and torn apart for profit.

"You wouldn't believe it, Nika. Over the years, my

mother saved thousands of shifters, and all under my father's and the rest of the barracks' noses."

It *is* hard to believe. The enormity of what one woman —Elias's mother—did has my head reeling.

"My mother said things began to change for her when she discovered she was pregnant with Peony. She didn't want to make the same mistake she'd made with me and raise another child in a barracks, so she set plans in motion to get Peony and me out. A few weeks after Peony was born, she had everything ready for us to leave."

Elias hesitates, and after a few seconds, I finish for him.

"But Stellan found out your mom was a sympathizer and made sure she wouldn't leave, huh?"

He tilts his head from side to side. "Yes and no. Remember the Sathoi I mentioned?"

"Yeah."

"Apparently he was my mother's lifelong lover."

My eyes widen. I didn't see that coming. A hunter being a shifter sympathizer is one thing, but a hunter having a romantic relationship with a shifter? You may as well sign your own death warrant in your own blood after slicing a dagger over your own throat.

Despite my shock, I remain quiet as Elias continues.

"The Sathoi and my mother did a lot of work together even before she inserted herself into our barracks. And you're right, my father did find out about the work my mother was doing, but the thing that tipped him over the edge was finding out about her love affair with the Sathoi.

"I also think that's his excuse for not having anything to do with Peony, regardless of the fact that a paternity test proved he is, without a doubt, Peony's father. He might have loved my mother, but him neglecting Peony just goes to show how much of a douchebag he really is."

"Sheesh, Elias," I say, trying to process all he said. "Why are you telling me all this?"

"I'm telling you because..." A few heartbeats pass as Elias collects his thoughts. "Even though I was brought up as a hunter, I always had a sense of revulsion toward this kind of life. When I found out what my mother was doing—helping shifters instead of harming them—I can't explain what happened. It was like something inside of me just clicked. I knew I had to follow in her footsteps, to pick up where she left off. There was a bit of a learning curve on my part, and it took time to prove myself trustworthy to the other sympathizers, but eventually, my mother's contacts became my contacts. Her role in directing shifters to safety became my role."

Elias swivels his body to face me head-on. Only then do I realize he isn't wearing a hunter's amulet. Come to think of it, I don't think he's worn one since he and the Ragefire entourage showed up that first night. Why did I never notice?

"The reason I'm telling you all this," he goes on, "is because the other night in the city, when you saw me with that woman—when she kissed me—I can only imagine what you thought to make you take off like that."

Immediately my cheeks burn, and the anger and hurt resurface in rolling waves. I shift my attention back to my knuckle-duster, rotating it around and around, unable to meet Elias's gaze.

"Nika, the woman you saw me with was a shifter I was helping. I met up with her to give her new forms and an ID to set herself up in a new life. I also informed her that her sister, whom she thought was dead, is actually alive and well, and I gave her an address where she could find her.

What you saw was her giving me a hug of relief and appreciation."

My knuckle-duster pauses in mid-rotation as I think back to that night in the city. Elias's revelation triggered a small detail I overlooked. When Peony and I approached the alley where Elias met with the woman, I recall her saying something right before she launched herself forward to hug him: *"Thank you, thank you. You have no idea how much this means to me."*

My shoulders sag as the shifter's emotion-fueled voice echoes in my mind. This time when my cheeks burn, it's with shame, mixed with a hefty dose of relief. If only I paid more heed to what she said earlier, I wouldn't have acted like a fool and fled like an OG Disney princess to go sulk in my room.

But why didn't Elias tell me earlier?

Because you didn't give him the opportunity to explain, chastises my logical voice.

"I feel like an idiot," I finally say. I brave looking at him, and my relief deepens when I don't see any rebuke in Elias's expression.

"Don't," he says, laying a hand on my forearm. "I'm the one to blame. I wasn't entirely up-front and honest with you."

I huff a derisive chuckle. "I'm not exactly up-front myself."

Again, with no sign of rebuke, Elias gives me a small smile

"Wait a second!" I round on Elias with an accusing glare when I recall another detail from that night. "Those holographic shoes the shifter was wearing. I thought I'd seen them before. She's the Meruvo I was hunting in that abandoned factory."

Elias's pursed lips are all the confirmation I need.

My jaw drops as a few other things become clear. "If that's the case, then it wasn't an accident when you sprayed me with Myst. You were trying to stop me from killing her."

His face morphs into a full-blown grimace.

"So me kicking your ass in the cafeteria was totally justified after all." I punch him in the arm. "You jerk."

"I suppose you don't hate me too much if you're punching me without that." Elias gestures to the knuckleduster in my other hand.

"Consider yourself lucky," I say with a goodhearted growl.

"So... am I forgiven?"

I take a few seconds to ponder his question. The guy deliberately sabotaged my hunt. I should be downright pissed that he thwarted my attempt to fill another vial on my amulet. But the funny thing is, I'm not pissed anymore. Not even a little bit.

I wave an indifferent hand. "Fine. But don't blame me for my knee-jerk reaction to throat-punch you the next time I see an atomizer in your hand."

Elias laughs, but there's a hint of regret in his eyes. "While we're doing this honesty thing, there's something else I should tell you."

"Oh?" Anxiety begins to churn in my stomach again.

He adjusts his position, taking a few seconds before continuing. "That night in the city, you asked what's stopping me from leaving the barracks. The truth is, I am leaving."

Whatever relief I felt earlier fizzles into a vapor. My insides turn to granite as dread engulfs me.

"My mother didn't want Peony growing up in the barracks. It was her last wish before she died. Peony is five now, and it's taken me a little longer than I would've liked, but I've got everything sorted to set her up in a new life away from all this. Perhaps in time, she'll forget her life among the hunters. And maybe when she's a little older, I can go back to helping shifters who need it."

I try to smooth my face into impassivity, but it's quite a challenge when I feel as though I'm dying inside.

"Nika? Are you okay?"

I go to nod yes, but my head shakes no instead. "I can't have children."

Elias blinks a few times; clearly he didn't expect me to blurt that little gem out. He gently lays a hand on my forearm. "What do you mean?"

As if the floodgates have been obliterated, my secrets pour out of me.

Elias listens, quiet and still, just as I did for him.

I tell him all about the hunt where I acquired my orange Jiovis blood sample—the fateful trip that ended with me being hit with a Luxium grenade. I describe the agonizing recovery and the even more agonizing fact that my uterus and ovaries were damaged beyond repair, then surgically removed.

I also babble about how I struggled with losing my own mother at an early age, about the heartbreak of not being able to follow in her footsteps to become a strong, caring, and empowering mother like she was.

With that truth laid bare, I blither on about how much it sucks that I've realized this far too late. I've wasted the majority of my life striving to hunt down shifters, only to pay the ultimate price of never achieving my soul-deep dream of becoming a mother.

"And all for what?" I exclaim. "All because I needed to work my ass off to prove to my deadbeat dad, my stupid brothers, and the rest of the morons back at the barracks that I'm more than... I'm more than..." I yank my amulet out of my shirt. "That I'm more than a bunch of glowing colors on a worthless chunk of metal. But it's all for nothing. I'm noth—"

I can't hold my tears back anymore. Turning my face away, I hold my breath, desperately trying to silence the sobs that ricochet through me. Even with my eyes squeezed shut, the tears stream down my cheeks, giving the rain outside a run for its money.

A warm hand appears on my cheek. Gently but firmly, Elias turns my face back to him.

My eyes remain shut tight. I try to turn away again, but my face is now cupped in both his hands.

"Don't do that." Elias's low tone is like a soothing balm.

I heave in a ragged breath, and thanks to the years of suppressing my tears, I regain enough control to avoid the incoming ugly crying. "Do what?"

His thumbs stroke away each rogue tear that escapes my closed eyes. "You don't need to hide your pain from me, Nika."

After a heartbeat, I slowly open my eyes to meet Elias's, which capture me in a gaze so genuine it feels as if I'm floating after being weighted down for years.

"You're right," he says. "You are more than a hunk-of-junk piece of jewelry. You're more than what the hunters want you to think. And dare I say it, you're even more than the ability to have children or not. There's so much more to you, Nika. And if you can't see it, then let me see it for you, until you can see it for yourself."

I've become immersed in Elias's eyes, in the look he's giving me—intimidating, intimate, and healing at the same time. Each of his words crashes like a boulder through the stronghold I've carefully constructed around my soul. Something inside of me shifts, and with it, so does my whole perspective—on the hunter world, the past I've endured, and the prospect of my future.

After a lifetime of fighting, hunting, and throwing myself into one dangerous situation after another, I manage to rustle up enough courage to do the scariest thing I've ever dared to do.

I lean in and press my lips to Elias's.

His response is instant. He kisses me back, matching my vigor, needing me as much as I need him.

After a few heated moments, I wrap my arms around Elias just as he pulls me onto his lap. My knuckle-dusters slips out of my hands and thuds onto the ground, where it lies forgotten.

I hold him tight, much as I did when we were tumbling down the ravine, but this time it feels even more as if my life depends on it. Elias embraces me just as firmly. Our kissing is on fire, but the strokes and caresses of his hands over my face, neck, and back are tender and reassuring.

Whatever heartbreak, pain, or hardship I've dealt with over the years fades away like a wisp, until all that remains in my world is Elias Ragefire.

Without warning, Elias pulls back, breaking our kiss and for a moment breaking the magic. He once again cups my face in his hands and captures my gaze.

"Come with me." His words are earnest, his expression fervid.

I blink a few times, taking a moment to understand what he's asking.

"When Peony and I leave the hunters for a new life, will you come with me?"

Chapter Eighteen

Elias opens the car door for me with a sweep of his arm and a small bow. "My lady."

Anyone else would have gotten an ass-kicking in return, but despite how cringey his gesture is, I can't get over the cheeky grin lighting up his whole demeanor. I find myself laughing.

With a lighthearted eye roll, I slide out of the Jeep. Before I've even taken two steps, though, Elias has me pinned against the car, catching my mouth with his.

The kiss that follows has me weak in the knees, my world once again revolving around Elias, and Elias alone. His heated caresses send tingles rushing up my spine and over my cheeks. My desperate need for more is on the verge of spiraling out of control when I suddenly become aware of where we are.

I dart my eyes around the parking garage, searching for signs of anyone else around. As far as I can tell, all of our hunting group's Land Rover Defenders are accounted for, along with a few of the Jeeps from Elias's barracks.

Back at our little ravine nook in the hinterlands, the

Ylixium didn't take long to heal Elias's leg enough for him to walk. But neither of us were in a rush to get back to the others. Instead we spent our time kissing, and talking, and kissing some more. Long after the rain cleared and the sun's rays broke through the predawn haze, we finally decided to hike back.

Of course, it was no surprise that everyone had gone; only Elias's Jeep was left waiting for us.

I scan the rest of the vehicles in the parking garage for good measure: a collection of other box trucks, four-wheelers, and a few motorbikes. I even glimpse the Ford Mustang I pinched from the city the other night, but thankfully there are no people in sight. No doubt everyone's in the cafeteria or has crawled into bed.

But it still isn't enough to give me peace of mind.

"Elias, I think we should go."

Ignoring me, Elias continues his trail of kisses down my neck and over my collarbone, to which my body blissfully responds. But the logical part of me won't let up.

"Elias, someone could walk in at any moment and see us."

Elias stops his kisses, and I immediately regret saying anything.

"I don't care." He places a hand on my cheek and looks me straight in the eye. "I'm not ashamed of the way I feel about you. Other than Peony, I don't care at all what anyone thinks. If they have a problem, they can all go kiss my ass."

I laugh, unable to explain the elation his words bring me. Never in my life has anyone gone out of their way for my sake, let alone been willing to damn it all to hell. If Elias isn't afraid to be with me, then I won't be afraid either.

I wrap my arms around his neck and give him a fierce kiss.

"Yes," I say, pulling away all too soon.

"Yes what?" But a split second later, Elias's eyes light up. "Wait a second. 'Yes' as in... yes you'll come with me?" The hope in his face is so substantial I could drown in it.

I nod.

"Really? Are you sure?"

"Yes, I'm sure."

He trails a finger along the black chain at my neck, then holds up my amulet. With his thumb, he traces each vial I've filled: silver, teal, magenta, and orange. "You've gained four colors, Nika. You're starting to make a name for yourself here. Who knows what more you could achieve—the status you could gain in a few more months or even years in the hunting community?"

I take the amulet from him and drop it; the familiar weight bounces on the end of the chain and comes to rest against my sternum. "I don't want a necklace to determine my worth anymore. You're right, it's just a chunk of junk jewelry."

"But what about what you have here?" Elias sweeps an arm overhead, his elation faltering. "Your life? Your brothers? The rest of your family and friends? Back in the ravine, I was caught up in the moment when I asked you to come with me. I hadn't thought through what I was asking. I know it was rash—"

"Elias, stop." I press a finger to his lips and give him a reassuring smile. "I've been thinking about it since you asked, and in the car ride back, I realized there's nothing here for me. Sure, my brothers are here, and my family. But my family's hunting legacy is no longer the future I want for myself. For the first time in a long time, I have no idea what my future holds."

I put a hand on his cheek. "Whether it turns out for the

better or for the worse, all I know is I want to begin the rest of my life with you."

Pure joy radiates from his smile. He places his hand on top of mine and turns his face to kiss my palm. "You have no idea how happy I am to hear you say that. In that case, I don't see any reason for us to linger any longer. We leave tonight."

I draw him closer and hug him tight. All words fail to describe my excitement for the next chapter in my life. As I give Elias another kiss, I hope he can understand how much I want to be with him. "I'd better go pack my things then."

We stroll through the hallways of the barracks, Elias's arm over my shoulders, mine around his waist. Periodically he looks down at me and plants kisses in my hair or on my brow.

I'm sure I'm grinning like an idiot the whole time.

We're nearing the sleeping quarters where my room is located when we come face-to-face with Quill and Hestus. Quill takes one look at Elias's arm around me before his face turns sulfurous. I know him well enough to recognize the furious restraint, thin as spider silk, in the shudder that ripples through him.

"What the hell are you doing with him?" Quill grits out through clenched teeth. It's clear his question is for me, but his venomous gaze never leaves Elias.

"What do you care?" I say.

"Branstones don't mix with Ragefires." Quill speaks as if he were quoting a commandment from the Bible. He stabs a finger at Elias. "We especially don't associate with the likes of him."

I roll my eyes. Clearly Quill's forgotten about all the

times we used to play with Elias as kids. "Back off. You don't get to dictate who I 'mix' with or not."

"Last I checked, you were beating Ragefire to a pulp in the cafeteria," says Hestus with a thoughtful frown. "What's changed?"

"Last I checked, that was none of your business," I growl. "And last I checked, you and Quill didn't give a crap about what I do. What's changed there, huh?"

Quill opens his mouth to respond, but Hestus holds up a hand. "We've heard stories about the Ragefires. Stories about what really happened to his mother."

An errant shiver of dread flutters through my chest. Elias's arm tightens around my shoulders, and his fingers dig into my bicep.

"I've told you before, you shouldn't believe every bit of gossip the Grimvast twins spew around the barracks," I counter, trying to sound as dismissive as possible. I don't know for sure what Hestus is referring to, but better for him and Quill to think it's a useless rumor.

Quill ignores me and takes a step closer to Elias. "We've heard about your mother," he hisses. "We've heard all about that traitorous shifter-shagger—"

In a flash, Elias has Quill slammed up against the wall, a handful of my brother's black shirt in his fist. "Don't you talk about my mother." His deathly quiet voice shudders with fury.

"Hey! Leave my brother alone." Hestus's warning lands on deaf ears.

I stand frozen for a moment, stunned. I haven't seen this kind of rage from Elias since we were children. Even when I attacked him in the cafeteria, he never once looked as if he wanted to rip my head off, the way he does now with Quill.

Quill's throaty laugh is dark and taunting. "If you ask me, that shifter-shagger got let off the hook too easy."

"Stop it, Quill." My words are drowned out by Elias slamming Quill against the wall again. The two men exchange glares with the ferocity of bears about to maul each other.

"You know, Ragefire, I don't recall ever seeing you bleed," says Quill. "But I suppose if I had a mother who was a shifter-shagger, I'd probably be careful too."

Only then do I spot the crystal dagger at Elias's throat.

"Quill, no!" I lunge at the same time Hestus does.

A fierce tussle ensues, but to my relief, Hestus is trying to break the guys up just as much as I am. I kick and punch at Quill, forcing myself between him and Elias until their grip on each other finally breaks. Elias and I go sprawling onto the ground, but we spring back up just as Hestus pins Quill to the wall.

"Elias?" I look over to find him clutching at his neck. My blood runs cold, then turns to ice when he removes his hand and looks at his palm.

Vibrant red trails down his neck and stains his hand.

Relief pulses through me, slightly thawing my dread.

"Damn it, Quill!" I bark. "We used to train with Elias as kids. I even gave him a bloody nose once. You know full well he's not a shifter."

Quill peers down at the tip of his Diamantium dagger, inspecting the glistening red as if he expects it to change color. After a moment, he hisses with frustration, but then a sinister haze eclipses his features. "Hmm, Ragefire might not be a shifter, but what do we know about that little sister of his?"

Elias erupts with vicious cursing, but I'm the one who lunges at Quill, brandishing my knuckle-duster.

"If you dare go near that little girl, I swear I'll kill you myself." Each of my words quavers with a fervid wrath I've never directed at one of my brothers before.

For a second, the bloodlust in Quill's expression falters. Even Hestus's eyes bug with shock at my reaction.

After a few tension-filled seconds, the venom returns to Quill's demeanor. This time he directs it at me. "If you side with a Ragefire over us, then as far as I'm concerned, you're a traitor—to our Branstone name, to our barracks, and to the entire hunter legion."

"What?" Hestus rounds his shock on Quill. "Don't say that, Quill."

My knuckle-duster digs into my hand with how tight I clench my fists. I'd be lying if I said Quill's words don't sting.

"What's it to be, Nika? Us or *him*?" Quill demands.

I bite the inside of my cheek to stop myself from crying. Back at the ravine, Elias asked me to leave the hunters and go with him, but never once did he frame the question in those stark "me or them" terms.

I flick my gaze to Hestus. His tortured expression tells me that even though he doesn't agree with Quill, he'd never go against his brother—against the Branstone legacy. Once again, I'm on my own.

Except... this time, that actually isn't true.

Elias places a hand on my shoulder, and I turn to look up at him. With his lips pressed in a firm line, he gives me a slight nod.

Whatever I decide to do, he is with me. Whether I want to kick my brothers' asses or turn my back and walk away, Elias is with me. Even if I decide to choose my brothers over him, I know—by the shadow of sadness in his eyes—he wouldn't begrudge me even that.

Before I voice my decision, a raucous shout echoes through the hallway, and we all spin. Deshawn and Jakai Grimvast are running down the corridor toward us, half a dozen hunters in their wake.

Reluctantly, I release Quill and step back.

"Hey, there you guys are," calls out Jakai when they're about ten feet away. He quirks an eyebrow in suspicion, clearly not missing the tension in our little group.

"What's going on?" Quill demands.

The Grimvast twins slow down, but the other hunters continue down the hall.

"Your Uncle Matthias and his posse are back from another whirlwind adventure," says Deshawn.

"So? What's the big deal?" I scan the hunters walking by; some appear a little bedraggled, with mussed hair and wearing sleeping clothes. A few hunters even crack wide yawns as they pass. Whatever's going on, it must be important enough to pull hunters away from their beds.

"Haven't you heard?" says Deshawn. "Word has it they've returned with the biggest Diamantium cache this barracks has ever seen."

"And apparently this time he has proof that the winged shifters really do exist," says Jakai.

I groan and roll my eyes.

"Here we go with the mythological winged shifters again," says Hestus.

"Come on." Jakai grins. "You guys aren't even a little bit curious?"

My brothers, Elias, and I shoot some guarded glances at each other.

"May as well go check it out," says Hestus. He follows after the twins, giving me a conflicted expression as he passes Elias and me.

A moment later, Quill trails after Hestus. "This isn't finished," he says in a low voice as he brushes past my shoulder. "*Traitor.*"

Elias takes hold of my hand, and I lean into him as my brothers walk away. "You okay, Nika?"

I nod in answer, then spot the wound still bleeding on Elias's neck. "Are you okay?"

He gives me a smile that doesn't quite reach his eyes. "Don't worry about me. I've dealt with worse things than an overzealous hunter."

Another group of hunters weave around us, heading in the same direction as the others.

Elias inclines his head at the procession. "Should we go see what all the fuss is about?"

I scrunch up my nose. "It's probably nothing. Just Uncle Matthias hyping up the barracks again over his obsession with myths and fantasies. Besides, I thought we had some packing to do?"

"I think the packing can wait." He rubs his jaw in deep contemplation as he watches more people pass by. "I've got a feeling we need to see what's going on."

* * *

Ten minutes later, the bulk of the hunters swarm into the cafeteria. It's one of the few communal areas big enough to fit us all at once.

Still hand in hand, Elias and I weave through the crowd to reach the front, where Uncle Matthias and a group of his goons are waiting with smug expressions. When I see what's on the floor next to them, my jaw nearly slams into the ground. Not one, not two, but five large wooden chests surround my uncle, each one brimming with Diamantium spikes of all sizes.

The crystal Veniri bones glister with myriad fractal rainbows, and at first glance, one might think it's just an obnoxious mound of crystal shards, but then I spot a crystal skull in the heap, then another and another. Each Diamantium skull possesses the triple set of crystal fangs distinct to the Veniri shifters.

"Told ya." Deshawn moves to stand beside me. "Ain't that the biggest cache of Diamantium you've ever seen?"

"How many sliths do you reckon it took to fill up that many chests?" Jakai asks from Deshawn's other side.

"In the hundreds at least," says Deshawn.

Elias's hand grips mine tighter at Deshawn's estimate. His face is void of all emotion, but I don't miss the scalding fury in his eyes.

Uncle Matthias raises his hands for the crowd to quiet down, then launches into the gripping tale of how he and his group scored such a bountiful loot.

Within a minute, I'm already holding back a yawn and wishing Uncle Matthias would quit the theatrics and get straight to the so-called proof that winged shifters exist. But on and on he babbles. If Uncle Matthias had been brought up in the mundane human world, no doubt he would have had a flourishing career in politics.

"Wait a second," Deshawn whispers. "I don't see Troy. Do you?"

I frown. "Troy?"

"Yeah, your uncle recruited him to go on this expedition," says Jakai.

"And now he's missing," Deshawn adds.

I scan the half a dozen hunters standing proudly behind Uncle Matthias. Dread seeps into my chest when I realize the Grimvasts are correct.

I recall the last time I saw Troy, when he caught me eavesdropping on Uncle Matthias and Axel—the viciousness of my hate toward him after his unfortunate aim with his Luxium grenade. Yet I still can't bring myself to think, *Good riddance to the guy*.

"Maybe Troy's at the infirmary." My voice sounds unconvincing even to myself.

"Nah, we passed it on our way over," says Deshawn.

"And it was empty," confirms Jakai.

I chew on my lip, turning back to the goons standing behind Uncle Matthias.

"Bandit and Mario aren't there either," says Elias.

I bristle at those two names, memories of my run-in with them flickering through my mind.

"Who's Bandit and Mario?" Deshawn asks.

"Two hunters from my barracks," explains Elias. "Matthias managed to also recruit them for this last mission." When I glance at him, he adds, "I know you didn't have the best introduction to them, but they're not all bad."

I *pish* my disagreement.

"I'm serious. Those kids have just been a little misguided. But they still didn't deserve..." Elias's frown deepens as he turns his attention back to my uncle's group.

I don't need him to finish his sentence to understand his meaning. Bandit and Mario didn't deserve to be led astray by my uncle. They didn't deserve whatever unfortunate circumstance is causing the hair to rise on the back of my neck right now.

"Just tell us about the winged shifters," calls a voice from the crowd, followed by a ripple of murmured agreement.

A hard expression flashes over Uncle Matthias's face as he pauses mid-sentence. Then his mouth curls into a big smile that shows off all his over-white teeth. "All right, all right," he says when the crowd quiets down. "I won't keep you in suspense about the winged shifters any longer. We have discovered the possible location of a map—"

The crowd erupts into booing and heckles.

"What kind of map?" someone yells.

"It's not a map," responds someone else. "He said they found a *possible location* of one."

"Trust Branstone to go on spewing about his fantasies again."

"What a load of slith crap!"

As the hecklers hurl more insults, I lean closer to Elias. "Like I said, it's just Uncle Matthias blowing smoke up people's asses again."

Elias only answers with a "hmm," his frown never faltering. He almost looks as though he's hanging on Uncle Matthias's every word.

"Now, now!" Uncle Matthias calls out over the crowd. "I know how this sounds, but I assure you, we are so close to finding these shifters. I just need some volunteers—"

The crowd erupts again, this time with a little more vehemence.

"What about the hunters who are missing? What happened to them?"

Uncle Matthias gives a smile he must think is assuring, but it has the exact opposite effect. "My recruits are very well aware of the dangers involved in these kinds of expeditions. They all knew the risks—"

The crowd jeers even louder. Insults and foul language are hurled at Uncle Matthias from all directions. But he waits, casually sliding his hands in the pockets of his gunmetal-gray suit pants, acting as if the furious crowd is calmly talking among themselves instead.

Then his eyes find mine. A sudden chill slithers down my spine as he studies me for a long second. Something shifts in Uncle Matthias's eyes as his gaze slowly pans down to where my hand is clasped securely in Elias's.

When Uncle Matthias's contemplative stare once again finds mine, the creep factor hits another level. A shot of fear sends rippling goosebumps over my flesh.

But in another second, he blinks, and his focus returns to the frenzied hunters.

"I say this!" Uncle Matthias shouts to be heard. "For those who wish to acquire not only riches but the glory of going down in hunter history, we leave for our next mission tonight."

Still a little taken aback by the ominous attention from my uncle, I almost laugh at the ridiculousness of this entire situation. How could anyone fall for something so ludicrous? With a smirk, I turn to Elias, half expecting him to be laughing too, but his face is still set in a mask of deep concern.

"I've got a really bad feeling about what's happened to those hunters," he finally says.

Chapter Nineteen

I PLACE my stack of black jeans into my large backpack, right next to a pile of folded black tops. Maybe I need to buy new clothes—something with a bit of color to suit my new life with Elias and Peony.

A thrill of excitement rushes through me as I check my watch. Only half an hour to go before the two of them knock on my door. I smile at the prospect of seeing Peony again. She is such a great kid. Despite the fact she's only five, I already admire her fearlessness and tenacity.

A knock sounds at my door.

I pause for a few heartbeats. Who is that? It's too early for Elias and Peony, and no one ever comes to visit me... It better not be Quill and Hestus coming for round two. I retrieve my knuckle-duster as I make my way over to the door.

Relief floods through me when I find Elias instead, but it instantly evaporates when I notice he's alone, not a backpack or suitcase in sight.

"What's wrong?" I ask.

"Can I come in?"

I step to the side. The moment I close the door, Elias sweeps me up into a hug. For that instant, wrapped securely in his arms, I can half believe everything is all right. I close my eyes and snuggle into him.

"We're not leaving, are we?" I say into his neck.

"Not yet."

My stomach falls.

"There's something I have to do first."

I pull back so I can look into his honey-brown eyes. Somehow—maybe by the way he's caressing my back with one hand and brushing his fingers through my tangle of curls with the other—I know what he's about to do.

Nausea roils in my gut.

"No." I forcefully shake my head.

"I have to."

"No, you can't. I won't let you."

"Listen to me."

"No, no, no. You're not going with Uncle Matthias. You can't."

"Hunters are going missing. Someone has to find out what Matthias is really up to. I have to do something."

"No, you don't. We can just leave. Someone *else* can—"

"Nika, my mother didn't just help shifters. She also helped hunters who needed to escape from this life. I don't know why, but I just... in my heart of hearts, I know she would want me to do this."

Deflated, I sag against him.

"That's not fair." A tear rolls down my cheek. "How can I argue against that?"

"I'm sorry." Elias pulls me back in for a tight embrace. "Believe me when I say I want nothing more than to turn my back on all this and run away with you right now. But I can't shake the feeling that this is one last thing I need to do before we leave. I've already arranged for someone to look after Peony while I'm gone."

"Fine, I'm coming with you," I say through my sniffles.

This time it's Elias's turn to shake his head with vehemence. "Absolutely not."

I narrow my watery eyes at him. "Elias, I am not a prissy girl who will just sit around and wait—"

"I know, Nika. You're the strongest, most courageous person I know. You're beyond capable of dealing with something like this. But I can't stand the thought of anything happening to you. I've only just got you in my life, and if I know for sure that you and Peony are safe, then I have way more reason to do what I need to do and come straight back to you."

I open my mouth to reply, but Elias quickly adds, "If I asked you to stay, just this once, would you do it for me?"

I close my eyes with a sigh, and two more tears roll down my cheeks. This "giving in to my emotions and allowing someone to see me cry" thing is still pretty new to me, but with the way this guy tugs at my heartstrings, I'm sure getting a lot of practice.

Even though every fiber of my being tells me to scream no, I nod yes.

Elias huffs out a breath, then his face breaks into a relieved smile. "Thank you. I know how hard that is for you."

"But what happens if you don't come back?"

Elias kisses my cheeks, following each trail my tears have made, before placing his lips on mine. He locks me in for a deep kiss—fierce, raw, and full of angst.

"I will come back for you, Nika," he says against my lips.

. . .

I don't recall in full detail the moment he left, but one thing I do know is Elias lied.

He didn't come back.

* * *

Days, nights, and then a week pass before Uncle Matthias, Axel, and the rest of the group of hunters return.

All but Elias.

At first I'm gutted.

And then I become enraged.

I kick and scream, demanding to know where Elias is. But again, Uncle Matthias's response is the same as that day in the cafeteria.

"Elias was very well aware of the risks this expedition entailed..."

I refuse to accept that as the only answer I get. I search every day, out in the field, within the barracks, in the city—everywhere! I question each hunter who went on the expedition with Elias, but no matter how hard I interrogate, no one says anything different from what my uncle said.

Much as I did when Sagan went missing, I go out every night and day, searching, searching, searching. Any little clue I got from grilling Uncle Matthias's followers, I relentlessly follow up on, only to always find myself at a dead end. Paranoia surfaces every now and then, with thoughts that someone must be covering Uncle Matthias's tracks.

Another week passes, then a month. My endurance never wavers, but everyone's tolerance of me reaches breaking point.

Ever since our little disagreement over my budding relationship with Elias, Quill and Hestus have avoided me. The Grimvast twins always do a one-eighty when they see me coming. Every other hunter skirts far around me and gives me side-eye, as if I have the bubonic plague.

The worst is when I find out that at some point during my fits of fury, Stellan Ragefire and the other members of his barracks packed up and left, taking Peony with them. I was so fixated on Elias I didn't even go check on Peony to see how she was dealing with the loss of her brother. I never got the chance to say goodbye to her.

After two months, I reach the stage of hopelessness, just as I did after searching months and months for Sagan. When I'm not out searching, I retreat to my room, spending hours either in a fugue state of grief or desperately trying to come up with a new plan to find Elias.

One day, there's a small knock at my door. If I wasn't already drowning in my sorrow, I'd have been beyond surprised to see Hestus waiting for me.

He puts his hands up. "I'm not here to cause a fight."

"Did Quill send you to lecture me more about how much I've betrayed the Branstone legacy?" I ask with narrowed eyes.

"No, he doesn't know I'm here."

After a bit of awkward small talk, Hestus finally says what he came to say. "Nika, it's a known fact that hunters go missing all the time. You have to accept the fact that Elias is gone. He's not coming back. So do yourself a favor and move on."

Whether or not it was Hestus's intention in telling me that, the fissures in my heart finally split apart, and my brother awkwardly leaves me in a crying heap.

Over the next few days, I try to reassemble my broken pieces, but the effort only forces me to realize one thing: if I can't find Elias, I need to get away.

I'm done with this barracks. I'm done with this life.

Once again I pack my things. Somehow I push through the emotional haze, trying not to think of how Elias should be here with me. While all the hunters are out searching for prey, I choose one of the remaining Land Rover Defenders, turn the engine on, slam the vehicle into drive, and squeal out of the garage.

Never once do I look back.

For the longest time, I have no idea where I'm going. I just continue to drive wherever the roads lead me. Eventually, I find myself in a forest near the old camping grounds where my family used to spend our annual vacations. Pulling the Defender into a clearing to park, I load up with my survival pack and the rest of my things, then begin a familiar trek through the forest.

Joyful memories encompass me as I wander the trails, and they swell into a flood the moment I set eyes on the cave my siblings, cousins, and I spent hours upon hours playing in. When I reach the cave's mouth, I know I've made it to my destination. The darkness within beckons me.

And the weight of my sorrow almost brings me to my knees.

There was once a time I thought I knew what I wanted. I had a purpose, a future that my family and ancestors had laid out before me. But that all changed when a Luxium grenade blasted through my abdomen. The final thing to send my life off its hunter trajectory was Elias asking me to leave with him.

And now, even that dream has been dashed to pieces.

I've come to the end of me. Grief and brokenness is all that remains.

How ironic that a brilliant flash of magenta light began the chain reaction that led me to the darkest moment of my life. I thought being the victim of a Luxium grenade was painful, but now I'd almost prefer that over the agony of my shattered heart.

Especially now that Elias is gone.

Staring into the abyssal black of the cave entrance, with the sunlight on my back, I find it hard to identify with the Nika I used to be: Nika the hunter. Nika the badass. The so-called Branstone Iron Maiden, tough on the outside and extra lethal on the inside. Nika with four vials filled in her amulet. Every title that I or others have placed on me no longer applies, but even the titles I want seem impossible now—daughter, girlfriend, mother. It's all empty. Meaningless, like ashes in the wind.

Elias may have seen beyond all that—beyond what everyone else saw in me—but I still can't see it for myself.

I'm as unsure as ever what my role is in this world. With everything shattered and stripped away, there's no point trying to reassemble the pieces. I need to forge new ones.

As I face the chasm of nothing my life has become, a small spark of surprise hits me when I realize I am certain of one thing. All I am is Nika, just Nika. And in this moment, that's enough, at least until I can find the strength to discover and reclaim my purpose in this world.

But for now, I step into the cavern, and the shadows engulf me with a wintry embrace.

Nika's story is not over. Find out what happens next when she makes a reappearance in **Flames of Mars,** *the second book in the Celestial Shifters series.*

Acknowledgments

It's hard to believe I'm already done and dusted with my third book!! This author journey is such a thrill. Each new book comes with its challenges, but again there's still so much more for me to explore in this adventure.

Once again, I owe my everything to my Lord and Saviour, Jesus Christ, and for Your amazing sacrifice. I'm so glad nothing can separate me from Your love. I give all credit to You, my Father in Heaven and the Holy Spirit for my life and all that is good in it. I have no doubts You've given me these stories, and it's been such an honour to collaborate in writing these stories with You. As much as Nika's story wasn't part of my writing plan for this year, You did warn me that book three in my series was gong to be delayed—I just didn't realise it would be delayed because I was about to go start *and finish* a brand new book 😄 Thank You for continuing to inspire me and giving me the words to write.

To Kevin, my wonderful husband, again your endless support is beyond what I can ever repay! A massive thank you again for encouraging me in this journey. Words cannot express how grateful I am, nor how much I love you! xxx

Annabelle, you are such a delight and you bring me so much joy. You are so creative and imaginative, and you always find inventive ways to make me laugh. I'm so glad I get to be a part of your life. Please don't grow up too fast!!!!

A big thank you Janeen Donovan, my Mum. Your support in more than just emotional and financial, has been truly grateful. It's an honour to be your daughter. Thank you for raising me, for being there whenever I need, for feeding my Enid Blyton addiction and for introducing me to authors such as Frank E. Peretti, C.S. Lewis, and J.R.R. Tolkien. I think I can safely blame you for sparking my wild imagination, haha! Another big thanks for taking time to beta read Nika's story and for you valuable input. Much appreciated!

A big thank you to the rest of my family! Oh, Wow! I'm so blessed to be a part of such a wonderful clan. The Hams, Donovans, Colemans, Evans', Drapers, McCuddens, Eveans', Youngs, and all the extended family. Thank you so much for your support in buying my first book and being my behind the scenes cheerleaders.

To my Alphas, the super talented Writer's Unite Group; Carleton Chinner, Julie Dickson, Tim Edwards, Suzie Eisfelder, Tarryn Mallick, and Katarina Smythe (a.k.a. Kaydence Snow), Stacy Sau, and Misty Clifford. You guys are AWESOME! I'm so glad I found you guys. Thanks for all the feedback, the support, the great laughs and the motivation to keep writing. Gosh, I cringe to think how many tears and whinging you had to put up with from me during the writing of this book. But, you guys have been such a solid and steady support in helping me to whip my work into shape, and find the courage to "suck it up" and move on with the next step. You're all such an inspiration and I'm so excited to see what the future brings for your own amazing writing.

A big shout out to all my beta readers who volunteered their precious time to read through my manuscript and to provide me with honest feedback. You all kept me on my toes and picked up several inconsistencies compared with the first book. Taking on a beta reader role is an epic job and I'm truly grateful. Thanks Heaps!

To my Hervey Bay bible study group and to the St George Sisterhood, thank you for remembering my writing journey in your prayers. Whether I'm facing the successes and the struggles, your prayers and spiritual support has been priceless. Thank you so much!

And to my editor, Kirstin Andrews. I've said it before, but I'm happy to say it again, I'm always so excited when I get to the editing phase of my books, I have such a great time working with you. Thanks so much for taking whatever rough-as-guts manuscript I send you way and for polishing it up into something I'm proud to share with the world. It's always an honour to have you as my editor. You're the BESTEST!

For the amazing cover, thanks so much to the amazing team at Deranged Doctor Design. I'm always amazed with the design work you door me. Thanks so much for making my books look so good!

I hope I haven't forgotten anyone. If I have, I'm so sorry! xoxo

About the Author

Tjalara Draper began her writing career at the start of 2016 when the stories in her crazy imagination kept growing. After an online course in Creative Writing, she was thoroughly convinced she needed to pursue her all-time dream of becoming an author.

She's wife to an amazing man who's made his own career change to become a doctor, and mother to a spitfire of a daughter, who becomes more creative and outgoing with each day that goes by.

When Tjalara isn't writing her next book or tackling laundry monsters and wrestling dishwashing shenanigans, she's bound to be somewhere flying on wishing chairs, frolicking with the mermaids, marking her skin with shadow hunter runes, raising dragons, or being a poison taster for the commander.

GET IN TOUCH:
    Website: www.tjalaradraper.com
    Facebook: Tjalara Draper Author
    Facebook Group: Tjalara Draper's Reader Lounge
    Instagram: @tjalaradraper_author
    Amazon: Tjalara Draper Author Page

Also by Tjalara Draper

Celestial Shifters Series:

Shards of Venus - Book 1

Flames of Mars - Book 2

Thorns of Neptune - Book 3 (**COMING SOON!**)

Celestial Shifters Spinoff Books

Nika

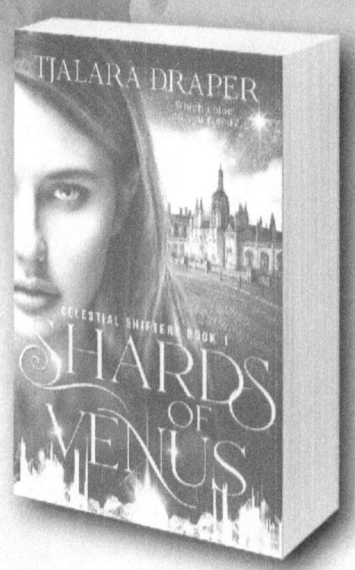
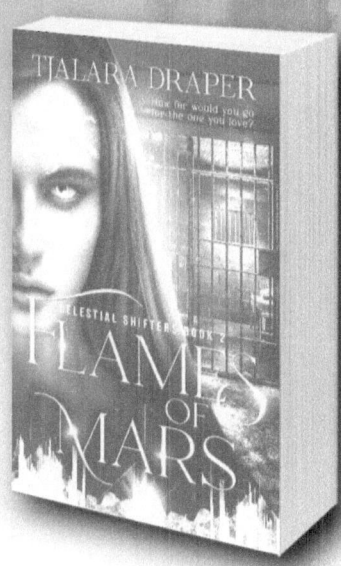

CAN'T WAIT TO READ CELESTIAL SHIFTERS?

TJALARA DRAPER

Which color do you bleed?

CELESTIAL SHIFTERS BOOK 1

SHARDS OF VENUS

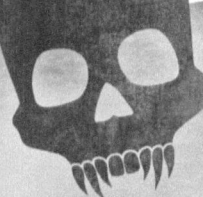

KEEP READING FOR THE FIRST FOUR CHAPTERS OF BOOK 1 -
Shards of Venus

Chapter One
Creating Cold Cases

Nathan Delano wandered through the dim cabin's living room, careful to watch his step. Police lights flashed garishly off countless crimson puddles and smears as he greeted each uniformed Erathi in turn.

Humans, he reminded himself, shaking his head. Even after all these years, the word *Erathi* still leaped to mind first.

Detective Judith Walker was inspecting a bedroom door's heavy bolt mechanism with a gloved hand. When she noticed him nearby, she waved him over.

"Hey, Jude," he said, sweeping his gaze once more over the room. "What's the situation?"

"Hey, Delano." She yanked off her glove with a *snap* and gestured to a black body bag being zipped up by a paramedic. "One deceased teenage girl."

"Do we know who?"

"Yeah. It's the missing Branstone girl." Jude handed him her phone. "Here, have a look. I took these when I arrived."

Nathan swiped through Jude's photos, immediately

recognizing the blonde victim, Lyla-Rose Branstone. In grisly contrast with the wide smile from the yearbook photo in her case file, her eyes were open and glazed. Four horrific grooves were carved into the side of her head, running from behind her ear to her chin. The ear itself had been sliced clean through in several places.

"Check this out." Jude reached across him to zoom into the area between the victim's neck and shoulder. "If I didn't know any better, I would have thought that was some weird bite mark."

Six bloodied puncture wounds formed an incomplete arc with a gap at the peak, which fell just below Lyla's left collarbone. The inner two marks were the smallest, while the middle ones were about the width of a ballpoint pen.

Nathan's chest tightened. *No. Not here. Not in Brookhaven.* Only one species made that distinct bite mark: his own race, the Veniri.

And he'd spent the last fifteen years hiding from them.

"Any weapons found?" Nathan asked, hoping Jude wouldn't notice the deflection.

She shook her head. "Nothing. At least, not yet. An abandoned vehicle was located down the road. I've sent an officer to go over it. I've yet to check out the surroundings myself."

Nathan nodded and handed back her phone. "What about witnesses?"

"The owner of this cabin lives farther down the hill. He and his wife were about to go to bed when they heard screaming coming from this direction. He came to investigate and dialed nine-one-one straight away when he found the victim."

A muscle twitched in Nathan's jaw. "Did he see anything else? Maybe catch a glimpse of who did this?"

She shook her head. "Whoever else was here cleared out by the time he—" A melodic tune from Jude's phone cut her off. "It's one of my kids," she said, glancing at the screen. She gave Nathan an apologetic look.

He gestured for her to answer. "I've got this."

"Thanks, Nathan." She patted his shoulder before quickly accepting the call and making a beeline for the exit. "Hi, sweetie . . . ?"

As the two paramedics with the body bag followed her out, Nathan turned back to the room. Time to set to work.

The quaint shack was likely several generations old, possibly built by one of the owner's ancestors. Knitted and patchwork throw rugs added a cozy touch, or at least, they would have if they hadn't been lying crumpled among splintered furniture. A decorative gun rack was mounted on one of the exposed timber walls, along with a collection of animal heads on plaques: deer, foxes, a bear, a zebra, and a tiger. Nathan had never understood the human desire for trophies, the need to display bits and pieces of their targets with pride.

With deliberate precision, he picked his way through the chaos, taking in the details of each gouge, splatter, and smear of blood and periodically snapping a few photos of his own. His boots thunked with each step on the timber floorboards. When he reached the open back door, a gust of icy wind bit into his face and neck, and he raised his collar and tightened his jacket. Peering into the darkness, he sucked in a deep breath of the cold night air.

A familiar tingle crept under his tongue.

He glanced back, ensuring none of the remaining officers were paying attention. The tingle grew into a fierce prickle as he allowed the simple transformation to take its course.

Within seconds, a forked tongue shot out from between his lips like a whip, then flicked back into his mouth. He assessed the night's aromas and flavors, a lingering bouquet of potent scents from the evening's activities.

The Veniri ability to scent someone's essence, or their soul-scent, was something Nathan heavily relied on for his Erathi work as a detective. Deducing the inner workings of a crime scene was so much easier when he could scent the residual intentions and emotions of the moment. But with all the extra cops, paramedics, and civilians traipsing through this area over the last hour, this time he would need more than his tongue to isolate the information he needed.

He scanned the stars. They were almost startlingly luminous, but none were brighter than Venus, sparkling straight ahead through the silhouetted tree branches. Nathan closed his eyes and took a deep breath, basking in the Venusian beams.

Beneath his closed lids, thin membranes glided over both his eyes. When he blinked them open again, the scenery before him was still drenched in darkness—until he flicked out his forked tongue. This time, the soul-trails illuminated like phosphorescent tendrils of smoke, gleaming wisps against the black of night. Each one glowed a different hue of the rainbow, leading into the forest beyond.

The leaf litter crackled and crunched beneath his feet as he stepped out of the shack. The trails started to fade but pulsed back to life with another flick of his tongue. With each taste of the air, he processed the flavors infused in each soul-trail, gathering valuable data.

After a few moments of walking, his boot kicked against something. He slid back the inner membranes of his eyes and pulled out his flashlight. The incandescent beam revealed a man in a hoodie and jeans, lying in a heap. Next to him, about a foot away, another person lay sprawled on the ground—a teenage girl. Patches of deep red speckled her clothing.

When his flashlight beam caught her face, he swore under his breath. Another kid from one of his case files. *Violet Chambers, 16 years of age. Legal guardians: Norman and Connie Hopkins. Address: 42 Daisy Crescent. Missing. Last seen approx 11:15 p.m. on Thursday, July 18.*

Her dark brown hair was matted with blood, dirt, and leaves. Compared to the photo, her features were hollow. Muddied cuts and bruises covered most of her face, and her right eye was almost indiscernible from the surrounding swelling.

Nathan hung his head, covering his face with his hand and wearily rubbing his temples. After a few breaths, he reached down to her neck to look for a pulse.

A faint beat tapped against his fingers.

* * *

Nathan hurriedly retraced his steps back to the shack, careful to avoid jostling the young girl in his arms. Violet gave a low groan.

"Hold tight," he said. "We're nearly there."

He barged through the back door and straight out the front. "I need a paramedic!"

Jude's attention snapped to him. She let out a gasp, eyes wide, then barked out some orders. Within seconds, two paramedics wheeled over a stretcher. Nathan laid down his bundle and stepped back, giving the paramedics space to perform their flurry of choreographed procedures.

Chapter One

The next few moments were a blur as he recounted to Jude what he'd found, leaving out his discovery of the second body. He'd hastily cleared it out of view, but he would have to clean that mess up soon—before anyone found it and started asking questions. Especially Jude.

His jaw tensed as he studied her. Her chin was resting on one hand in her signature thoughtful pose. He could almost see her mental processes breaking down and analyzing the new pieces of evidence he'd provided. Her intelligence and intuition always impressed him; it was what made her such a great cop. It was also what made him work overtime to keep her in the dark. She could never know who was responsible for this hellish mayhem. Her life would be in danger, not to mention his own.

He scoffed. Who was he kidding? His life had been in danger for years now.

His derisive snort broke Jude's trance. She shook her head and focused back on him. "Sorry for zoning out. Just thinking."

He gave her a knowing smile but didn't reply.

"Here." She reached into the car Nathan was leaning on and pulled out a red vacuum flask. "Have some coffee. It might still be hot."

He took a sip, cringed, and forced himself to gulp down the bitter, lukewarm liquid. "Ugh, maybe a little sugar next time." He wiped his mouth with his sleeve.

"No time for sugar," said Jude, drawing a long mouthful from the flask.

Over her shoulder, Nathan noticed one of the paramedics waving to him. "Coffee break's over. We're being summoned."

They headed over to the ambulance, and Nathan

nodded a greeting to the paramedic by the stretcher. "How's the vic?"

"She's awake and stable for now. We've given her a dose of morphine to help with the pain until we can get her to the hospital."

Nathan nodded. "Mind if I ask her a few questions?"

The paramedic shrugged. "You can try. You might be able to get something out of her, but maybe not much tonight."

Nathan stepped closer to the girl. "How ya doing, kid? You warm enough?"

She looked up at him with wide, glassy eyes.

"Your name's Violet, isn't it?"

After some hesitation and a quick glance at Jude, she nodded.

"Violet, can you tell me what happened?"

No answer.

"Can you tell us who did this to you?" Jude asked.

Nathan's stomach churned at her question. Violet's expression grew distant. Finally, she shook her head and looked away.

Nathan relaxed. "It's okay, Violet. You're safe."

One of her hands clenched the top of her silver foil blanket. Dry blood was caked under her fingernails, and half the nail of her index finger had been completely torn off. Her knuckles were shredded and bloodied. Whatever had happened to this kid, she'd certainly fought hard to defend herself.

Nathan's mind raced, imagining the horrors she must have faced as she screamed and begged her attacker to stop. A fiery rage boiled in the pit of his stomach. His elbows started to burn as the screams in his mind grew louder and louder. A slicing sensation replaced the burning in his elbows, and he felt the sleeves of his jacket beginning to tear. He needed to regain control of himself, *fast*.

But the female face screaming in his mind was no longer Violet's. It morphed into—

Stop it! Nathan slammed his eyes shut and turned his face away from Violet. He took a few deep breaths, forcing himself to relax until the blades in his elbows melted back into his flesh.

He turned back to the girl. "Violet—"

"He had a tattoo," she said in a raspy voice.

Shock gripped him. Her gray-blue eyes captured his with sudden, sharp intensity.

"A tattoo? What kind of tattoo?" Jude asked, taking out her phone.

Violet's next words were slow and deliberate. "He had a tattoo of a crystal scorpion, right here." She pointed to the side of her neck.

Nathan furrowed his brow and scratched his head.

"Are you sure?" Jude asked, tapping more notes into her phone.

Violet nodded.

"Was he a friend of yours?" asked Jude.

"I . . ." She screwed her face up, clamping her eyes closed. After a few heartbeats, she let out a quiet sob. "I . . . don't . . . I can't remember."

"That's okay," Jude said gently.

Violet turned toward Nathan, a tear rolling down her swollen cheek. "I don't know who he is," she whispered.

"It's okay, Violet." He gave her a soft pat on the shoulder.

Silver foil crinkled as she gripped the thermal blanket with both hands, her whole body shaking with silent sobs. Tears carved clean trails through the blood and grime on her face.

"That's enough for now," said the paramedic. "We've kept her here too long already. We should get her to the hospital."

Nathan and Jude stepped to the side as Violet was wheeled into the back of the ambulance. The lights flashed on, and the engine roared to life.

Jude let out a heavy sigh. "I suppose we should go process the area where you found—" Once again, her ringtone cut her off. She checked her watch and clicked her tongue. "It's my kid again. She's been really sick, and with the long hours I've been doing lately . . ."

"It's okay, Jude. If you need to head home, just go."

Jude pursed her lips. "I really shouldn't."

"Yeah, go on. Your kids need you." He patted her on the shoulder. "You've been here longer than me anyway. I'll deal with this mess."

She hesitated. "You sure you don't mind?"

"Not at all." He steered her toward her car. "Get home and kiss those kids goodnight."

Jude gave him a weary smile and stood up a little straighter, as if a heavy burden had been lifted off her shoulders. "Thanks, Nathan. I can always count on you."

Two hours later, Nathan stood at the side of his car, watching the last police vehicle pull away from the scene. As soon as its taillights drowned in the night, he ducked under the police tape and walked back toward the cabin.

Time to shut this investigation down.

As much as he hated tampering with the evidence, cases involving shifters were better left to go cold. What Jude didn't know couldn't keep her and her kids awake at night.

He needed to get rid of the second body, but first, there

Chapter One

was something else he needed to do. Violet had remembered a tattoo, and if she saw it again, all hell would break loose.

The wind whipped around him as he squinted into the inky blackness of the cabin. Nothing. Blinking, he raised his face to the heavens and, like before, sought out Venus. The radiant evening star sang to him in a faint melody only he could hear, and his body responded, his inner eyelids once again hazing into existence.

He flicked out his tongue, and the darkness flooded with colored phosphorescent mists, each hue of the glowing rainbow alive with its own collection of flavors. The ethereal light began to fade but, with another flick, pulsed back to vivid clarity.

Like a bloodhound, he followed the trails, veering left or right according to the prompting of his forked tongue. But unlike a bloodhound, instead of odors, he followed emotions and intentions, desires and interests, the distinct medley that makes up a being's very soul.

He gradually filtered out the familiar scents of Jude and the other officers and paramedics, reducing the rainbow to fewer colors. Soon he'd isolated Violet's and the deceased girl's scents as well and also filtered them out. Only a handful of trails remained.

He called on his internal Venusian energy and, like blowing out a foggy breath in winter, expelled some of it into the remaining trails, brightening and sharpening them against the dark. Clouds of the subtle light had gathered in various areas. These were echoes of moments past—snapshots of the subject's strongest emotion. With another gust of Venusian energy, he channeled his attention on these places until misty faces came into focus within. He inspected each one until he found what he was looking for.

Chapter One

Nathan released a burdened sigh. Right there, in the vaporous echo of the man's neck, was a tattoo of a crystal scorpion.

Ignoring his rising emotions, Nathan continued to follow the trail back out into the night.

Chapter Two
Assaulted Taste Buds

Violet jerked awake; someone had taken hold of her arm. Strobing memories of her abduction flickered through her mind, and she yanked away.

"It's okay, Violet," said a female voice. "I'm just checking your vitals."

Violet's panic subsided when she recognized the nurse by her bed. She relaxed back into the pillows and rubbed her eyes.

"I'm going to check your blood pressure, okay?"

Before Violet could reply, the nurse slipped on the blood pressure cuff and switched on the electric pump. The squeeze on Violet's arm had just passed uncomfortable when the nurse released the pressure and noted down the reading. Then she briskly moved on to checking Violet's temperature and heart rate.

Violet silently berated herself. She should be used to this routine by now, considering a nurse checked her vitals roughly every six hours. She'd been well looked after by the nurses and doctors at Brookhaven Hospital, but that didn't do a thing to change how much she hated being there. As far as she was concerned, all hospitals were odious, with their stark white walls, the promotional "Ask your doctor" medical posters, and the nose-pinching aromas of infected bodily fluids mixed with the sharp tang of antiseptic.

But even the smells and ambience were infinitely more bearable than the lifelong ache of what hospitals meant to her—the stinging reminder that her mother had abandoned her in one of these cold, lonely buildings shortly after she was delivered. Violet had long ago given up on the idea that her mother would one day return to claim her, but that didn't stop her grief from resurfacing every time she was forced to step into one of these godforsaken places.

"Hmm," said the nurse, jotting down some notes on the clipboard at the end of Violet's bed. "Your injuries are healing beautifully, but you're still showing a low-grade fever. I'll make sure you get another dose of Tylenol."

Violet nodded, blinking away the sting of tears, and swallowed the growing lump in her throat.

Despite the heavy weight of emotions, staying at the hospital was still preferable to the alternative. A slight shudder raced through Violet's body at the thought of being sent back to her foster parents.

The nurse frowned. "Are you cold?"

Violet responded with a small nod. It was better than giving the real explanation. How could she stand to face her "home" now that Lyla-Rose was gone? Lyla had been her lifeline, the spark in the darkness, the breeze under her broken wings. Lyla had kept Violet going, her only friend in the world. And now she, too, was gone.

"I'll get you a warm blanket." The nurse gave her a reassuring smile and left the room.

Violet stared up at the bland pattern of ceiling tiles, trying to breathe through the growing tightness in her chest.

Chapter Two

Dead. Lyla's dead.

This time, she didn't even try to blink the tears away. They cascaded down her cheeks, and she turned her face into her pillow. The aches and pains that hadn't fully healed roared back to life as her body shook with sobs.

The last few days had been a blur, clouded by pain and tangled up in a constant string of nurses, doctors, social workers, and police officers. The police had questioned her for every detail. *What happened? Who?* But no matter how hard Violet tried, she still couldn't remember anything— except for one blazing image. A neck tattoo of a crystal scorpion.

Violet squeezed her eyes shut and dug her fingertips into her skull. *Come on. Think! Try to remember.* It didn't change a thing. Her memories remained locked away. For the space of a few heartbeats, fear shoved aside her frustration. What was wrong with her? Why couldn't she remember?

Faint chatter cut through Violet's thoughts. As it grew louder, Violet recognized the baritone voice of her doctor and the lighter voice of her social worker, Miranda. Judging by the tone of their conversation, they were discussing something serious.

Violet quickly nestled into her pillows and feigned sleep as the two paused outside her door.

"We can't keep her here forever, Miranda."

"I know, I know... I was hoping to have another home ready for her by now, but at her age it's becoming next to impossible."

A slight panic began to churn in Violet's chest.

"I understand, but she's been here for almost two weeks, and that's only because we aren't overrun with patients at the moment. She's more than ready to be discharged. I'm not running a halfway house here."

"You're right. I get it. And I can't thank you enough for keeping her in longer than necessary. I just can't stand the idea of taking her back to those god-awful people."

"I wish there was more I could do to help. Really, I do. But for now, all I can give you is the rest of the afternoon. You need to take her today."

"Thanks, I really appreciate it. That should be enough time for me to make some more calls."

"Great. For now, we'll leave her to sleep. I'll make sure one of the nurses gives you the discharge forms."

Footsteps tapped away on the hospital linoleum.

Violet's eyes flew open.

Today. Miranda was taking her home *today*. Her eyebrows pinched together as she analyzed her options. Sure, she didn't have anywhere else to go, but she was sixteen. She wasn't a child anymore. She could fend for herself—hitchhike to the city, find a job, lie low until child services forgot about her. The plan wasn't foolproof, but there was no way she was going back to a foster home. Of that, she was sure. She was done.

She threw her blanket off and winced. Another thing she was sure of was that she needed some painkillers for the road.

A few moments later, Violet was dressed, and her small denim bag, packed with the few belongings Miranda had retrieved for her, was slung over her shoulder. She poked her head into the hallway and checked both ways before leaving the room.

Over the years, she'd become a pro at sneaking around. She stayed clear of the nurses' station and ducked out of the hallway whenever someone passed by who might recognize her. With a bit of luck, she made it to the hospital pharmacy without any problems.

The patient roller window was shut, as was the access door around the side. The pharmacist was either doing ward rounds or out to lunch. With a casual glance around to make sure no one was watching, Violet dug into her bag and pulled out some hairpins. Wedging one in her teeth, she bent the metal out of shape, then stuck her makeshift lock-picks into the pharmacy door handle with a finesse gained from hours of practice.

Click.

Perfect. She eased the door open.

"You know," said a deep voice behind her, "it's one thing to run away from the hospital, but stealing meds is a shortcut to juvie."

Violet froze. She barely had the door open an inch. In her periphery, a guy leaned against the wall next to the pharmacy door—one of the cops who had frequently visited and questioned her about Lyla's murder. He wasn't looking at her. Instead, he casually inspected his nails.

She glanced toward the hospital exit at the opposite end of the hallway.

"I wouldn't if I were you," he warned. "I'll have you crash tackled and handcuffed before the sliding door sensor even registers your existence."

Violet frowned. With her ribs, thigh, and ankle still not one-hundred-percent healed, he was probably right.

"But what I *would* do," he continued, "is contemplate very carefully which decisions to make next." He looked at her from the corner of his eye. "If you make some wise decisions, then it's likely I'll forget to say anything to my partner and the hospital's superintendent. Not to mention Miranda.

She'd be crushed if she knew what you were up to. She's been singing your praises the whole time."

Violet hesitated, but the steel in his tawny eyes warned her to act soon, or he would. With a juvenile huff, she removed her hairpins from the lock and let go of the door, which slowly closed with a pneumatic wheeze. All her adrenaline had dried up, leaving only shame. The cop was likely to snitch anyway, and Miranda was going to kill her.

"This way, kid," said the cop. He headed down the hallway, in the opposite direction of the hospital exit. Violet shot a mournful look at the door to freedom. She could still make a run for it; the cop hadn't even bothered to check if she was following him.

She winced. *Who am I kidding?*

With a defeated sigh, Violet trailed after the cop, but after a few paces, she frowned. He wasn't leading her back to her room. Instead, he pushed through a glass door and held it open for her.

"This isn't my room."

"I know" was all he said as he gestured for her to enter.

The world she stepped into was a complete contrast to the sterile hospital: the facility's botanical gardens. Trees towered high above. Instead of stark white walls, every hue of green imaginable tumbled and climbed in all directions, broken up only by a vast spectrum of bright flowers. Water trickled musically down a rocky feature wall by the door, and a gentle breeze, heavy with the scents of rich earth and flowers, chased away the smell of antiseptic.

Other patients were wandering along the weaving path or sitting on the benches provided. A nurse pushed an elderly lady in a wheelchair, but she stopped to allow her patient to stroke a low-hanging flower with her wrinkled hand.

Chapter Two

"What are we doing here?" Violet asked.

"Remembering for a few minutes that life isn't always crap."

He walked up the path a few paces and settled on a bench overlooking the pond, which was fed by an artificial waterfall.

Violet frowned. What was this guy's deal? He'd just busted her for trying to steal drugs, and instead of gloating, he wanted to zen out in nature?

After a few moments, Violet sauntered over and plonked down on the opposite end of the bench. She peeked at him from the corner of her eye. He had his eyes closed, and his face was tilted up, catching patches of sunlight that speckled through the leaves. She figured he was maybe early forties, judging by some silver streaks in his dark hair and the salt-and-pepper stubble along his square jaw. The creases around his forehead, eyes, and mouth gave him resting I'm-about-to-kick-your-ass face, and his towering height and muscular build only added to his edge of intimidation.

Still, Violet didn't feel scared around him the way she had with previous cops—the ones who liked to use their badge and brawn to bully culprits into so-called justice. Something about him felt soothing.

"So, kid, you wanna tell me why you were trying to run away?"

Violet picked at the ends of her sweater sleeves, glaring at the orange koi fish gliding leisurely through the water. "I wasn't trying to run away."

"Oh, really? Then what would you call it?"

She folded her legs up onto the seat and hugged her knees. "I was..."

A few silent moments passed. She couldn't bring herself

to finish the sentence. There was no point. The cop was probably mentally rehearsing his lecture, including threats to use his taser to make her go back to her awful foster parents. Because it was the right thing to do. Because she wasn't old enough to take care of herself. Blah, blah, blah...

Instead he unzipped his jacket halfway, reached in, and pulled out a white paper bag. He opened it and held it out to her, revealing some kind of candy in the shape of black discs. She took one. He took one too and popped it in his mouth before putting the bag back in his jacket.

Violet inspected both sides of the disc. One side was smooth, while the other had an embossed impression of some kind of European coin. With a small shrug, Violet put the disc in her mouth. Immediately, her tongue wanted to commit suicide. Her whole face screwed up as the intense flavor of salt and licorice coated her mouth.

"What the—?" she exclaimed right before involuntarily spitting the rubbery gunk into the garden behind her. Warbled sounds of disgust followed as she tried to hack out the lingering flavor. When that didn't work, she rubbed her tongue with her sleeve.

"What a waste," said the cop. His expression held a hint of amusement.

"What *is* that stuff?"

"In this part of the world, it's called Dutch licorice."

Violet's whole face twisted in revulsion. "Ick! Remind me never to put one of those in my mouth again."

His amusement spilled into a smile. "Aw, c'mon. It's not that bad."

"Are you kidding? I'd rather lick the road! *Ew!*"

He chuckled at that, a bass resonance from deep in his chest.

"Violet, there you are!"

Violet turned to see Miranda barging through the door a few feet away. Her face was calm, but her eyes were blazing. *Uh-oh, she's pissed.*

"What is the meaning of this?" demanded Miranda. "Please tell me you weren't trying to run away *again*? Do you seriously think living on the streets is a better option for you? It's bad enough that one girl has died already, and now you—"

"It's okay," a new voice cut in. Another cop Violet recognized, a middle-aged woman, came up behind Miranda and touched her shoulder. "We found her."

Violet curled into a ball and hugged her legs again. Her eyes stung with fresh tears.

"Come on, Miranda," said the lady cop, steering her away from Violet. "How about we have a chat? Nathan, do you mind?"

"I'll be back, kid." He patted her on the shoulder and went to join the ladies.

They huddled a few feet away, close enough that they could keep an eye on Violet—and close enough that she could still hear their conversation despite their hushed tones.

"I'm sorry, Jude," said Miranda.

"There's no need to apologize to me."

"I know. I'm just... I don't know what to do. I understand why she's running away. I get it. I would be doing the same thing in her situation. I've been making calls for days to try and get her into a new home, but even all my emergency housing is over capacity. I just..." She dropped her head into her hands and gave a restrained groan of frustration.

"I hear you, Miranda," said Jude. "I don't like the idea of her going back to those people either. Hell, if I wasn't already raising two kids of my own, I'd offer her a bed in a heartbeat."

"Thanks, I appreciate it. And you too, Nathan. Thanks for making sure she didn't take off. I don't know what I would've done if she'd disappeared again."

"Can she stay here for another night?" Nathan asked.

Miranda shook her head. "I've already tried that. Violet has stayed past her welcome. I have to take her today, and the best I can do for the moment is a group home back in the city—at least, until I can find a home willing to take on a sixteen-year-old. If only she were ten years younger."

Violet dropped her head against her knees.

"Well, I do happen to have a guest bedroom that isn't being used," said Nathan.

"Oh my gosh! Would you?" exclaimed Miranda.

"Look, I don't know whether it's appropriate or not for a cop to take her in, but—"

"Don't worry," cut in Miranda. "Leave it to me. It would only be temporary. I promise."

"Nathan, are you sure?" said Jude. "It's not like taking in a puppy, you know."

"Yeah, I know. But the kid's had a rough ride. I can at least give her a bed for a few days. Besides, you can give me some pointers, can't you, Jude?"

Jude scoffed. "I've yet to experience the teenage mood swings. It might be a case of the blind leading the blind."

"So what else is new?"

"Great, it's settled." Miranda rattled off a list of forms she needed to prepare before bringing Violet around to Nathan's place.

"Hey, Violet," said Jude.

Violet raised her head to see Jude looking down at her,

Nathan at her side. Miranda was already making a phone call behind them.

"Some temporary arrangements are being made for you to stay in Nathan's spare room until better accommodations can be found." Jude inclined her head to Nathan. "Do you think you can handle putting up with this guy for a few days?"

Violet gnawed on the inside of her cheek. The idea of staying with a cop was a foreign concept. But what other option did she have? As far as cops went, he wasn't too bad. He certainly hadn't needed to give her a chance after busting her for breaking into the pharmacy, and he hadn't snitched on her. Yet. In fact, so far the worst thing he'd done was assault her taste buds with that tar-flavored disc.

"Yeah," she said, giving them a slow nod, "I think I can handle it."

Chapter Three
Stupid Rose

THREE YEARS LATER

Nathan sighed with relief when he spotted a vacant parking spot near the college entrance. "Must be my lucky day," he said in a low voice.

The jeep rolled to a stop, and Violet's sleeping form jolted in the passenger seat. Her arms flailed, smacking against the dashboard, and she cried out, eyes still clenched shut.

Nathan leaned over and took hold of one of her arms. "Wake up! It's just a dream."

She released a strangled growl, fighting his grip.

"Violet!"

Her eyes flew open and harried pants replaced the screams. She looked around, brow furrowed in confusion. When she spotted Nathan, she slumped back in her chair and groaned. "Sorry, I must have fallen asleep. Was I screaming again?"

Nathan nodded, his lips in a tight smile. "Same dream?"

Violet rubbed at her eyes with the heels of her hands. "Yeah, the faceless man with the neck tattoo."

The familiar wave of guilt surged through Nathan's chest. *That damn neck tattoo.* Violet's trauma had latched so fiercely on to that image that it was impossible to erase. He sucked in a breath and held back his sigh. "No need to worry, Vi. It was just a dream."

"Yeah, I know." Her tone was edged with a chronic frustration. She turned her attention to the buildings outside. "Wow. We're here."

They hopped out of the car and gathered up Violet's things from the back.

A guy with greasy blue hair and a black metal-spiked vinyl jacket bumped into Nathan, causing him to drop the cardboard box he carried. The kid didn't stop or even apologize. Nathan growled a string of choice words as he bent to gather the box's scattered contents. He stopped mid-curse when Violet came to stand next to him.

"Damn, kids these days," he gruffed, rummaging through the hastily repacked items with one hand. "If he's broken your camera, I swear I'll—"

"Don't stress. I have it here." Violet held up the camera, which was suspended from a strap around her neck.

Nathan secured his grip on the box, still scowling. "If anything's broken, you can blame the blue-haired punk over there." He jutted his chin toward a cluster of college kids with freakish colored hair. Along with the shiny black vinyl, several wore studded dog collars, and he winced when he spotted one guy sporting black lipstick.

Violet looked over, adjusting her hold on her pillow and suitcase. "I'd say they're goths, not punks."

Nathan snorted. "What's the difference?"

Violet bit her lip. He knew it was her way of holding back a smirk. "Well, if you put on some spectacles, old man, you'll notice the lack of safety pins and mohawks."

Chapter Three

"Mohawks or not, they're lucky I'm not going over there," Nathan deadpanned.

This time Violet did smirk. "Why? Afraid they'll figure out you smell like mothballs?"

"For the record, it's not mothballs. It's Old Spice."

She threw her head back and laughed. "Seriously? You're wearing something that literally has the word *old* in its name."

Nathan smiled. She had such a great laugh—a recent development for the girl who continued to bloom and shed the husks of her old life. The image of her from the night he'd first found her would always be seared into his brain, but the girl standing before him was a complete contrast. Her gray-blue eyes—stark against the frame of her dark brown, shoulder-length hair—held more sparkle and amusement. When she smiled, her defined, angular cheekbones became plump and rounded—proof of how a healthy diet and exercise had filled out her previously gaunt frame.

She'd had her nineteenth birthday a few weeks ago, and as per her request, it was a low-key barbecue with just Jude and the kids. As much as Nathan held concerns about her moving out into the world, he knew she was more than ready. He'd done the best he could to prepare her to look after herself. Her instincts were killer—as long as she didn't panic first.

He nudged her with his elbow. "Yeah, yeah. Come on, this stuff's getting heavy."

They took several steps, then Nathan stopped short. "Almost forgot." He balanced the box with one hand and fished a set of car keys out of his jacket pocket. "The last thing I want is some greaser stealing my new ride." He pressed the lock button on the remote.

Violet smirked again.

"What?" He put on a defensive tone. "I've only had it a week."

She laughed and shook her head. "Come on. Your jeep will be fine."

A wide stone staircase led from the parking lot to the college entrance, which consisted of two red brick pillars with white cornerstones, standing a couple stories high. At the top rested a decorative black arch bordered with gold. The college emblem, an open book backed by a shield, was situated at the top, and beneath it was MONARCH GROVE COLLEGE spelled out in silver. The tall black gates hinged open, inviting newcomers into the college grounds.

Violet paused at the entrance, her forehead creased. Her expression reminded Nathan of the first day she'd arrived at his place three years ago, not long after she was discharged from the hospital. Back then her skittishness was clear even during the tour of her new room.

He leaned in and gave her a gentle nudge. "You know that blank canvas life you keep talking about? It's through those gates."

She sighed. "I know." She still didn't move.

"It's not here on the steps, Vi."

He didn't receive the sarcastic reply he expected. Instead, her eyes became more agonized. "I don't know if I can do this, Nathan."

Nathan blinked a few times and scratched the top of his head. "Um . . . well . . ." It was times like these he wished he was more of a "pep talk" kind of guy. "Look, the way I see it, you can give up now and spend the rest of your life wondering 'what if,' or you can walk through those gates with your head held high, knowing you damn well deserve to be here. You'll make friends, you'll go to parties, you'll study hard, then you'll leave with your hard-earned diploma. Either way, it's up to you."

She nodded a few times, chewing on her lower lip. "But I've never done anything big like this before."

Nathan shrugged. "Yeah, well, you'll never know whether you're capable if you don't try."

She snorted, and to his relief, the corners of her mouth twitched up into a smile.

"So, Violet. What's it going to be?"

"Okay." She nodded. "I'll give it a go."

"Great! I'd hate to think we drove two hours for nothing."

She laughed and gave him a playful punch before stepping through the gates.

Sunlight glittered through the leafy canopy arching over the path, and the manicured greenery beneath thrived with hundreds of bold flowers. Benches were scattered around the gardens, most of them already occupied. The campus buildings, which generally followed the red brick and white cornerstone design, could be seen beyond the trees. Dormitories were easy to spot by the bay windows that waved in and out of the buildings' facades, contrasting with the linear lecture halls and community establishments.

Violet's room was on the second floor of one of the dormitories. They navigated through the countless students, parents, and college welcomers, making sure not to trip on any of the boxes and bedding that hadn't made it into rooms yet.

Finally, they stood outside room number 2052 of the west wing. The door was ajar, and Violet hesitated.

Nathan laid a hand on her shoulder. "Blank canvas, remember?"

When she turned to him, he was relieved to see her

expression wasn't fearful. Instead, her eyes held a glint of excitement. With a smile and a nod, she shoved the door open.

"Ouch!" yelped a male voice from inside.

"What the—?" Violet stumbled back into Nathan, and the box he carried toppled and spilled for the second time that day.

The door slowly swung back open, revealing a guy clutching his face. A few agonized groans escaped from between his fingers.

"What happened?" asked a female voice from farther in the room.

The guy just moaned.

A petite girl with chestnut dreadlocks that hung down to about mid-waist came into view. She wore an oversized heavy-metal band shirt with blue denim shorts edged with white lace. Her skin was golden, either sun-kissed or spray-tanned; she looked as if she'd just stepped off a beach.

"Show me." She yanked the guy's hands away from his face.

"Ouch! Careful, Autumn."

"Quit being a baby and show me." After a moment of inspection, she released him and whacked him on the shoulder. "There's no blood. You're fine."

His reply was a groan of derision. Then he pointed to Violet. "I think your roommate is here."

Dreadlocks fanned out as the girl spun around.

Violet's eyes bugged. Her hands covered her mouth and her cheeks turned red. "I'm so sorry. I had no idea that—oh my gosh. Are you okay?"

The girl smiled. "Don't worry, he's fine." She put her hands on her hips. Her slender nose crinkled as she looked

Violet up and down with dark brown eyes. "So... you're my new roomie."

Even though the girl was a few inches shorter than Violet's five feet and eight inches, she radiated an intensity that made Violet shrink back against Nathan.

"Yep," said the girl after a few heartbeats. "I think you'll do."

The guy behind her groaned and rolled his eyes. "Don't mind Autumn. You'll eventually get used to her overbearing ways." He stepped in front of her and held out a hand. "Hi, I'm August."

He was taller than Violet, but he still had a few inches to go before he would reach Nathan's eye level. His dark brown hair was styled in a messy quiff. Faded, ripped jeans were matched with a low-cut white V-neck and about a half-dozen necklaces made from black thread, gemstone beads, copper, and silver.

After a slight hesitation, Violet shook his hand, which sported a faded turquoise wrist cuff adorned with a few bracelets that matched the guy's necklaces. "Hi, I'm Violet."

"Awesome." He grinned.

"I'm sorry again for hitting you with the door."

August waved his free hand; the other hand still held Violet's. "Don't mention it. No permanent damage done. It'll take a lot more effort to ruin this pretty face."

The handshake continued for what Nathan figured to be the longest handshake in history. Finally, he cleared his throat, and the boy dropped both his grin and Violet's hand.

Violet inclined her head. "This is Nathan."

"Cool." August nodded in a manner that reminded Nathan of a bobblehead doll. He held out his hand. "Nice to meet you."

"You too," Nathan replied, making sure his tone held a

note of warning. He restrained the temptation to crush the boy's hand but still went for a firmer than normal grip. The boy hid his wince of pain pretty well, but his relief was obvious when Nathan released the handshake.

"So," Nathan said after a pause, "Autumn and August?"

"Yeah, you can blame our hippie mothers," said August. He put his hands in his pockets, rocked back on his heels, and donned a tight grin.

Autumn gestured between herself and August. "We're cousins, born a week apart. Our mothers are sisters and thought it would be so cute for their babies to have semi-matching names."

August forced a laugh and attempted an indifferent look. "It obviously didn't occur to them exactly how cute it would still be once we reached adulthood. And in case you were wondering, I was born in May, not August." He paused a moment. "And yes, to be honest, I am actually glad that my mother didn't call me May. But if you ask me—"

"You can just call him Gus," Autumn cut in.

"Right. Yes. Gus is fine." His head bounced in a nod again, and he crossed his arms. "So, Violet, what do you think of your new room?"

"She hasn't seen it yet," said Nathan.

Autumn snorted a laugh, and Gus's cheeks turned a little red.

They all picked up Violet's things from the spilled box, and the cousins ushered Violet into her new home. Two beds, two bedside tables, two desks, two desk chairs, and two wardrobes mirrored each other on either side of a bay window seat. To the right of the entryway, a door led into a small bathroom, and to the left was a kitchenette with a mini fridge and microwave.

Autumn had obviously already claimed the right side.

Clothes, shoes, power cables, power boards, and a number of other items were strewn all over that half of the furniture. Violet dropped her bedding on the free bed, and Nathan set his box on the desk.

Autumn planted herself on the bay window seat, her legs folded beneath her, and patted the space next to her. "Come on over and make yourself at home, roomie."

Violet flicked her gaze to Nathan. He mouthed, *Give it a go.* She gave him a slight smile and crossed the space between the two beds to sit next to Autumn.

"So, Violet, what brings you to Monarch Grove University?" Autumn asked.

"Uh, nothing special." Violet picked up a cushion and placed it on her lap. "I'm just doing photography."

Nathan folded his arms. He hated it when Violet downplayed her talents. Since the day she picked up his dusty old camera, he knew she had a keen eye for photography. He would never forget the smile on her face when he bought her a new camera, one with enough buttons and functions to rival a spaceship. His walls back home were lined with her framed handiwork.

"What about you?" Violet asked.

"I'm studying cybersecurity and program engineering," said Autumn, lying back and snuggling deeper into the cushions. She selected a dreadlock and twirled it in her fingers. The sun streamed in through the window and enhanced the girl's golden skin.

"Oh." Violet stroked one of the cushion's tassels. "What's that?"

"It's just a fancy way of saying 'hacking.'" Gus had slumped into Autumn's desk chair and was swiveling from side to side. "She just wants to learn what the regular people of internet land are doing these days to secure themselves against the likes of her." He jabbed an accusatory finger at his cousin.

She rolled her eyes. "Shut up, Gus. You know full well you wouldn't be here if it wasn't for my 'hacking,' so drop your high and mighty attitude and show a little gratitude."

He shook his head. "Nope. I still maintain I worked hard for those pitiful grades. You just ruined my bad boy rep. Seriously, not *everything* needs to be manipulated to get your way." He gestured to her laptop. "You treat that thing like it's a genie that grants wishes."

Autumn rolled her eyes. "Whatever. Just admit how glad you are to be rubbing shoulders with college girls right now instead of flipping burgers."

"Pfft. Don't pat yourself on the back yet. I haven't rubbed shoulders, or any other body parts for that matter, with any college girls."

Autumn sniggered.

"Wait, hold up," said Violet. "Are you serious? Did you really hack into your school's network to change his grades?"

"*Hack* is such a crude word," said Autumn. "I like to think I was doing the world a favor. Not only was I helping a cousin out, but I also discovered our biology teacher was using his school computer to stash his disgusting collection of taboo porn. Let's just say, after an anonymous tip to the cops from me, he's no longer teaching biology." Autumn shuddered in disgust. "Ugh!"

"Damn, girl," said Violet. "Where were you when I needed help with my grades?"

Nathan cleared his throat and gave her a pointed look.

"What? Totally joking," she said, stifling a smirk. "And what about you, Gus? What are you studying?"

"Nothing major. I've taken up a few random classes until I figure out what I want to do."

"Such a waste," Autumn scoffed. "I keep telling you that if you just applied yourself, you could be a doctor like your mom. I've already fixed your high school grades, so no one will know you were trying to make out you were a slacker."

"Just leave it, Autumn." The tone in his voice suggested this was an old argument.

"Come on," whined Autumn, "it's not too late for me to change your status to 'med student.' Seriously, you're wasting your time with Greek poetry and textile classes."

"You never know. The textile class might come in handy with helping Aunty Skye with her hemp-weaving business."

"Quit joking around," growled Autumn. "I'm not going to let you give up on medicine. I just don't know why you—"

"You *do* know why," Gus said through gritted teeth. "Now drop it." His cold glare could have turned water into ice.

Autumn's mouth clamped shut, but her own glare matched Gus's level of severity.

Nathan and Violet exchanged an awkward glance.

Gus groaned and rocked his head back to look at the ceiling. "Can we please discuss this later when we're not trying to make a good impression on our new friend here?"

"Fine," Autumn relented. "But this isn't finished."

Gus rolled his eyes. "Of course. Why would I ever think you'd let this go?"

Autumn *hmph*ed and crossed her arms.

Gus gave Violet and Nathan an apologetic smile. "Sorry for the drama."

"It's fine," said Violet.

Nathan just gave a tight-lipped smile and waved his hand indifferently.

"So..." Gus floundered through some small talk with Violet until the tension started to ease up. Autumn eventually dropped her attitude, and the three of them commenced a lengthy discussion about their anticipation for their college careers, the towns they moved from, and other trivial things like movies and fashion.

Nathan watched as Violet smiled and responded to whatever Autumn and Gus were saying. He hadn't seen her look this content and confident in a long while. In fact, come to think of it, the whole time he'd known Violet, he'd never seen her act like... well... like a teenage girl.

"Oh my gosh!" Autumn exclaimed. "I can't believe you don't know who The Wanderers are."

"Uh, sorry." Violet's lips compressed into a half wince, half smile.

Gus groaned. "Brace yourself. You're about to be baptized into one of Autumn's obsessions whether you like it or not."

"It's not my fault you haven't developed a taste for great music, cuz," retorted Autumn.

"It's not your *taste* in music I'm opposing, *cuz*. It's the time, place, and consistency. Violet, I suggest you invest in a decent pair of earmuffs if you want to get any sleep."

Autumn tossed a cushion, which smacked him square in the face.

Gus yelped. "Autumn! Door! Hurt! Remember!" He wiped at his nose with his shirt collar. "Sheesh! What's it take for a guy to get a bloody nose around here?"

Autumn leaned back into her cushions, her hands behind her head and a victory smile on her face.

Violet hid a laugh behind her hand.

Nathan shook his head. He didn't envy Violet putting up with these two. His phone buzzed, and he pulled it out of his pocket to read the message, then noticed the time.

"Damn! Dinosaur alert!" Gus pointed at Nathan's flip phone, a ghost of a smirk playing on his lips. "I had no idea people still carried those antiques around."

Nathan gave him a stare he reserved for the perps he interrogated. After a moment, Gus awkwardly folded his arms and dropped his gaze to the floor. *Ha, that was too easy.* He wished the people he grilled cracked as easily as this kid.

He closed his phone and put it back in his pocket. "Violet, sorry to interrupt, but I gotta go."

"No problem. I'll walk you out."

A few paces down the hallway, a young man holding a stack of flyers approached them, flashing a big toothy grin at Violet. "Hi, am I right to presume you're new here?"

Violet nodded. "Uh, yeah. Just arrived."

"Awesome!" The guy very enthusiastically held up his thumb. "Welcome to Monarch Grove College, or MGC, if you're into acronyms. I can guarantee you're gonna love it here. And in honor of your first day, we're having a party." He handed her a flyer.

"A party?" said Violet. "Already?"

"Of course! What better time than the present to show off our amazing school spirit?"

"Because all we have is the present right?" Violet gave him her own toothy grin.

"Right! A girl after my own heart."

Nathan inwardly cringed. Peppy guys like this grated on him, but he couldn't overlook his appreciation that this kid was giving Violet a warm welcome.

Violet scanned the flyer and pointed to the name of the venue. "Um, sorry, but where is this?"

"Oh, it's super easy to get to." The guy turned and pointed, explaining the directions. In doing so, he exposed a tattoo of a rose on his neck.

Nathan felt Violet stiffen beside him. Her breaths grew shallow and uneven. The flyer crinkled as her hands clenched into fists, her knuckles going white.

When the guy turned back, neither Nathan nor Violet responded, and his toothpaste-commercial grin faltered.

"Ah, like you said, super easy to get to," Nathan blurted. "Thanks for your help."

Violet nodded and smiled, although not as bright as before. Instead it was the tight smile Nathan knew so well— the one that held no joy behind it, only masking the turmoil rising inside her. He took hold of her shoulders and gently guided her away.

"Breathe, Violet," he said in a soothing voice only she could hear. "It was a rose. It's not him. Just breathe, okay?"

Her anxiety, triggered by something as unassuming as an unfortunately placed tattoo, was plain to anyone who cared to look closely enough. It was evident in the tightness of her shoulders, in the way her eyes darted around, in her uneven breathing, in the way she fidgeted with the flyer.

Nathan directed her outside, hoping some fresh air would help. They found an empty bench under one of the ancient trees in the garden.

"I'm sorry, Nathan. I know you have to get going," said Violet, taking a seat. "Don't worry about me. I'll be fine."

"It's all good, Vi." He sat next to her and patted her back. "I can spare ten minutes."

He remembered when Violet first started showing her post-traumatic stress symptoms, not long after she'd been found. The numerous episodes at school had ranged from catatonic to frantic screaming. Nathan promptly had her referred to a psychiatrist and the school counselor.

It took some trial and error, but as soon as she began working with someone specialized in trauma, Violet's mental health improved in leaps and bounds. Over time, she'd learned to recognize her triggers and developed methods to cope.

He was proud to see how well she was handling this one. Some triggers were worse than others, and even a year ago, the sight of a neck tattoo would have resulted in a full-blown panic that would have had Violet reaching for the switchblade tucked securely in her back pocket. Now she managed the situation like the trooper she was.

She took several more deep breaths, regulating her breathing and lowering her heart rate. Slowly, the tension in her shoulders released, and she sat back against the bench with a little less rigidity.

He knew she had this under control, but he added some words of encouragement just for good measure. "Violet, you're safe. No one is here to hurt you. You're not in any danger. And you're doing great at managing this anxiety."

That made her chuckle. She nodded and took a few more measured breaths as Nathan released a quiet, grateful sigh. The worst of it was already over.

It had been a few months since she'd had a full-blown panic attack—the last, Nathan hoped, she would have to experience. But he couldn't help worrying about how she would cope on her own, at a new and unfamiliar place, by herself.

He stopped reviewing his mental list of worries when Violet stood up.

"Okay, I'm all good now." She forced a grin, but it didn't quite reach her eyes. Even though her expression was calmer, the flyer still shook with the slight tremor in her hands from the residual adrenaline rush.

Nathan had half a mind to grab her wrist and take her back to the car. And if he was reading her expressions correctly, she was afraid he was going to do just that.

He forced his own smile. "So, you got everything you need?"

"I think so." Her voice shook a little, but she raised her chin and said in a bolder tone, "Yes. I have everything I need. I'll be fine."

He had to give her credit, she was determined to prove she wasn't going to let one little near attack break her on her first day of college. With a genuine smile, he gave her a nod of approval.

"Good. Oh, and before I forget"—he pulled out the keyset for the jeep and placed it in her hand—"these are now yours."

Her eyes bulged and her jaw dropped. "What? No way. That's your new car. I can't take your car." She attempted to give the keys back.

He shook his head and closed her hands around them. "You've already used all your savings on school fees. Think of this as a late birthday present."

She shook her head.

"Fine. If you can't take it for you, then at least take it for me. This old man wants to sleep at night knowing you have a safe way to get home from off-campus parties and shopping sprees in the city and whatever else you college kids get up to these days. I'll be honest, I don't fancy the idea of you catching trains or buses and especially walking home in the dark."

She gave him an *are-you-kidding-me* look. "Really? And what about from the parking lot to my dorm? It's still a good ten-minute walk, and there are lots of dark places attackers could be lurking, you know."

"I know, but that's what this is for." He pointed to the place where her switchblade was hidden. "Don't tell me you've already forgotten all your self-defense training from the past few years. In case you have, a swift kick to the balls should do the trick."

Violet put her hands on her hips. "And what if it's a girl who's attacking me?"

"I... um..." Nathan frowned and rubbed the back of his neck. "I don't know, kick her in the teeth and yank on her hair, or something."

She laughed. "Or something?"

He smiled. "Anyway, I'll let you get back to your new friends." He patted her on the shoulder. "And don't forget, you can call me whenever. Day or night, no matter the time."

She nodded.

"I mean it, Vi."

"I know." Her teasing smile dropped into seriousness. "Thanks, Nathan."

"Don't mention it."

"No, really. Thank you. For everything. I wouldn't have made it here without you."

He waved a hand. "Ah, someone had to drive you. It beats catching the train with all the stuff you had to carry."

She hit him on the arm. "You know what I mean."

He nodded, and before he could react, she hugged him. He hesitated for a second, then hugged her back. "You know, I think you're going to do great here." He didn't have to see her face to know she was smiling. "I'll catch you later, Vi." He turned and walked down the path.

Chapter Three

"Wait," she called after him. "How are you getting home without a car?"

Without stopping, he called over his shoulder, "I bought a train ticket. The station is only a few minutes' walk from here."

"But the train station back in town is still a twenty-minute drive to your house."

"Jude's picking me up."

"What? Are you telling me you finally—"

"Bye, Vi. Enjoy your first day."

Chapter Four
Angry Pixies

Violet sat alone on the bench for a few minutes once Nathan was out of sight. After her near attack, all she wanted was to curl up on her bed and go to sleep.

Living in Nathan's spare room for the past three years had been a godsend. It was only meant to be a temporary arrangement, but even after three months, her social worker hadn't been able to find her a suitable housing situation. A few discussions later, Nathan had offered to have her stay on a permanent basis, and without a lot of hesitation, Violet had agreed. After all, Nathan was about as chill as a guardian could be, and having her own space—a place to hide away whenever she felt the need, no questions asked—had given her a safe haven, somewhere she could heal and recharge after losing Lyla.

Living with someone else in the same space wouldn't be an easy adjustment. She wasn't one to trust people easily, if at all. Still, Autumn and Gus *were* the kind of people she would like to get to know. Given a little time, maybe she would even come to call them friends.

She fidgeted. Something in her jeans pocket was

digging into her. She pulled out her switchblade, another gift from Nathan. He had given it to her not long after he started training her in self-defense. At first he'd just taught her the basics—things like how to break free from headlocks and choke holds—but after a few weeks, he'd moved on to how to defend against someone with a weapon, starting with a knife. Not only had he trained her to defend against a blade; he'd also taught how to use one effectively.

When he'd presented her with the switchblade, claiming it had been in his family for several generations, of course she'd refused to take it. She'd never owned anything so valuable. But he had insisted.

She twirled it in her palm. There was no denying how beautiful it was. When she pressed the button, a double-edged blade glided out from the center of the handle with a *shnik*.

She held it up, the handle fitting snuggly within the contours of her hand. The sun reflected subtle changes of color along the pearlescent hilt, and a crest of some sort was ornately carved on the topside of the pearl finish. Along the back were ten embedded black gemstones.

On either end of the pearly white handle, both the bolster and guard were mostly teal, but when she rotated the knife from side to side, veins of emerald green and magenta glistened in the sunlight. They matched the blade itself, where the emerald and magenta glimmered through the teal in an organic whirled pattern right up to its deadly tip.

She pressed the button again. *Shnik*. The blade disappeared back into the handle.

Violet switched her attention to the keys in her other hand, shaking her head. Nathan's generosity was staggering. A part of her had wished over and over again that he'd shown up much earlier in her life, but another part knew he'd arrived at the perfect time.

She'd spent most of her life watching her world be destroyed piece by piece, and Lyla's death had been the final Armageddon. But Nathan had shown her how to rebuild, helped her claw her way out of her wretched abyss and learn how to fight her demons. He'd become her beacon, a reason to trust not only in him but also in herself. He was there when she'd needed someone the most.

She took in a deep breath and slowly exhaled. Now she was at college, by herself. He was no longer just down the hallway. The thought of doing this next chapter in her life without him almost brought on a new wave of panic.

She squeezed her eyes shut. *Stop it!* She couldn't do this anymore. She couldn't keep falling to pieces and waiting for Nathan to mend her. *Come on, Violet, get yourself under control. It's going to take a little adjustment, that's all.*

She needed to grow up, embrace her new reality, remember that this college life was what she wanted. She just needed to take it one day at a time.

For now, maybe caffeine would help. Earlier she'd seen a quaint little coffee shop near the parking lot outside the college grounds. The walk there and back might give her enough time to clear her head and prepare herself to face the dynamics of her new home life.

About twenty minutes later, she pushed through the glass doors of the café and placed an order for a chai latte with extra foam. She then leaned against the wall, out of the way of the other customers, and twirled a tassel on her scarf while she waited.

Glossy wallpaper and various artworks decorated the café's walls. A television mounted in one corner played a black-and-white Marilyn Monroe movie with the volume on low. People came and left with Styrofoam cups, steaming croissants, and other snacks-to-go. A barista called out an order, and a woman with blonde wavy locks and a tan jacket moved past Violet to collect her latte.

Violet's heart skipped a beat. *That woman... Was she... ?*

The woman turned and happened to catch Violet's eye for a second on her way out. Violet's shoulders sagged. What was wrong with her? Of course that woman wasn't Lyla.

A lump formed in her throat.

She'd lost count of how many times she'd wished she could remember what happened the night Lyla died. She only knew what Nathan and Jude had told her, but none of it explained *why*. Why were she and Lyla kidnapped? Why did Lyla have to die? Why was she still alive? Lyla was more deserving of life than she was. Lyla had a family: a mother, father, and brother who missed her.

Self-loathing clung to Violet like gelatinous goo. No matter how hard she tried to scrub it away, a sticky residue always remained—just like how the tattooed man from her dreams remained. The faceless one with that stupid tattoo she saw every time she closed her eyes.

Violet inwardly cringed, replaying how she'd reacted to the guy handing out the flyers. *It was a stupid rose tattoo, for crying out loud!* Rubbing her eyes, she let out a sigh.

"Miss? Excuse me, miss."

She blinked a few times. The young female barista behind the counter was waving at her. "Your chai latte is ready."

"Oh, sorry." Violet walked over and handed the barista a few bills from her wallet. "Here you go."

"No worries, love," said the barista, taking the cash.

Love? Violet hated it when younger girls called her

"love." She offered a tight smile, picked up her latte, and turned.

And crashed right into someone.

For a second, brown liquid and white foam blocked Violet's vision. The aroma of cinnamon and other spices overtook her senses.

She froze in horror.

A man about her age looked down at his scarf, jacket, pants, and shoes, now covered in a murky tinge. She regretted asking for extra foam. Both he and she watched as a white glob smeared a trail down his scarf, then splattered into the milky puddle at his feet.

He looked up at her.

Her heart pounded, her cheeks grew warm, and her eyes couldn't open any wider. Her whole body tensed, preparing for what was about to come next. The rage. The shouting and screaming about third-degree burns and ruined clothes. Memories flashed through her mind's eye, each one more violent than the last. She braced herself.

Then he grinned.

She blinked.

He was actually grinning at her.

Her panic hitched.

His smile was lopsided but genuine. A hint of amusement twinkled in his golden-brown eyes.

"You know," he said, wiping a few specks of white foam from his blond goatee, "when I figured some coffee would warm me up, this isn't exactly what I had in mind."

"I'm sorry?" Was she missing something? Was this usually how people reacted after being baptized in hot chai?

He shrugged, still smiling at her. "Apology accepted."

Apology? Violet gasped. *Oh, right!* She threw her hand over her mouth. "I'm so, *so* sorry."

She turned and grabbed a nearby stack of napkins. She should probably help him wipe down his clothes, but the idea of touching a stranger made her slightly uneasy. Instead, she stooped and attempted to sop up the pool at his feet.

He chuckled and bent down to her level. "Here." He reached a hand toward her, and his fingers grazed her wrist. "Let me hel–"

On instinct, Violet flinched away and stood up. A look of horror instantly replaced his grin, and he stood up with deliberate slowness, both palms held out.

"I'm sorry... I didn't mean... I just... " His eyes darted over and around her. He took half a step back as if preparing to flee.

"Oh!" *He was just reaching for the napkins in my hand.* "No, I'm sorry." *Sheesh, soon this guy is going to think that the only word I know how to say is* sorry. She offered an apologetic smile just as she realized her other hand was resting on the switchblade hidden in the back of her jeans. She forced herself to relax and let her hand drop to her side. *It's fine, Vi. He wasn't actually going to—*

She blinked. Going to what? Attack her in the middle of the coffee shop? Latch on to her wrist and drag her out to his white van and stuff her inside?

She gritted her teeth and gave a slight shake of her head. *Seriously, get a hold of yourself. Not everybody is a kidnapper.*

"Um, you just... startled me. That's all." She held up the napkins. "Here."

His eyes narrowed at the napkins. He still had his hands raised, palms out.

Gosh, this guy is acting like I'm pointing a gun at him instead of holding a stack of napkins. His focus on her was

248

intense. Violet's cheeks grew warm. Could she blame him? Her recoil had been a little over-the-top for an accidental graze of the wrist. From his reaction, she may as well have yelled, "Stick 'em up, homie, and give me all your money!"

He took a step back and started to turn.

She cursed herself. It was the second time she'd overreacted that day. Did she have to act like a psychotic jerk every time a cute guy tried to be nice to her?

"Let me pay for your coffee," she blurted out before he could completely turn away. He paused, but when he didn't say anything, she added, "...for the whole week."

He still didn't respond, but his intense expression relaxed a little.

She glanced at his scarf. "I can also replace your scarf, if you like. I'll get you one with, um..." She winced. "...less milk stains."

"Hmm..." He tilted his head to one side, then to the other, making a show of considering her offer. To her relief, he dropped his hands; the act made her feel less gangster.

At last he nodded, a half smile appearing on his face. "I think I'll take you up on that free coffee. But don't worry about the scarf. I've never liked it anyway." He held up a soppy tassel with his finger and thumb. "In fact, I think you've improved it."

Two new lattes and an extra stack of napkins later, Violet and the guy stood at the door of the café. She put her hand on the door handle, then hesitated. The wind had picked up, tugging with greedy tendrils at the coats, jackets, and scarves of the people who passed by. Clouds covered the sun, blocking any of its efforts to shed some warmth.

She sighed and hugged her chai latte close.

"If you're not in a hurry to leave," said the guy, "why don't we sit for a few minutes and see if the sun is willing to show its face again today?" He gestured to an empty table with two chairs by the floor-to-ceiling windows. Before she could respond, he held up a warning hand. "Just promise that you won't throw another latte at me." A corner of his mouth twitched, amusement twinkling in his eyes.

Violet couldn't help smiling, despite the remaining butterflies of embarrassment in her stomach. She took one last look at the dreary view outside. It was going be a good twenty-minute walk back to her dorm, and all she planned to do when she got back was take a nap.

"I promise I won't bite," he said.

The butterflies in her stomach fluttered harder. Not butterflies—more like angry pixies buzzing and banging to get out.

He smiled at her.

Her nap could wait.

She nodded and followed him over to the table.

Once settled, he shed his still damp jacket. Violet's embarrassment flared again at the blotchy latte stains that had bled onto his long-sleeved shirt. He adjusted his scarf, then took a sip of his drink.

Violet dipped her head, hoping her red cheeks weren't obvious. She took a sip of her latte, relishing the scald and the decadent flavors dancing over her tongue.

"So, I didn't catch your name." The guy turned his cup in a slow spin on the table.

"My name?"

Again, a corner of his mouth twitched. "Yeah, you know. The word that people use to get your attention. I figured if a lovely lady such as yourself has offered to buy me coffee for the rest of the week, I should at least know her name."

She raised an eyebrow. "'Lovely lady'? That makes me

think of an elderly woman with poodles."

He chuckled. "All right, how about I change that to 'beautiful lady'?"

Violet's cheeks and neck grew warm. She dropped her gaze to the lid of her drink, at the four raised domes labelled *White*, *Capp*, *Latte*, and *Choc*. The dome for *Latte* was pressed in, and she circled her thumb in its dip. "It's Violet."

"Violet." His voice was velvet.

She bit her lip.

"So, are you a student?" Violet asked.

He shook his head. "No, thankfully I'm all done with my degree. I now work from home."

"Oh, really? What do you do?"

"I'm a marketing consultant."

"That sounds fancy."

He let out an amused sigh. "Not really. Basically, I assess a business's marketing strategy and develop a plan that outlines proposals for improvements."

"Nice."

"Yeah, it's not a bad gig. I'm my own boss and I get to choose my hours. At the start I didn't have the luxury of picking and choosing my clients, but I've developed a bit of a rep, and I can now take on the ones that interest me."

"Wow, that sounds awesome." Earlier, she'd guessed he was about her age, but if he'd finished a degree and was already running his own business, then he had to be at least twenty-three. It made sense; his masculine features easily outpaced the pubescent boys from her high school, who were still growing out of their delicate childhood phase.

"So, Violet, if you don't mind my asking, why chai?"

Her brow crinkled and she tilted her head. "What do you mean?"

"I mean, forgive me if I'm wrong, but you don't strike

me as someone who would like... chai."

"Oh." Violet shrugged. "I don't know, what's not to like? It's like drinking a cup of Christmas. All of those festive flavors—ginger, cloves, vanilla, star anise, and cinnamon. Now, who doesn't like cinnamon?"

He crinkled up his nose.

Violet's jaw dropped. "Don't tell me you don't like cinnamon?"

He pursed his lips and shook his head. "Sorry. Not a fan."

"Come on, man, what about cinnamon doughnuts? Freshly cooked."

He crinkled his nose again. "I prefer glazed."

"What? You're kidding? There's no way that glazed doughnuts are better than cinnamon ones."

He laughed and held his hands up. "Okay, okay. How about we agree to disagree? I'll leave you to your chai preference, and you leave me with my glazed doughnut preference."

Violet laughed and nodded. "Okay, deal."

He smiled. "Great."

The distance between them was short over the tiny table. From this proximity, she could see his eyes were actually deep chocolate with dazzling flecks of gold, which together emitted the golden-brown hue from a distance. His trimmed goatee, now free from foam, matched the sandy blond of his hair, which was streaked with vintage gold and sun-kissed white. His scarf hid his neck and most of his chest, but his gray sleeves were tight enough to showcase the muscles in his shoulders and arms.

She realized he was studying her as she was him. Once again, her cheeks flushed, and she dropped her gaze to her coffee lid.

Chapter Four

"So, I don't suppose I get to know your name?" she asked. "Because, you know, I figured my friends would want to know who the poor unfortunate soul was that got assaulted by my chai."

He laughed. "Ah, in that case, we can't let your friends down."

"No, we can't," she said, biting her lip.

"Well, you better tell them my name is Thane."

* * *

Violet walked back into her room, the remainder of her chai latte in hand.

"So, your dad's pretty cool." Autumn was sitting in her desk chair, twirling a dreadlock around a finger. Colored thread and beads decorated a few of her locks, and silver bell earrings reflected sparkles of sunlight onto her face. They tinkled when she moved her head.

Gus sat in Violet's chair, casually swinging from side to side. "Yeah, he's also kinda..." He half squinted an eye, searching for the word. "...intense."

Violet dropped onto the bay window seat, smiling. She shook her head as she wrapped her arms around a cushion. "Nathan's not my dad."

"Oh," said Gus. "So, what, he's your uncle? Much older brother?" He gave Violet a conspiratorial grin and waggled his eyebrows. "Is he your sugar daddy?"

Violet scoffed and threw the cushion at him. "He's just a friend."

Gus *ooph*ed when it hit him in the face. "For the love of doughnuts, would you girls please stop attacking my beautiful face? I'm starting to think you're jealous of my good looks."

"If that were true, I would have thrown my chai at you instead."

Gus laughed. "From now on, I'll keep an eye out for flying hot beverages."

Violet laughed and drained the rest of her chai, then set the empty cup down on the windowsill. Chai always triggered her small cluster of happy memories—most of which involved Lyla.

"So," said Autumn, "other than carry boxes, what does your friend do?"

"He's a cop."

"Oh," said Autumn at the same time Gus exclaimed, "A cop!"

Gus smacked himself in the forehead and groaned. "Why, oh, why did I have to mention Aunt Skye's hemp business in front of a cop?"

Autumn rolled her eyes. "It's not illegal, doofus."

"Maybe *he* doesn't think that. And what about you? That was a great time to bring up your illegal online activities. He's probably already on his radio requesting backup."

"Stop making it sound so shady," Autumn ground out.

"I knew you'd be caught one day!"

"Nathan's cool," said Violet. "Trust me, he doesn't care about stuff like that."

"Says you." Gus stabbed an accusatory finger at her. "How do we know you aren't a plant sent here to report on Autumn's hacking activities?"

"A what?"

"You know, a *plant*. It's cop language for 'spy.'"

"Umm, actually, I don't think it is."

Autumn groaned. "She's not a spy, Gus."

"How do you know?"

"Because I just know."

"How? You think you can just do a little *clack-clack*"—he motioned typing on a keyboard—"and you know everything?"

Autumn kicked his chair. "Shut up, Gus."

"I'm serious. You're going to cross a line one day and find yourself seriously screwed."

"You're freaking out over nothing."

"You're not freaking out enough!"

Autumn gritted her teeth and let out an exasperated grunt. Gus just glared at her. For a few moments, the two stared each other down.

Violet was starting to think she'd come back too soon.

Then, as if snapping out of a trance, Autumn said, "*Anyway*, moving on to more important matters"—she held up a flyer like the one Violet had been given earlier—"some guy came by to give us one of these. We're totally going, right?" When Violet didn't answer straightaway, she turned to Gus. "Right?"

Gus sighed and threw his hands up. "Sure, let's go party."

Autumn squealed. "How 'bout it, Vi?"

"Um..." Violet hesitated. When she'd received the flyer earlier, she'd been keen to go try it out. But parties meant people, lots of people, and after her near panic attack, the idea of pasting on a cheerful demeanor for the rest of the night was too overwhelming to think about.

Plus, she'd had her fill of meeting new people for the day. There were sure to be more parties later. This was college, after all.

"You two should go. I think I'm in need of an early night. I want to be fresh and ready for tomorrow."

Autumn put on a pout.

"You're kidding, right?" said Gus. "This is college!

255

Now's the time we get to let our hair down and party till we puke. And seriously, we don't need to worry about classes until at least the week before exams anyway."

"Yeah, I know," said Violet, trying not to cringe. "But I've had a long day. I'll postpone the puking until later."

Autumn and Gus gave up trying to convince her after a few more attempts. They stuck around for a little longer, then to Violet's relief, they left to set up Gus's room, which was in the south wing of the building.

Violet curled up on the window seat and hugged a cushion tight, overcome with exhaustion.

Outside, the final rays of the setting sun tinged the world a warm yellow. Below, she could see the network of paths cutting through the garden from each dormitory. Every path was filling up with students, the majority of them headed in the same direction.

They were all going to the location of the impending party, based on the directions the guy with the flyers had given Violet earlier. That guy probably thought she was a moron. He was probably telling all of his friends right now how much of a freak she was.

She groaned and buried her face in the cushion.

It was a rose tattoo. A stupid, stupid rose!

With a huff she leaned on the windowsill, propping her head up on one hand. Hopefully, tomorrow would be a little better. Although the day hadn't been *all* bad.

Cinnamon and spices still lingered on her taste buds, and her thoughts drifted to Lyla. A fierce, familiar ache stabbed through her chest and clutched at her throat, and before she could stop it, a tear rolled down her cheek.

"I've done it, Ly. I've made it to college."

Read the rest of SHARDS OF VENUS on Amazon.